Soft. That was Shelby's first sensation.

How could a man this tough feel so soft? There was solace and comfort and safety here, and an unbearable, nearly inconceivable tenderness. She caught her breath and sighed.

Jake's work-hardened palm cupped her cheek gently, as though she were something precious, something to be cherished. The brush of his mustache was softer than black velvet as his mouth melded with hers, not demanding, a simple offering of human understanding and compassion.

Soft. The kiss was like a cloud, and she was drifting, dreaming.

Suddenly she froze. Confusion and suspicion filled her. Already she'd revealed too much, let this man see her vulnerable and wounded side. What man wouldn't be tempted to press his advantage of that weakness?

If she let him....

Dear Reader,

The holiday season has arrived—and we have some dazzling titles for the month of December!

This month, the always-delightful Joan Elliott Pickart brings you our THAT'S MY BABY! title. *Texas Baby* is the final book in her FAMILY MEN cross-line series with Desire, and spins the heartwarming tale of a fortysomething heroine who rediscovers the joy of motherhood when she adopts a precious baby girl. Except the dashing man of her dreams has no intention of playing daddy again....

And baby fever doesn't stop there. Don't miss *The Littlest Angel* by Sherryl Woods, an emotional reunion romance—and the first of her AND BABY MAKES THREE: THE NEXT GENERATION miniseries. Passion flares between a disgruntled cowboy and a tough lady cop in *The Cop and the Cradle* by Suzannah Davis—book two in the SWITCHED AT BIRTH miniseries.

For those of you who revel in holiday miracles, be sure to check out *Christmas Magic* by Andrea Edwards. This humorous romance features a cat-toting heroine who transforms a former Mr. Scrooge into a true believer—and captures his heart in the process.

Also this month, *The Millionaire's Baby* by Phyllis Halldorson is an absorbing amnesia story that's filled with love, turmoil and a possible second chance at happiness. Finally, long-buried feelings resurface when a heroine returns to unite her former lover with the son he'd never known in *Second Chance Dad* by Angela Benson.

All of us here at Silhouette wish you a joyous holiday season!

Sincerely,

Tara Gavin,
Senior Editor

Please address questions and book requests to:
Silhouette Reader Service
U.S.: 3010 Walden Ave., P.O. Box 1325, Buffalo, NY 14269
Canadian: P.O. Box 609, Fort Erie, Ont. L2A 5X3

SUZANNAH DAVIS

THE COP AND THE CRADLE

Published by Silhouette Books
America's Publisher of Contemporary Romance

With thanks to Kay Anderson
and for Penny Richards

 SILHOUETTE BOOKS

ISBN 0-373-24143-7

THE COP AND THE CRADLE

Books by Suzannah Davis

Silhouette Special Edition

The Cop and the Cradle #1143

Silhouette Desire

A Christmas Cowboy #903
The Rancher and the Redhead #947
Gabriel's Bride #1041
Dr. Holt and the Texan #1067

*Switched at Birth

SUZANNAH DAVIS

Award-winning author Suzannah Davis is a Louisiana native who loves small-town life, daffodils and writing stories full of love and laughter. A firm believer in happy endings, she has three children.

Chapter One

"Hellfire and damnation!"

Wiping a bullet of sweat from his dark mustache, Jake Lattimer urged his skittish horse into a canter toward the Lazy L's well-tended redwood barn and corrals. Electricity crackled in the sultry, afternoon air, and thunder rumbled with heavy menace from deep within the dark clouds roiling northeast across the rolling Texas pastureland. But nature's fury was nothing compared to the wrath simmering inside Jake.

What a devil's hind end of a day.

First, two ranch hands quit without notice, leaving him shorthanded just when he'd planned to finish the vaccinating and the haying was due to start. Then, the minute Jake's father took off on a golfing jaunt in Florida—to de-stress his sixty-two-year-old body after a too-eventful spring, he'd said, but actually Jake knew Ben wanted to lie low until the smoke cleared after his only son's latest debacle—every attorney and oilman and broker the Lattimers dealt with had developed a sudden dire business crisis and demanded a decision *today*. Not to mention cattle prices were at an all-time low, and the stock they'd planned to sell wasn't going to bring half the expected revenues.

To really top things off, the June storm that hadn't dropped so much as an ounce of rain on the Lazy L's thirsty pastures had taken an expensive toll nonetheless. The Lattimer spread boasted over two thousand acres southwest of Ft. Worth near Aledo, so *of course* lightning had to strike the one lone mesquite bush where gentle Tinkerbell had taken refuge, turning the ranch's prize fifteen-thousand-dollar Charolais bull into a ton of grilled hamburger.

Shadowed by the white straw brim of a Charlie One Horse cowboy hat, Jake's expression hardened. Of course, the way his luck was running these days, that was all good news.

Bad news was coming face-to-face in just the past few weeks with an identical twin brother he hadn't known existed, learning after thirty-five years of ignorant bliss that he'd been adopted, and then finding out said newfound sibling, upright law enforcement officer Texas Ranger Zach Rawlings was making a play for Jake's very own sweet-faced fiancée!

Really bad news was having the two of them run off together on his very wedding day a mere two weeks ago, leaving him literally standing at the altar in a rented monkey suit with egg on his face in front of the whole damn county!

Despite the fact that to Jake his usual calm, soft-spoken Texan demeanor was a matter of pride and good breeding, and despite the fact that maybe deep down somewhere he'd had his own doubts about his feelings for sweet Georgia, it was hard to be philosophical about being made a public laughingstock. With no alternative but to hold his head up and return a houseful of wedding gifts, his mood was murderous, and after a day like today, he wasn't too particular about his choice of victim!

Grinding his teeth, Jake reined the roan mare to a halt at the barn's dusty entrance and swung down from the saddle. Down the line of corrals, Lucy, his favorite mare, wickered a soft greeting. Overdue to foal, even she wasn't cooperating. With his luck, what else could happen?

Sweat dampened his pearl-buttoned chambray shirt as he released the girth and tugged off the saddle. He pictured a long bourbon and a short swim. His mother—all right, his *adopted* mother, Retha, but the only one he'd ever known and the only one who mattered—had insisted on building the pool ten summers ago, just before her heart condition had finally taken her from her menfolk. Time had eased the grief, and now the memory of his sweet mother's smile improved his mood a notch. Yeah, that was the ticket. A quick dip, then one of Rosalita's world-famous mesquite-grilled steaks....

A streak of black lightning whizzed between the mare's hooves and pounced on Jake's calf. Sharp claws penetrated his worn Wranglers, drawing blood. At Jake's surprised yelp, the already-nervous horse launched into a bucking frenzy. Cursing, Jake dived for safety, and the startled mare galloped down the lane toward the sprawling, white clapboard main house. With a triumphant yowl, the ebony demon disappeared inside the barn.

Spitting dust, Jake rolled to his feet with an oath on his tongue and fire in his dark brown eyes. "Dammit! That's it for you—*cat!*"

Too furious to appreciate the fresh sweet tang of new

hay, Jake strode into the barn, grabbed the old Browning shotgun he used for killing snakes and loaded it with rat shot. Dubbed Attila, in tribute to his winning personality, the mean-tempered, randy old tomcat belonged to Zach, which only added insult to injury. The animal had made Jake's life a living hell since hitching a ride from Ft. Worth and hopping off for some country living at the Lazy L.

A hiss of pure disdain sounded from the rafters over Jake's head. Black as the underbelly of Hades itself, the animal sported a bitten-off ear and scarred nose from innumerable street battles. Jake raised the gun, found a pair of evil yellow eyes in his sights and pulled back the hammer. The alley cat had lived fast, loved hard, and by golly, if Jake had anything to say about it, the vile-tempered son of a Hun was going to die young!

But then another's throaty, seductive wail wafted downward, and Jake stifled a groan of pure frustration.

A regal, pug-nosed Persian appeared on the rafter, tiptoeing as daintily as a prima ballerina around Attila, rubbing and purring, back and forth, twirling her fluffy tail in a veritable frenzy of feminine enticement.

"Good grief, Elizabeth, you hussy!" Defeated, Jake lowered the gun.

He could no more endanger the offspring of his mother's prized and pampered pussycat than he could sprout wings and fly to the moon. Nor could he callously massacre Attila just because he was the meanest, orneriest critter this side of Amarillo, either. With a sigh, Jake uncocked the gun. Unlike his brother Zach, Jake wasn't the type to come between a happy couple. Which, in some uncanny fashion, Jake was sure Attila knew.

He glared at the tom, whose expression he could have

sworn betrayed an almost human smugness. "Next time, buddy..."

"Talking to yourself, Jake? That's one trait we don't have in common, thank God."

Jake pivoted on his heel. A rangy figure, whose six-foot, three-inch frame was a carbon copy of Jake's own, materialized in the barn's double doorway. Jake's jaw throbbed with instantaneous tension. He would never grow accustomed to seeing this other self, he decided. He would always feel this shock of both recognition and disbelief, like gazing into a magic mirror and having his own reflection come to unexpected life with a wicked and betraying will of its own.

It was Jake's own thick black hair under that black Stetson, his unique curve of an inky mustache and strongly marked brows. How utterly unnerving to see oneself in a familiar pair of dark brown eyes and the same lean jaw and square, cleft chin Jake shaved every morning. His own wide mouth and carved lips grinned back mockingly at him.

Jake blinked, still amazed that twins raised apart, not even aware of the other's existence, could end up so much alike, from both playing linebacker in high school and wearing the same jersey number to favoring the same brand of aftershave. Under Zach's white dress shirt were shoulders just as wide as Jake's, and there was the same muscular strength in long legs covered by blue denim. Yes, they were two peas from the same pod physically, Jake acknowledged, but in the ways that truly counted in a man, in terms of honor and integrity, they were as different as day and night.

Jake broke open the shotgun and removed the shells, his movements controlled. "You've got a lot of nerve showing your face around here, partner."

Zach chuckled. "Now you sound like a bad Western."

"Just state your business and get the hell out."

"Trying to run me out of Dodge before sundown? Hoss, you need a better line than that." Zach straightened with a grin and gestured at the weapon. "Though it looks like you're ready for a showdown. Hunting varmints?"

Jake jerked his chin in the cat's direction. "I was two shakes from blasting that menacing pet of yours to kingdom come."

Above their heads, Attila yowled a greeting—or a warning?

"Hey!" Zach raised his hands in protest. "He's not *my* cat!"

"Then maybe I should just concentrate on the two-legged vermin around here."

Zach's smile faded, and he jammed the flats of his hands into his jeans pockets, the first sign that he wasn't as confident as he looked. His expression sobered. "Look, I can't blame you for being mad as hell at me, but aren't you going to ask about Georgia?"

Jake stiffened. Carefully he replaced the gun on its rack, making his face a mask of indifference. He'd be dad-blamed if he'd show the remotest flicker of his hurt and humiliation to this man, this brother he couldn't quite muster any affection for. "She's not my business any longer. You saw to that."

"She's upset that you won't take her calls. She needs to explain, to apologize."

"What's the point?"

"You're a stubborn cuss, you know that?"

"I don't think it's my character that needs scrutinizing," Jake replied pointedly. "Frankly, it's been a hell of a day, so if you don't mind, haul your sorry butt off my property. I got nothing to say to you or Georgia."

"I make her happy, Jake," Zach said, his voice soft.

God, that stung! He'd loved Georgia—at least he'd thought he did—even if he wasn't exactly *in love* with her. He'd known she'd longed for more excitement in their relationship, but they were comfortable together, good friends, and wasn't that important, too? So maybe he was predictable, with a tendency to suppress his emotions, especially where women were concerned, but he was solid and dependable. *Boring,* a tiny voice whispered inside his head. He squelched the inner wince of self-doubt with a shake of his head. Hell, they'd planned a good life together. It would have worked out just fine.

But Georgia had made her choice, rejected him and all that he offered in the most public and mortifying fashion, showing the world he was a failure as a man and a lover. Well, he could take just about anything, but to have his nose rubbed in it, salt poured into the wounds of his failings and insecurities by this man who shared his own blood—it was too much.

"Be honest," Zach advised. "You know deep down you aren't what Georgia needed. She deserved better, and so do you."

"I guess if Georgia thought 'better' was a lying, conniving son of a bitch, then that's what she got." Jake didn't like the bitterness in his own voice but was helpless to contain it. "Congratulations to you both."

"Jake—"

"Get out of my sight, Zach." Grabbing a bucket of sweet feed, Jake brushed past his brother, his voice rough and dangerous. "We might have shared the same womb, but I don't make peace with skunks and scalawags."

Zach followed him out of the barn, his expression turning harsh with regret and embarrassment and anger as he watched his twin open the corral gate. "I didn't come to make peace, or even to ask your blessing, you bullheaded galoot!''

The afternoon light was still fitful—brilliant, arrhythmic shafts of sunlight stabbing through the purple curtain of thunderheads in blinding pulses. Jake gave a sharp whistle to call up the spooked mare, squinting against the glare, his eyes narrowed suspiciously on the other man. "Then what do you want?"

"A couple of things." Zach hesitated. "I thought you ought to know I found Dad…Dwayne, I mean. Turns out my gut feeling was right. I wasn't adopted, at least not by Mom. Oh, hell, what I mean is that from everything I can learn, Abby Pickett was my—*our*—birth mother.''

A jolt went through Jake, and his hand stiffened around the gate railing at the implication. He didn't want to think about Dwayne and Abigail Pickett Rawlings. What kind of parents would give away only one of their twin sons? What had it been about Jake as an infant that had made him their sacrificial choice? Not that he really cared, of course, he told himself fiercely. Growing up the highly favored only son of a successful, wealthy rancher and his delicate, beautiful wife hadn't been a hardship by any means. In fact, he counted his lucky stars daily for Ben and Retha Lattimer's love and the quest for a family that had brought them to a private adoption arranged by a young lawyer named Tom Barnette.

Still, some mild curiosity about his parentage and the circumstances of his abandonment was understandable, only there wasn't really anyone left to ask. According to Zach, Abby had passed away some years back—so not having a mother was another thing they had in common—and Dwayne was a trucker with too great a fondness for fists and fifths of Wild Turkey, who had a long-established habit of dropping out of sight. Only now, it seemed, he'd risen to the surface like scum on a pond.

Jake wondered if he really wanted to delve into secrets over three decades old. He knew who his true father was. What purpose would it serve to meet the man who'd sired him, then cast him off?

Jake's jaw clenched, caution warring with curiosity. With feigned disinterest, he sauntered into the corral toward a wooden feed trough attached to a railing. "What did Dwayne have to say?"

Zach followed him across the corral, his boots making identically sized indentations in the dirt beside Jake's tracks. "We had a real interesting conversation. Since you haven't had the dubious pleasure of making Dwayne's delightful acquaintance, this probably won't mean as much to you, but he had no idea I had a brother, let alone a twin."

"What?" Taken aback, Jake scowled and faced his brother. What kind of conniving female had his birth mother been that she'd been able to conceal such a thing from her own husband? "How could that be?"

Zach's lips twisted ironically. "Easy, since he's not our father at all."

"What the hell does that mean?"

"Just what I said. Dwayne Rawlings isn't our biological father. He told me he and Mom got married when I was about five months old."

"My God, why?"

Zach shrugged. "He loved her, I guess. You've seen her picture. She was pretty as an angel back then. And her folks were real religious. Grandpa Pickett was a preacher, and you could almost smell the brimstone after his Sunday-morning services. For her to have a child—"

"Children," Jake corrected tersely.

Zach nodded. "*Children* out of wedlock must have been unacceptable. Dad...er, Dwayne said they put a lot of pressure on her. And he promised to raise her kid like his own. After the wedding they moved away to get a fresh start." Zach's gaze turned inward, looking at memories that still provoked a flicker of pain in the depths of his dark eyes. "It wasn't much of a marriage, Jake. And it wasn't much of a childhood, either. I guess Dwayne did the best he could, but maybe the reason things went sour so early was because he couldn't forget his beautiful wife had carried another man's baby. And they never were able to have any of their own. I guess looking at me every day was an insult to his manhood or something."

Jake glimpsed an inkling of the bleakness of Zach's youth compared to the richness of his own. But he didn't want to feel any empathy for his brother, this man who'd betrayed whatever bonds of blood they might have developed between them by stealing the woman he'd loved. But there was one other thing he wanted to know. He cleared his throat. "Did Dwayne say...?"

Zach cocked an eyebrow. "Who our real father was?"

"Yeah."

"He never knew. Abby refused to tell him."

"He must have some idea—"

"One of the football players she'd been dating, maybe. Laura has a few ideas about how to track down that kind of information. She's keen to keep on it for us, says it'll make a great sidepiece to the big adoption story she's been working on."

Jake frowned. Zach's good friend, Laura Ramirez, was an investigative reporter who already had a reputation for tenacity and being able to ferret out long-buried secrets. But who could guess if her investigations would open up a Pandora's box that could never be closed again?

"I don't think that's such a good idea," he said cautiously.

"We need to know," Zach replied.

"Why? What difference will it make?"

"All right, dammit, *I* want to know who he was." Zach grinned suddenly. "Just think, we must have gotten our athletic ability with the pigskin from him. And Mom was a cheerleader, you know. Pretty, popular, just an all-American girl."

Jake laughed, a bitter bark with no humor in it. "Who made the biggest mistake of her life behind the bleachers with an oversexed jock."

"You're in no position to judge her like that," Zach retorted angrily. "Mom was the kindest, sweetest woman I'd ever known until I met Georgia. Whatever her reasons for separating us, they must have been good ones."

"I guess she hoped our paths would never cross again." Jake's eyes were as dark and angry with turmoil as the clouds rolling overhead, and his voice was cold and caustic. "Well, I'm sorry she didn't get her wish."

"And I'm sorry you feel that way, because I don't."

Jake stared hard at his twin, his gut in such a knot he couldn't begin to know how to respond. Was it a challenge or a peace offering? His jaw tightened. It didn't matter. He didn't want or need to have anything to do with Zach Rawlings. "Was there something else?"

Zach chewed his mustache a moment, then admitted, "I need a favor."

Dumbfounded, Jake's jaw dropped. Then new fury heated his cheeks under his tan. "You've got the gall of a loco mule, Rawlings. You know I wouldn't spit on you if you were on fire."

"It's not for me." Zach jerked off his hat and jammed

a hand through his hair, muttering. "I knew this was a bad idea."

"Then hop along, Cassidy," Jake sneered. "You were right."

Exasperated, Zach scowled. "Look, I've got a girl in trouble—"

"What!" Thunder cracked overhead. With a matching roar, Jake flung the bucket to the ground and latched both fists onto Zach's shirtfront. "You sorry bastard! Another woman already? I swear, if you hurt Georgia—"

"No, you don't understand." Zach struggled under Jake's irate hold. "Get a grip, man! I love Georgia more than my next breath! It's Shelby."

"Who?"

"Shelby Hartman, my old partner. She stayed with the Dallas force when I joined the Texas Rangers."

Jake eased his grasp, his eyes narrowed suspiciously. "What about her?"

Zach's dark gaze shifted away. "She had an... accident."

"What kind of accident?"

"Ever heard of Gus Salvatore?"

Puzzled, Jake shook his head. "No."

"Not surprising. He keeps a low profile, but he's got fingers in just about every nasty racket in the Dallas-Ft. Worth area. Shelby volunteered to work undercover, but someone ratted on her—maybe someone within the department, but that's another story." Zach grimaced, the idea of a dirty cop making his features harsh. "Anyway, Salvatore found out and tried to silence her—permanently. It was sheer luck backup arrived before he could finish the job."

"Rough business." Jake unclenched his fists and released his twin. "So she's all right?"

Straightening, Zach shrugged, his expression reflecting his uncertainty. "They let her out of the hospital, but that doesn't mean she's okay, not by a long shot. She's on the edge, Jake. She needs someplace quiet, safe, someplace she can be pampered, not have to lift a finger while she gets better."

Understanding dawned. Jake's mouth hardened. "Not here."

"Just for a few weeks."

"No."

"Dammit, Jake, word on the street is there's a price on her head. Salvatore's gone underground, but he isn't taking any chances on letting Shelby testify against him before the Grand Jury."

"And you want to bring her here? Why, for God's sake?"

"It's perfect. No one in the department knows except the division captain and me. It's secluded, peaceful, and who'd guess I'd have the nerve to stash my old partner with a man who hates my guts?"

"You got that damned straight!" Jake agreed. "So forget it. The Lazy L isn't a hideout, and I'm no baby-sitter! Find some other pigeon."

"Look, it's either this or a safe house, and that'd be worse than a prison. If you'll just hear me out—"

Shaking his head at the sheer audacity of the man, Jake turned away. "Go to hell."

Zach caught Jake's shoulder. "Wait a damn minute! What happened to that noble, unselfish pillar of the community? Georgia says your hobby is bailing out damsels in distress. She sang your praises till I thought I'd go nuts. What's happened to the man known for never turning away a soul in need?"

Jake jerked free, and his hands clenched in mounting

fury. "He gave up Christian charity as a bad deal two weeks ago on his wedding day."

Zach glared back at him. "That's what this is all about, isn't it? Not that you won't consider helping a good cop who's had a rough time, but that you won't help *me*."

"Bingo, bright boy."

"Well, get over it, Jake," Zach shouted. "I didn't steal Georgia, she *ran* away from you."

Jake's knuckles connected with Zach's chin before his brain even registered the message that he'd thrown a punch. It was a satisfying, solid smash that numbed his fist and reverberated all the way up his arm to the shoulder socket.

It knocked Zach flat on his butt in the dusty corral.

In the next instant Zach tackled Jake's knees and they both went rolling and tumbling, fists flying, all the pent-up anger spilling out as they pummeled each other.

Zach landed a blow to the rib cage, and the air whooshed from Jake's lungs. In retaliation, he caught Zach a glancing slam across the temple. Equally matched in size and strength and temper, they battled in silent ferocity. What Zach possessed in superior training, Jake more than made up for in justified indignation. Dust flew, boots scratched for purchase, grunts of effort and pain and the fine spray of blood filled the thick, sultry air.

"Hey! That's enough! Knock it off! What do I have to do, call the cops?"

The sharp sound of an angry feminine voice cut across the free-for-all with the precision of a blade. On his back in the dirt, Jake froze, one hand twisted in Zach's collar, the other raised in a balled fist. Similarly paralyzed, Zach's next punch halted halfway in its flight toward Jake's jaw. As one, their heads rotated toward the blonde standing in the corral gate, her sandaled feet spread belligerently, her white-knuckled hands clenched around the roan mare's leather reins.

"Good Lord!" Disgust laced her husky, Lauren Bacall voice with ice as she eyed each man through gold-framed aviator sunglasses. "You call this *peaceful?*"

Zach made a move to rise, and Jake followed him up, both men using each other for support as they lurched to their feet like drunken sailors. Chagrined to be discovered tussling like a second-grader on a playground, Jake pushed away from his brother, dusting his grimy shirt and jeans and looking around for his hat, as guilty as a school-boy caught by the teacher.

But this woman was no sweet-faced schoolmarm like Georgia.

Her features were even, unremarkable when taken in-dividually, yet something exotic and mysterious when set in an oblong face whose jaw should have been too square to be attractive in a female but somehow wasn't. Her straight, sandy blond hair was streaked with honey by nature or the sun, and she wore it simply, parted on the side and just shoulder length. It looked as though it never got more than a brief finger combing, but the haphazard way the golden strands lay against her cheek and the curve of her neck reminded him of a woman after a long night of loving, tousled and sexy and touchable. Jake knew in-stinctively that the look was probably deceiving.

Of medium height, she was wiry and athletic, slim legs encased in form-fitting denim jeans that molded the curve of her hips like a lover's caress. She wore what looked to be a man's white singlet undershirt and nothing else be-neath a hundred-year-old denim jacket bleached nearly white with age and use. When she removed her sunglasses and hooked the stem in the scooped neck of the shirt, the soft cotton fabric stretched revealingly over small, firm breasts and a shadowy glimpse of dusky tips.

Jake sucked in an involuntary breath at that careless movement and the answering tingling in his groin. With his tongue he probed the split in his lip under his mustache, savoring the coppery tang of his own blood to regain his equilibrium. He forced his gaze upward, past the blue cotton bandanna she wore twisted around her slender neck to her eyes.

Those orbs were a mysterious mixture of green and gold, like gilded pine needles. Defiant and challenging, yet shadowed and tense with the reflections of some unnamed suffering, they raked the two men—bruised and battered mirror images of each other—and in that flicker of scathing assessment, they both came up short.

Zach's left eye was beginning to swell. He snatched up his hat and took a step toward the woman. "Shelby—"

Jake's attention jerked from the visitor back to his twin, his dark eyes burning with accusation. "You didn't tell me you brought her with you!"

"You didn't ask," Zach snapped, jamming his hat on. "Shelby, you should have waited in the car."

"I'm not the patient type." She jerked on the mare's bridle. "And then Bossy here came along—move, you dumb nag!"

To save the mare's mouth and possibly this city girl, who obviously didn't know horseflesh from Holsteins, from getting stomped, Jake picked up his own hat, whipped it across his thighs to knock off the dust, then went to her and took the reins. She stepped aside with an affectation of nonchalance that made him wonder if it were him or the horse that made her jumpy.

Shelby Hartman seemed as tightly coiled as an overworked watch spring. A whiff of her soap mingled with a whisper of hospital antiseptic to tickle his nose, a re-minder that her being wired wasn't surprising after what she'd been through. Now that Jake was close to her, he could see the faint purplish shadows under her eyes, the lines of strain tightening the corners of her remarkably lush mouth. Setting his hat to the back of his head, he removed the bridle and, with a slap, sent the mare can-tering into the corral where she immediately began to nuz-zle at the spilled bucket of horse ration.

"Thanks for the help." Jake nodded to Shelby, indi-cated for her and Zach to step out of the corral, then latched the gate behind them. The courtesy that was an ingrained part of him reasserted itself. "Sorry to have bothered you, ma'am."

"Ma'am?" Shelby laughed, a brittle sound, like the hum of a guitar string stretched to the point of snapping. "What century did you drop in from, cowboy?"

"Pardon me?"

She scoured Jake with that green-gold gaze, assessing and cataloging every detail of his appearance and attire with her cop's expertise, then shook her head. "Jeez Lou-ise," she muttered, "you really are twins. This is creepy."

"Take it easy, Shel," Zach said with an uneasy chuckle. "You've just been on the streets too long."

"Easy for you to say with your cushy office job, part-ner." The smile she flashed held no humor, and her tone sizzled like acid on metal.

Zach raised his hand in a pacifying gesture, trying to defuse the electric aura of tension that crackled around her with a teasing smile. "I simply mean it's past time for some R & R when you don't recognize a quintessential Southern gentleman like Jake here."

"Since the buckaroo is your spitting image, and since you, Rawlings, are no gentleman and never have been, no wonder I'm a little confused." Her lips were peachy, bare of lipstick, and they curled in a cynical twist. "Besides, gentlemen usually don't pound each other senseless."

Zach shuffled his boots. "Er, just a minor difference of opinion."

"Sorry you had to witness that, ma'am," Jake added gruffly.

"That little piddlin' boxing match? I've seen worse, believe me. Besides, I couldn't respect a man who didn't at least *try* to beat the snot out of the bastard who took his woman." She winked at Jake. "Good work, cowboy."

Angry heat rose up Jake's neck. God, she really knew how to go for the jugular! What else did she know about his humiliation? "The name's Jake, ma'am," he growled.

"Well, Jake, you've got blood on your mouth."

Automatically, Jake lifted a skinned knuckle to wipe at his lip, then gave an inward curse at Shelby's brief, disdainful smile. This woman was as tough as they came, with a viper's tongue and an ability to throw a man off balance and tie him up like a calf in a roping contest. Such talents might make her a capable law enforcement officer, but they were beginning to annoy the living hell out of him.

"Cut it out, Shel," Zach ordered, his own irritation showing in the unhappy curve of his mouth. "You aren't helping."

She shrugged. "This wasn't my idea. I told you wide-open spaces make me nauseous."

"Look, it's for your own good."

"I don't think the buckaroo appreciates the idea of an uninvited houseguest—only, his mama must have raised him to be too much of a gentleman to say so."

Jake latched a hand around Shelby's upper arm, holding her still while he glowered down into her face. "My mother taught me a lot of things, but if you call me that again you're going to find yourself flat on your keester, lady.''

Shelby lifted her chin, her eyes flashing molten gold with hostility. ''You can try—*buckaroo*.''

The tilt of her chin shifted her bandanna, and Jake's gaze dropped to her neck. What he noticed peeking over the edge surprised him into a perplexed scowl.

''For crying out loud, Shel!'' Zach moved to step between them, but faltered when her glare impaled him.

''Stay out of it, Zach,'' she said furiously. ''I can take care of myself.''

''Sure you can.'' Jake's sarcasm lashed like a whip. ''And you've got the bruises to prove it.''

He hooked a finger on her bandanna to expose the small discoloration he'd noticed, but the loose knot gave way and suddenly he was holding the square of cotton in his hand. What he saw made his belly clench, and an oath slipped from his lips, low and vicious, damning not only the man who'd done this to her, but himself for losing control and exposing her pain.

The bruises were an exquisite rainbow necklace of purple, green and yellow. Jake knew without counting that there would be exactly ten rosettes in the deadly circlet marking her creamy throat, one for each murderous finger of an enemy who'd done his best to choke the life from her and very nearly succeeded. What had gone through her mind as the world went black and her lungs screamed in silent agony?

Jake felt sick. He'd never taken out his ill temper on a woman in his whole life. Retha's fragile health had trained him from an early age to revere and comfort and protect the feminine gender. Now look what he'd done. He was lower than dirt. Jake's fingers went slack, dropped away from her arm.

"Ma'am, I'm so sorry."

And he knew in that moment he'd made an even bigger mistake. Shelby Hartman could give as good as she got, could no doubt knock his block off with a karate chop and plug him through the heart with her service revolver if she had to. But what she couldn't stand was to be pitied, and he had no doubt that was exactly the emotion now written all over his face.

"Damn you." Her breath caught, and she went white with fury, sweating and shivering at the same time. "Don't you dare…"

Zach shot his brother a killing look and reached out a comforting hand. "Shel, it's okay—"

Her face, so stark and devastated, yet so unyieldingly proud, silenced him, stopped him dead. Thunder grumbled. A fat raindrop hit the ground, then another, hissing at it slapped the arid dirt. Shelby started at the faint sound, swaying slightly as the rain slid down her cheeks, mimicking tears Jake was certain she'd never shed. With a gesture of contemptuous dismissal, she turned her back on both men, muttering, "Hell, I don't need this."

Then, to Jake's horror, she crumpled at his feet like a discarded rag doll.

Chapter Two

Shelby came to with the startling and utterly mortifying realization that she'd passed out cold for the very first time in her life, but here she was, being carried in someone's strong arms, her cheek pressed against a very hard, very broad male chest, swooning and namby-pamby like some kind of simpering, tight-corsetted Southern belle.

It was the most galling moment of her life.

She opened her eyes, peering upward beneath her lashes at the lean-jawed face bent just inches from her own, the brim of his hat tilted to shield them both from the worst of the afternoon cloudburst. Tanned masculine skin with a bloom of late-day stubble, velvety black mustache framing a hard, no-nonsense mouth that could just as easily smile—*Zach.*

Relief washed through her. He'd been a real brick throughout this whole mess. God, he'd even postponed his wedding night to be with her in the hospital—what greater sacrifice could you ask of a man? So maybe he wouldn't rib her too hard.

She allowed herself the briefest moment of self-indulgence to take comfort from her best friend's closeness, the familiar woodsy scent of his cologne mingled with male musk and—what? Something niggled at her awareness, and a perplexed frown pleated her brow. Her senses reached out, instincts grappling, but she knew she was frayed and overwrought. Surely that accounted for the almost electric sensation as skin brushed skin, the unnatural heat of his large hand gently clasping her shoulder through her damp denim jacket.

Then he looked down at her through thick lashes, piercing her with dark, penetrating eyes—*not* her friend at all, but a stranger. A vastly disturbing stranger. Shelby caught her breath, inhaling the indefinable essences of leather and horse.

"Put me down, cowboy," she croaked. "Haven't you heard? Chivalry's dead."

"Not on the Lazy L," Jake Lattimer replied grimly.

She pressed her palm against his chest, struggling. "You're not listening—"

"Be still." Hefting her a little closer, quelling her squirmings with no more effort than if she were a two-year-old, he took the back steps of the rambling white farmhouse two at the time, shouldered his way through the double doors and headed down a long corridor faced completely with glass French doors on one side and floored with glossy Saltillo tile the color of ripe apricots. His bellow reverberated against the hard surfaces. "Rosalita! Rosalita! Where the heck are you?"

Shelby caught brief, dizzying glimpses of her surroundings as he pounded up the hall: beyond the French doors, a rain-drenched terrace and sea blue swimming pool; opposite that, doors that opened into tastefully appointed bedrooms; then a gigantic country kitchen with burnished copper pans hanging over a central island.

Lord, she thought muzzily, *it's a flipping mansion!*

A petite, well-rounded woman in her thirties appeared from a laundry room set off the kitchen. Her raven hair fell from a neat French braid down her back and she wore jeans and a T-shirt. "*Madre de Dios,* Jake! What's happened now?"

Jake didn't slow down, just threw a request over his shoulder for dry towels and continued through a wide foyer past a broad staircase and into a spacious living room. Shelby barely had time to register that the room was elegant, warm and comfortable with an ease that spoke of many cozy family evenings: a discarded newspaper, favorite books and family pictures, a beloved, well-worn chair in front of the television. Jake laid Shelby down on a leather sofa the color of ancient mahogany as carefully as though she were made of the finest Dresden china, then plumped a beautifully handcrafted needlepoint pillow behind her head.

"I'm all right," she said irritably, embarrassed as much by such unaccustomed male attention as by her fainting spell.

Rosalita bustled into the room, concern marring her olive-skinned features. Jake turned to take the towels she offered with quiet thanks, then began blotting at Shelby's damp face and hands as if she were a child. Rosalita's anxious gaze focused on Jake's swollen lip, but when her attention slid to Shelby, her eyes widened in shock. Shelby automatically put a hand to her tender throat.

"Here." Jake pulled her blue bandanna from his shirt pocket. "Sorry."

"So you said." Snatching the scarf, Shelby defiantly stuffed it into her jacket along with her sunglasses.

Although Salvatore's strong fingers had nearly crushed her windpipe, she was recovering, the rasp of her voice improving daily, her bruises blossoming colorfully as they healed. The physical wounds would fade; it was the psychic trauma of coming so close to death, the helplessness and utter despair she'd felt when she'd realized that for once she couldn't protect herself, that undermined her confidence and courage and kept her nerves on a perpetual hair-trigger. But at twenty-eight she was street tough from a checkered childhood in a series of Tarrant County foster homes and worldly-wise from having made her own way through two years of college, the academy and the still-primarily male domain of law enforcement.

She would handle this just as she'd handled every other challenge in her life—alone, depending on no one but herself. She'd covered her battle scars for other people's comfort, not her own, but now Shelby didn't care if the sight of her bruises made Jake Lattimer uncomfortable or not. She met his regard unflinchingly, scorn smoldering in her eyes like emerald fire.

In turn, Jake's dark brown gaze never left her, never faltered, and although hostility crackled between them like summer lightning, his tone was cordiality itself. "Rosie, this is Ms. Shelby Hartman. Would you fix our guest some hot tea, please? Plenty of sugar."

"Sure thing, Jake." Rosalita scurried away, visibly relieved to leave a room practically pulsing with animosity.

"Where's Zach?" Shelby demanded.

"Don't worry, he hasn't deserted you." Jake gave a nod in the direction of the circular driveway out front. "He's getting your things out of the car."

"Uh-uh." Feeling increasingly trapped, she ignored her

light-headedness, struggling up on one elbow. "He's not pulling this on me! I knew I should have ridden the hog."

"You're in no condition to ride any kind of animal," Jake said. Without asking permission, he skillfully shucked her out of the wet jacket and pushed her back down.

She glared up at him, hating her weakness, hating him. "Not a pig, country boy, my Harley. I'm not staying here."

"No one's forcing you to." His expression bland, he tossed his hat onto a coffee table, then used the same towel to dry his own face and wipe the glistening raindrops from his dark mustache.

Shivering at not only the whisper of air-conditioning on her damp skin but also the subtle intimacy of that act, Shelby felt her nipples contract against the thin knit of the undershirt. To her continued mortification, Jake noticed the transformation, his eyes narrowing in a way that was distinctly male, clearly predatory. Shelby hurriedly crossed her arms over her breasts. He was just trying to annoy her. Her chin firmed. Well, she'd be damned if she'd let this cowboy get to her. If he disapproved of a female cop who owned a motorcycle and was dressed like an out-of-work hooker, he gave no outward indication, and yet prickles of antagonism danced over Shelby's taut nerves.

"You don't want me here," she challenged.

Jake shrugged his broad shoulders. "That seems hardly relevant at the moment. And it's not my habit to boot helpless females out of my home."

"Helpless?" Incensed, she struggled to a seated position. "Forget it, I'm outta here."

"The hell you are!" Zach stood in the foyer doorway holding a small athletic duffle and her shoulder bag.

With both men in the room, Shelby blinked at an eerie, vertiginous sensation of double vision. Identical on the outside, but what about inside, where it counted? While she and Zach had always been easy compatriots, there radiated from Jake Lattimer a level of masculine virility and dominance that immediately raised her feminine hackles. What was it about him that rubbed her the wrong way so vehemently?

It couldn't be his looks—they were exactly the same as Zach's, but his rangy rancher's physique was enough to produce palpitations in any woman who appreciated tight jeans. While she and Zach had been friends from the start, however, with never any element of attraction or friction between them, Jake Lattimer unnerved her in ways she couldn't readily identify. It must just be that he was angry as hell at his newfound brother and Shelby was responding to all that free-floating male aggression with an instinctual defense of her friend.

When Zach had first revealed he'd found a brother quite by accident—and an identical twin, at that—Shelby, who'd never had a real family of her own, had been enchanted by the miracle and even felt a tad envious. But who could have guessed Zach would whisk his brother's fiancée away on her wedding day? Shelby had met Georgia and liked her. She was a real sweetheart, perfect for Zach. The two of them were obviously crazy in love, so such impetuosity could perhaps be excused, but it must have been a bitter pill for Jake.

That had to be it, Shelby thought; she was picking up on the understandable tension between the two brothers and it was making her jumpy as a cat. The strain was getting to her, obviously. She had to get a grip. She had to get away before she lost total control.

Frustration tightened her features as she glared at her

former partner. "This is ridiculous, Zach. You said we'd just have a look-see, and I've definitely seen enough. Besides, I've got work to do—"

"You went on 'extended personal leave' the minute we sneaked you out of the hospital." Setting the bags down in the doorway, he cocked her a hard look. "Or have you forgotten why you had round-the-clock guards?"

"The captain overreacted," she muttered resentfully. "I'd rather go home, anyway."

"It's not safe right now. Besides, that hellhole you call an apartment is no place to get your strength back."

"I like my place," she said defensively. All right, so her apartment was an airless box with no character, and the drunk who lived upstairs liked to play his jazz harmonica at 4:00 a.m. It was clean and convenient, and she wasn't there that much, anyway. Her lower lip jutted out belligerently. "It's...homey, that's all."

"Homey? It makes a condemned tenement look like the Hilton."

"Well, the Black Hole of Calcutta would be better than staying where I'm not wanted." She glared at him mutinously. "You didn't tell me your brother was a flipping millionaire!"

"What difference does it make? And as for not being wanted—you've obviously misunderstood." Zach shot a look at his twin. "Hasn't she, Jake?"

"I apologize if anything I said led you to believe you wouldn't be welcome here, Ms. Hartman." His voice stiff with formality, Jake watched Shelby carefully, as if she were an interesting specimen under a microscope. He draped the towel around his neck, saying, "Of course we'd be delighted to have you at the Lazy L for as long as you like."

She cast him a skeptical look, sure that since she'd

keeled over on his property he was just feeling guilty and obligated somehow to "do the right thing." Well, she didn't need his damned charity.

"Yeah, right," she drawled. "Your sincerity absolutely underwhelms me, cowboy."

Zach gave a snort of pure aggravation, then winced and gingerly tested the swelling around his eye. "Cripes, put a cork in it, will you, Shelby?" He raised open palms toward Jake in apology. "I swear she's not normally so mouthy, Jake. Usually quiet as a mouse, can't get a word out of her. Makes her great on stakeouts. You'll have to excuse her. That hospital stay has her rattled, but with a little tender loving care she'll settle down and be such an ideal houseguest you won't even know she's here."

Shelby gulped in outrage. "Zach Rawlings, don't you dare talk about me as if I weren't in the room!"

Zach began to look a little desperate. "Look, Shel, I can personally vouch for the hospitality around here. I had a sample of it when I got that knot on my noggin, remember?"

Zach's head injury in the line of duty had produced a bout of temporary amnesia, leading Georgia to mistake him for her then-fiancé, Jake, and bring him back to the Lazy L to recuperate. Here, the brothers had met for the first time since their birth, and whether that had been a good or a bad thing was a question that was still up for grabs.

Shelby nodded. "I'm sure you had a very nice time, but I should have known you were up to no good the minute we left the city limits. All this fresh air—I'll probably break out in a rash." She stood up, making an extra effort not to wobble, and flashed a crooked grin. "Nice try, Zach, but no deal. Let's go."

Zach's mouth compressed, then he gave a short nod. "All right, Shel, you win."

"Now you're talking." She grabbed her jacket and started toward the doorway, aiming a quick, sardonic smile at Jake. "See you around, buckaroo."

"I hope you have a pleasant stay at the safe house, Ms. Hartman," he replied.

Shelby frowned, and her gaze whipped back to Zach's too-innocent face. "What's he talking about?"

"Oh, didn't I mention that?" Zach crossed his arms over his chest. "Captain said if this idea didn't work out, he wants you in protective custody. The safe house off of Alameda, I understand. But don't worry, Shel, I hear the last fumigation got rid of most of the roaches. The rats, however, are another matter."

Her fists clenched and she took an angry step forward. "Why, you dirty, low-down..."

"It's either here or there, Shel. Take your pick."

"But this place is more isolated than outer Siberia."

"So? Peace and quiet is just what you need."

A breath of panic tickled the back of Shelby's throat, and her tension level skyrocketed. Her control of her own destiny was slipping between her fingers like sand, and there was nothing she could do to stop it. "You want me to play 'Home on the Range'? With *him?* I'll die of pure boredom inside a day."

Jake started, then a flush of red crept up his lean cheeks, and he crossed his arms over his chest in a stance identical to his twin's. His deep voice dripped with sarcasm. "But we've got satellite TV, Ms. Hartman. You can do your nails and watch soaps till the cows come home."

"Oh, joy." Self-consciously, she hid her well-bitten nails behind her back. No doubt he was accustomed to well-bred, soft-spoken women who had a manicure twice a week and couldn't say "boo" to a mouse. Well, she could outrun a suspect, wrestle him to the ground and then disarm him in twelve seconds flat, so breaking a nail wasn't high on her list of concerns.

She shot Jake a poisonous look, then turned her furious countenance toward Zach. "Don't think you're going to get away with this, Zach Rawlings. I won't be manipulated."

"You forget someone wants you dead."

Shelby choked back a gasp at his blunt words, lifting a hand to her throat. "But—"

Zach shrugged. "Your choice. Stay in seclusion here until the trial and have a little freedom and breathing space, or spend the next few weeks in a ten-by-ten bedroom in the heart of the city—no walks, no rides."

Shelby felt an almost suffocating sense of claustrophobia at the image of the safe house. But would a sojourn at the Lazy L be any less stressful? She chanced a look at Jake's unreadable expression, then swallowed hard. "This isn't fair."

Zach shook his dark head. "Not fair is what Dr. Psycho will do to you if you don't take some time off."

Shelby jumped. "Dr. Psycho" was the nickname given to the department shrink. "Patterson wouldn't—"

"He'll pull your badge so fast your head'll spin if you try to spite him on this call. Is that what you want? To risk your career, everything you've worked for?" Zach's expression softened. "Admit it, Shel, it's been a rough assignment. Tougher nuts than you have cracked, so what's the harm in taking it easy at Club Med, here? You can lie by the pool and Jake will bring you margaritas."

"Every hour on the hour," Jake quipped. He looked up as Rosalita appeared with a tray. "But maybe you should start with that tea first."

Rosalita set the tray down on the coffee table, "tsking" between her teeth at the sight of Zach's eye. "You boys. If you were mine, I'd take a switch to you both."

Ignoring her, Jake took Shelby's elbow, firmly and expertly guided her back to a seat on the couch, then pressed a hot mug of tea into Shelby's cold hands.

"Drink up. It'll do you good," he said quietly. His fingers seemed as hot as flames against hers. "Mom always said there was no problem that couldn't be solved with a good cup of tea and a long think."

"So what's it going to be, Shel?" Zach demanded.

The fragrant steam from the mug warmed her face like a lover's kiss, but it could not squelch her dismay at the corner she found herself in.

"It seems I don't have a choice," she said between clenched teeth, feeling betrayed and, worse, *helpless.* Dammit, she was the victim here, and they were acting as though she were the criminal with no rights. Well, maybe she couldn't wiggle out of this predicament at the moment, but she'd accept the arrangement on her own terms or not at all.

Resolutely she lifted her chin. "I'd be pleased to accept your hospitality, Mr. Lattimer, if it's not too much trouble." She took a calming sip of tea.

"No trouble at all. But call me Jake." His dark eyes gleamed with a daunting spark of wicked devilment. "Or if you say it just right, I might even answer to 'buckaroo.'"

Shelby nearly choked on her drink. Did the cowboy have a sense of humor? Or was he merely needling her? She shivered, suddenly apprehensive.

Zach beamed with relief. "Thank God that's settled."

"Let's get some ice for that eye of yours, Zach." Rosalita shooed him toward the doorway. "Want some Mercurochrome for that busted lip, Jake?"

"In a minute. I should show Shelby to her room so she can get out of those wet clothes." His gaze dropped again briefly to the erect buds of her breasts poking against the damp knit shirt. Shelby's shivers dissolved in a flash of unexpected heat. His voice was gruff. "Maybe you'll want to rest a while before dinner."

At the mere suggestion, a wave of exhaustion washed over Shelby. To lie down, to be alone, to have the chance to wrestle the nightmare images that danced on the edges of her consciousness back into submission—it was a glimpse of paradise she couldn't resist. "Yes, I'd like that."

She rose unsteadily, and while she didn't protest when Jake again placed a supporting hand at her elbow, she couldn't prevent the tiny quiver that coursed through her body at his touch. She knew that he felt it, too.

Zach paused at the door, a relieved smile on his lips, but his eyes serious. "Thanks, Jake. I owe you."

Jake's hand tightened almost painfully on her arm, and his expression was suddenly so fierce Shelby quailed with foreboding.

"Brother," Jake said, his voice deadly quiet, "this makes two."

The sun was just going down after a very long, eventful summer day when Zach opened the front door of his Ft. Worth apartment. Neatly labeled boxes of Georgia's belongings stacked in unsteady towers filled the tiny entrance way. The appetizing smell of sautéed onions and the mournful twang of his favorite country music station drifted from the kitchen. Married life was wonderful.

"Zach?" A slim strawberry blonde in a dropped-waist

madras sundress rushed into the living room to meet him. She came up short, the hope in her blue eyes dying when she saw him. Then she threw herself into his arms. "Oh, Zach."

He kissed his new bride thoroughly, tasting the sweetness of her mouth. Breathless, she drew back, biting her lip in sympathy as her fingers gently touched his swollen eye.

"I guess this shiner means that Jake wasn't in a forgiving mood," Georgia said unhappily. "Oh, I'm so sorry—"

"Hush, sunshine, it's not bad." Zach dropped a kiss to her freckled nose. He grinned. "Nothing that a dose of your tender loving care can't cure."

She gave him a melting smile and stroked his mustache tenderly. "With pleasure, Officer. I just wish..."

Perching his chin on the top of her head, he wrapped his arms around her, longing to protect her. "Yeah, I know. But it's early days yet. Jake's still mad, but he'll get over it eventually."

"I tried to tell him, I really tried." Georgia's voice wobbled. "I never wanted to hurt him, Zach."

"I know, but it's me he's really sore at, not you."

"But to come between brothers—I can't stand it."

Zach pulled her down on the sofa, catching her shoulders so that he could look her in the eye. "We did the only thing we could do, you know that, don't you?"

"You're right, of course." Georgia drew a shuddering breath. "I think—I hope—that deep down Jake knows he didn't love me the way married people ought to. We were just a...a habit, like an old pair of boots."

"He'll figure out that his pride is bruised more than his heart. It's just going to take some time."

"And if he doesn't ever forgive us?" she asked.

"Then it's a price I'd pay a hundred times over to have you in my life, Georgia Lee Rawlings." Zach touched her silky hair with reverence and pulled her against his shoulder. "Jake will come around soon enough. Besides, he's got Shelby to contend with now." He shook his head, chuckling. "Man, she really gave him hell. This ought to be very interesting."

Georgia's peach-colored mouth made an O of amazement. "You're kidding. He punched you in the eye, then agreed to take her in?"

Zach grinned. "You didn't see what I did to his lip. He'll be eating soup tonight for sure. And, yes, Shelby's going to wait things out at the Lazy L. Neither she nor Jake were too happy about it when I left, though."

"I know you thought this was an ideal solution, but Shelby's still so rocky, Zach. Will she be all right?"

Zach sighed, trying to squelch the same niggling doubt. "She's safe, sunshine, and for the moment, that's all we can ask."

"So it's chicken noodle soup. What? You thought I was going to make you chew a steak with that fat lip?"

"No, soup's just fine, Rosie."

Fresh from the shower, Jake ducked his damp head to miss a copper skillet hanging from the overhead kitchen rack and peeked into Rosalita's steaming stock pot. Chunks of white chicken and fat homemade noodles floated in the golden, richly aromatic broth. Rosalita Perez would never stoop to serving something out of a can.

She and her husband, Earnesto, and their daughter lived in the housekeeper's apartment connected by a breezeway at the back of the house. Earnesto took care of the landscaping and maintenance chores around the ranch house, while Rosalita saw to the cooking and housekeeping for the Lattimer men and worked toward her history degree part-time. Earnesto had confided to Jake long ago that when his sweet *chica* was in one of her moods, you didn't go complaining about her dinner menu, not if you knew what was good for you.

But damn, Jake thought, his mouth was watering for a piece of red meat. Feeling much abused, he shook his shaggy head, and his shoulders slumped under his worn-out University of Texas football jersey. After the day he'd had, he wished he was back playing college ball for the Longhorns, but he'd have to settle for what he could get and be glad of it.

Trying not to look too morose, Jake picked up the tumbler holding the two fingers of bourbon he'd been nursing—the only thing in his original plan for this evening that he'd been able to accomplish—and walked around the kitchen island to perch on a heavy oak bar stool. Through the French doors, he could see that dusk had gathered, a single star appearing to announce the storm front had moved on. Dim security lights illuminated the lush shrubbery surrounding the terrace, and the underwater lights in the pool turned the water to translucent sapphire. Jake shifted his bare feet on the cool tiles and let a trickle of bourbon slide down his throat to heat his belly.

Yes, sir, he couldn't wait for this day to be over and he could turn in with last month's *National Geographic* or maybe his newest true crime novel. He grimaced at where his thoughts had taken him. He was a real live wire, all right. No wonder Georgia thought he was too dull to marry.

"Should I set supper in the dining room tonight?" Rosalita asked.

Her question brought Jake back to himself. They kept

up the formality when Ben was home, but Jake actually preferred eating in a more casual manner at the kitchen table in front of the big bay window. He shook his head. "No, I don't think so. Ms. Hartman…Shelby, that is, looked too worn-out to make a big deal out of supper. She might even prefer a tray in her room."

He'd given Shelby the upstairs guest room. The other bedroom and adjoining sitting area on that floor had been his parents', but they hadn't been used since Retha's death. Ben now preferred a downstairs room on the rear wing, one of the many improvements and additions that had been hammered on to the original modest Lattimer homestead through the years. Since Jake's own room adjoined the new downstairs office just off the living room, he'd opted to let Shelby have the entire second floor to herself for quiet and privacy.

She'd been surprisingly subdued when he'd shown her the room and brought up what he considered to be woefully inadequate luggage for even an overnight stay. But, standing in what she clearly considered to be defeat, her strained face nearly as white as the Battenburg lace coverlet covering the cherry four-poster bed, for an instant Shelby Hartman had looked more like an abandoned child than a tough cop.

A tremor of compassion touched Jake then, eliciting the age-old instinct to protect and defend. It certainly wasn't Shelby's doing that Zach had stabbed Jake in the back, and Jake knew it was wrong of him to take his hostilities out on her. He tasted regret, sorry that he'd been so hard on her, but was uncertain how to apologize without risking her ire again. Then she'd gathered herself up, thanked him curtly and closed the door in his face, leaving him with the impression of forest-colored eyes that were more than merely haunted. They were almost dangerous.

Jake thoughtfully fingered his split lip. What did he know about this strange woman he'd taken into his home under duress? Just that she was a valued friend of Zach's, which wasn't exactly a sparkling endorsement of her judgment or character in Jake's estimation. Other than that, all he knew was that she'd survived a traumatic assault and looked on the brink of either an explosion or a breakdown. Well, he'd given his word, and he'd see things through. Hopefully her stay at the Lazy L would be just as boring as she feared. Jake certainly hoped so.

Rosalita carefully set her stirring spoon onto a cow-shaped spoon rest. "What's she doing here, Jake? She's not really an old friend of the family's, is she?"

Jake decided Rosie had a right to know the truth. While he had his everyday duties to attend to, she would most probably be the one who'd have the most interaction with their "guest." Briefly, while Rosalita prepared a salad, he sketched the story Zach had told him.

"So you see the situation is pretty sensitive, Rosie," he said at last. "You'll have to keep this to yourself. If anybody asks, she's just someone visiting for a few weeks and that's all you know."

"Of course." Rosalita's dark brown eyes were luminous with sympathy as she carefully arranged wedges of tomato on top of an assortment of lettuce. "The poor thing. No wonder she's slept away the afternoon. Maybe we should just let her rest."

Jake took another sip of his drink, grimacing slightly at the liquor's burn. "No, she asked me to wake her about now. She made it clear she didn't want to disturb the household routine, so let's do our best to oblige her."

"Mama, is it supper yet? We're hungry."

Jake turned with a smile as four-and-a-half-year-old

Leza Perez appeared at the kitchen entrance, a limp cat caught in the loop of each arm.

"Almost, sweetheart," Rosalita replied. "Why don't you give the kitties their dinner then go wash your hands?"

"Okay. Hi, Jake."

"Hello, yourself, punkin."

The little mophead had a halo of raven curls and the biggest, brownest eyes Jake had ever seen. Dressed in tennis shoes and a cotton shorts set, Leza handled Elizabeth and Attila with no more concern than if they'd been two of her baby dolls. Surprisingly, the long-suffering cats allowed the child every liberty. While Elizabeth merely endured with an air of royal disdain, Attila actually had the temerity to purr, a sound like gravel in a tin can, but he broke it off with a silent hiss the moment he spotted Jake.

Jake bared his teeth back at the ornery animal. Leza carried the cats into the laundry room to their feeding dishes, and Jake heard the child's crooning answers to the animals' demanding yowls, then the rustle of the dry cat food bag. Within moments, Leza reappeared, darted across the kitchen and crawled up in Jake's lap for a hug.

"Did you have fun today?" Jake asked, situating her on his lap.

"Uh-huh." Leza's eyes gleamed. "Mama let me go swimming, and I played house, and Buddy Lester came and we ran races and watched videos and had popcorn. It was the best!"

"A fine day," Jake agreed solemnly, smiling at the way Leza cuddled against him, chattering like a little squirrel.

Jake felt a constriction around his heart. He liked all kinds of baby critters, especially kids. Children had been a big part of his and Georgia's plans. He wanted a family to fill up this big old house and someday inherit the Lazy L and the Lattimer legacy. If he'd married Georgia two years ago when the subject of marriage had first come up, instead of letting their engagement drag on and on, he might even now be sitting here with his own little girl on his lap. Now that dream was, at the very least, postponed. Just another black mark against Zach Rawlings.

Rosalita set the salad bowl on the table and began to take soup bowls down from the cabinet. "We need to call your Papa to the supper table, Leza," she said. "Jake, I suppose you should go wake Ms. Hartman."

"Is the lady still asleep, Mama?" Leza asked. "I *never* have to take a nap that long, even when I've been bad."

"I guess she was pretty tired, huh?" Jake laughed, ruffling the kid's curls and then setting her to her feet. "I'll go call her."

"Let me, let me!" Leza hopped in excitement. "I can do it."

"Okay. Just knock on her door and tell her it's time to eat."

"Okay." Leza disappeared toward the stairs in a minor thunder of sneakers.

Rosalita set bowls on the table and began to arrange crisp gingham napkins and silverware. She cast Jake a sly look. "I think it's pretty generous of you to help out this way, considering everything."

"You know I'm just a pushover for a damsel in distress," he said, his lips twisting. "Although Shelby would probably try to skin me alive if she heard me call her that. Actually, I've never met a woman who needed help less."

Rosalita made a small sound of disbelief. "And I think you've still got a lot to learn about women, my friend."

"Obviously. Just ask Georgia." Jake laughed harshly

and then downed the last of his whiskey in one gulp. "Listen, I'm so hungry I'll even eat noodles, so—"

A shrill shriek from overhead cut his words to slivers and turned his blood to ice. It came again and again, even more chilling, a child's cry wrought with absolute terror.

Jake stopped breathing, then his breath burst from him and he bolted for the stairs, Rosalita on his heels.

"God, no—Leza!"

Chapter Three

Shelby slammed the sides of her fists against the barn's exterior walls, echoes of the child's screams still ringing in her ears. Her hands were bleeding from the rough boards. It didn't matter. She couldn't feel anything except the rage and anguish that bubbled up from deep inside her. A cry of remorse tore from her throat, shattering the dark silence of the starlit sky. Down in the corral, phantom horses stomped and nickered uneasily.

Her heart thundered, and her breath roared in her ears, harsh, rasping, as if she'd run a thousand miles instead of just the short distance from the house into the sheltering shadows just beyond the barn's security light. Unable to form even the words of a curse, she made another guttural sound, pounding her hands against the splintery wood in an agony of frustration and deep regret.

To rise from a nightmare and spring like a tiger at the sinister presence threatening your very existence, only to realize—Shelby moaned. The child. Oh, God, the little girl!

"Don't." Large hands came from behind her, grabbing her fists, halting her self-inflicted punishment.

Shelby turned with a snarl born of pure, instinctual fear, pounding Jake Lattimer's broad chest with everything she had, bucking and jerking to free herself from his grasp. She hadn't heard him at all. He'd sneaked up on her, proving again she was a failure, unable to perform the job she'd been trained for. Adrenaline surged, overwhelming her already overloaded system so that she was only barely cognizant of who he was, all her survival energies focused on one thing only...escape.

"Stop it." The words commanded, yet contained no anger, no violence. Still, she flew at him. In an instant he turned her, clamping her back against his chest, enclosing her in a firm embrace, containing her struggles within the circle of well-muscled arms that could have been cast from steel. The feeling of helplessness was too much like what she'd felt during Salvatore's attack, and hysteria snapped at her, flinging her further into chaos. With a hiss, Shelby kicked at Jake's shin with her bare heels, tried to bite him.

"That's enough." Lifting her off her feet, he staggered, thrown off balance by her frantic struggles. His back connected with the barn wall, and he slid them both down to a seated position on the ground, pinning her half in his lap, his chin caught in the curve of her shoulder, his lip against her ear. "She's okay. Shelby, she's all right."

His words seemed to come from a great distance. Shelby's body heaved with dry, racking sobs, great gasps of air that left her unsatisfied, panicky.

"Breathe," he murmured. "Slowly, now. Leza's okay. Just scared her a bit, that's all. Wasn't your fault."

She wanted to believe him, but the picture of the little girl, her face blank with terror, thrown to the carpet by Shelby's instinctive self-defense, was an image that burned her brain with remorse. She hadn't even known there was a child in the house. When Rosalita and Jake arrived in answer to the little one's screams, Shelby had been too groggy, too stupefied to do more than watch the child rush into her mother's arms, before she'd fled Rosalita's angry, accusing eyes.

She had sworn to protect and defend, and yet Shelby knew she could have done irreparable harm to an innocent. The horror of it caused a painful quiver. She had to admit it; she was strung out, farther out on the ledge than she'd cared to admit, or even realized.

And that was the scariest thing of all.

Another shuddering breath racked her. She'd changed to a dry T-shirt and cutoffs earlier, and now her breasts strained against the Harley-Davidson eagle on the black cotton knit as she struggled against the iron-hard arm circling her rib cage. Her efforts to free herself were half-hearted, the emotion draining from her in an exhausting torrent, her throat constricting with tears, but her eyes dry.

"Easy there, angel face." Jake's voice was low and soothing. "There you go. Any more ruckus is liable to upset Lucy, you know. She's due to foal soon. Had a heck of a time breeding that little quarter-horse mare last year, that's why she's so late, but she ought to have a prize-winner. If it's a colt, I thought about calling him Little Ricky, 'cause I named his mama Lucille Ball on account of her having such a red coat. 'Course if it's a filly, maybe I'll call her Ethel...."

Jake's gravelly baritone was like a honeyed balm flowing over her frayed nerves. Her breathing grew deeper, slower. She caught the faintest smoky hint of whiskey as his lips pressed against her ear, and the warm bulk of him against her back cradled her protectively, his long legs framing hers, their bare feet brushing as they sat together on the fragrant, rain-dampened earth. By infinitesimal degrees, her tension began to dissipate, and his hold gentled, his arms folding around her to comfort now instead of control, his low words rambling.

"...see Orion's Belt there, Cassiopeia, Ursa Major. Did you know there's a nebula out there shaped like a dadgum horse's head? That's what they call it, the Horsehead Nebula, and—look there! A shooting star."

He pointed, using his chin to aim her face in the right direction so that just in time she saw the silvery trail of sparks before it vanished against the navy blue sky.

"That's good luck," he said, his beard-shadowed skin rasping pleasurably against her temple. "Make a wish on a falling star, my mama always told me, and it's sure to come true. Lot of things out there we don't know about, but probably none of 'em more powerful than wishes."

Listening to the calming cadence of his words, Shelby wasn't even aware that she'd quit struggling. Lying quiescent in Jake's arms, her heart found a regular tempo again. Her brain, so lately spinning out of control in crash-and-burn hysteria, now spiraled gently toward a soft landing.

A cowboy who believed in wishes. How bizarre. But her interest was captured, her thoughts distracted from the incident that had brought her here, and she listened intently, concentrating on words that somehow expelled demons even as they fascinated.

"Did you know some scientist actually created antimatter in his lab? Now they're saying there are whole universes of the stuff out there. Put matter and antimatter together, and poof!—pure energy. That'll be all she wrote for fossil fuels." A chuckle shook Jake's broad chest. "Pop will have a conniption fit if it makes our oil wells obsolete."

"He will?" she murmured. The conversation had been so one-sided, Shelby felt almost obligated to participate, but her gaze remained fixed overhead as if the blue-white sprinkling of stars was a signpost pointing the way home.

"Well, wouldn't you?" Jake replied. "Won't please the Campbell brothers, either. Of course, Logan has his New Orleans law practice, but Campbell Drilling is Russ's baby, now that their dad, Jack, is nearing retirement. Jack and Pop have been business associates for—well, gosh, since we were all in diapers."

"A long time."

"Hell, they're almost family, like cousins, I guess."

She sighed at the thought. Family, even an unofficial extended one, was something she'd desperately wished for as a kid, but no magic stars had answered her childish prayers. Limp with reaction, she floated in Jake's embrace, absorbing the essence of his maleness as she drank in the details of his family, luxuriating in the sensation of feeling protected, whole.

"Russ is the redheaded hell-raiser," Jake continued, "but it was me and Logan who used to butt heads most often. Had to teach the rich city kid a thing or two. He busted me a good one once in a while, though."

"About like Zach did today?"

"Naw, this little ole split lip is nothing, though maybe I could have used a stitch. Did you ever hear tell of that African tribe that uses giant ants for sutures? Just let the critter bite the wound closed, then pinch his head off and—"

Shelby found herself shaking her head in helpless amazement. "I was all wrong about you, cowboy."

"How's that?"

"You may be strong, but you're hardly the silent type, are you?"

A whisper of velvety mustache brushed her ear, and she sensed, rather than saw, his wide smile.

"Talking soft generally settles a restless herd of heifers."

"Should I moo?" she asked sweetly.

He laughed, his breath warm against her cheek. "Feeling better, are you?"

The world came back into focus with a crash. She was suddenly very conscious of the intimacy of their positions. Her backside nestled against his lap in a perfect fit, and his forearm brushed the underside of her breasts, raising a tingle that puckered her nipples and shot electricity to a place low in her belly. Worse than the involuntary physical chemistry that his blatant masculinity stirred, he'd seen her out of control, vulnerable in ways she found intolerable both as a cop and a woman. That he'd been the one to haul her back from the brink was vastly mortifying.

She stiffened, trying to draw away. "You can let me go now. I'm not going to fly apart again."

"It's okay if you do. Nobody around here to see you but me, and I think I can handle it."

If she found the seductive comfort of his embrace incredibly disturbing, his acceptance of her frailties was even more so. She was stronger, prouder than that. She straightened her spine. "Let me go."

"Yes, ma'am. Anything you say."

Jake released her and they both climbed to their feet, Shelby eyeing him warily in the shadowy light. She jumped when he took her hands, turning them so that he could inspect the scraped skin.

"Rosie's got some antiseptic in the kitchen."

He touched a splinter, and Shelby drew a careful breath, her fingers clenching. "The little girl—she's really all right?"

Jake let go of her hands. "Just had the wind knocked out of her."

"I—I'm sorry. I was dreaming—"

"Must have been pretty bad."

The horrific images rose again inside her mind's eye, and she shuddered violently. "The worst."

Jake brushed her hair aside and ran a fingertip along the necklace of bruises peeking from under the crew edge of her shirt. "About this?"

As badly as she hated to reveal such weakness, there didn't appear to be any way to deny it, so she nodded, her throat too thick to articulate an answer.

"No wonder you came up fighting," he murmured.

Her short bark of laughter was self-denigrating. "You didn't bargain for a crazy female, did you, cowboy? I shouldn't be here. I tried to tell you and Zach—"

"Not your fault, I said." His tone was firm.

Shelby swallowed hard, then admitted her worst fear. "It could happen again. What if I really hurt someone next time? What if—?"

"Look, I sent Leza up without thinking. My mistake entirely. You're entitled to be a bit jumpy, and anyway, even half-asleep, you had enough presence of mind not to really hurt her. You'll find a way to make it up to her, and Leza's not the type of kid to hold a grudge. So no harm done, angel face."

The careless endearment brought an uncomfortable warmth to her cheeks. Finding herself a danger to the household was almost as unsettling as the unwelcome tug of attraction she felt in the pit of her stomach. Besides, it was too weird. She'd never experienced this kind of chemistry with Zach, so how could his mirror image have this effect on her? She had better sense than to acknowledge any such ridiculous notion, much less act on it. No sir, she wasn't jumping from the frying pan into the fire like that. "I should leave."

"We've already covered this territory." Jake cupped her elbow with old-fashioned, courtly courtesy. Golden bars of light beckoned them from the ranch house windows, a picture-perfect image that in Shelby's mind represented all that was unattainable.

"Come on, Shelby. A bowl of chicken soup and some downtime on the Lazy L is just what the doctor ordered."

She tipped her chin at him, dredging up the last of her defiance to issue a warning. "Or a prescription for even more trouble, cowboy."

"Well, ma'am," he drawled, undaunted, "sometimes a girl just has to take her chances, doesn't she?"

A mockingbird with an attitude drove Shelby from her bed the next morning. The noisy intruder fussed and harangued on the windowsill overlooking the detached carport until in self-defense Shelby abandoned her rose-strewn pillows and headed for the guest room's adjoining bath. She could tune out all kinds of city noise—sirens, cursing motorists, trash cans being slammed to the sidewalk—so how come one boisterous little featherbrain had the power to drive her slap crazy?

Shelby threw cold water on her face, then glared at her bleary-eyed reflection in the mirror. It was clear country life was not agreeing with her. To hell with nature. She needed a fix of exhaust fumes and man-made noise.

By the time she pulled on jeans and the same black T-shirt she'd worn previously—her wardrobe sadly lacked in variety—and ran her fingers through her hair, her head was beginning to pound from hunger. She hadn't exactly been interested in food or further company after last night's episode, so she'd taken up Jake's offer of a tray in her room. It now sat on the cherry dresser, the half-eaten bowl of chicken soup cold, the noodles congealed in unappetizing clumps.

But the thought of facing Jake Lattimer again, not to mention Rosalita and her daughter, was so daunting she toyed with the idea of simply finishing the soup. With another glance at the gelatinous mass, she shook her head. No, even *she* wasn't that brave.

It didn't do her battered self-esteem any good to realize that she'd totally lost it—again. Shelby wandered around the room, straightening the white, embroidered comforter and shams, stacking the books on the bedside table. She folded the soft-with-age Lone Star quilt, then sat on the foot of the four-poster bed with the blanket clutched to her chest like a shield. But nothing could shield her from her own self-castigating thoughts.

She knew that she wasn't herself. Had she ever been so argumentative, so loud-mouthed, uncivil and downright insulting? While she wasn't afraid to voice her opinion, she generally was able to do so tactfully, diplomatically. She rubbed the tender place at the base of her throat. Salvatore's attack had changed her, and she didn't like the manic woman who flew off the handle at the least provocation and whose lack of emotional control made her dangerous not only to herself but to others. She couldn't perform as an effective law enforcement officer like this. That, in and of itself, was reason enough to put the bastard away for good.

She prayed to God that these changes within herself were only a temporary reaction to trauma. Surely if she were good enough, strong enough, she could put these feelings behind her?

But could she blame everything on Salvatore? Somehow, she'd made a miscalculation, done or said something—she had no idea what—that had tipped him off. Had she been overconfident when she'd convinced her partner, Harve Spaulding, as well as the captain not to end the surveillance, arguing that she could handle it, finally winning out against her superior's better judgment? Or had she been too timid, not forcing her hand that final time, failing to call for backup and make the arrest when she could have? Had she had something to prove that clouded her judgment at a critical moment? Some lunatic notion of showing she could do a better job than any man, could gutsy it out to the last with the best of them? Well, she'd gotten her comeuppance in a big way.

Shelby massaged her throbbing temple, unable to come up with answers. But at least that part of it was done. Now the only way to bring Salvatore to justice was to keep herself safely out of the line of fire until it was time to testify. She had to quit raging like a spoiled kid at the circumstances in which she found herself and buckle down to do the job. Zach had her best interests at heart, or else he would never have brought her here. And Jake had been kind in his own way, despite his obvious reluctance to become involved. The least she could do was cooperate.

That was it, Shelby told herself. Just think of it as another undercover assignment. She'd played the part of barmaid at Salvatore's favorite watering hole, she could just as easily put on the role of grateful guest. She'd keep her distance and her nose clean. Come hell or high water, there'd be no more panicky incidents and certainly no more close encounters with the hunky rancher, even if he could resurrect her libido with that slow, knowing smile. Not even if within the protection of his strong arms she'd felt safe for the first time since the attack.

Shelby shook off that memory, telling herself it was just another aberration perpetrated by her overwrought nervous system. Jake certainly had better things to do with his time and energy than to mollycoddle a beat-up cop. Besides, they were really from different worlds, the dissimilarity in privilege and family and lifestyle an insurmountable obstacle. She hadn't even been good enough for a middle-class fiancé, so what could she possibly have in common with a man who'd been born with the proverbial silver spoon in his mouth?

Men! Shelby blew out a harsh breath. *That* was a complication she certainly didn't need. Hadn't she learned her lesson with Gary? He'd been in the class ahead of her at the academy, swept her off her feet with roses and all kinds of romantic to-do, promised her his eternal devotion, talked about houses and kids—then left her flat for someone with a better pedigree. It had taken her a long time to get over the devastation of that betrayal, but she'd learned a valuable lesson about never letting her guard down, and it had served her well since.

Shelby placed the quilt on the bed and went to pick up her tray. Hunger was a great incentive, and she couldn't hide out in this room forever, no matter how pleasant and comfortable. Since a thoughtful guest bussed her own dishes, she could at least start making amends in this small way.

Out in the upstairs hall, Shelby paused. The house was quiet, only the peaceful chirr of the air-conditioning disturbing the silence. Curiosity, a detective's stock in trade, pushed her toward the other door opening onto the landing. She balanced the tray on her hip and peeked inside, finding a small sitting room furnished with wing chairs in front of a tiny fireplace and a black-bordered floral needle-point rug. Through an archway lay another larger bed-room, immaculately furnished, but with an air of disuse. Satisfied, Shelby turned to pull the door shut again, then gasped in surprise and delight.

"Oh, my goodness." She heard the awe in her own voice.

Without conscious volition, her feet carried her inside and she absently set the tray aside on a small side table, her eyes never leaving the wall of glassed bookcases. But it wasn't books that filled every crevice and cranny, it was dolls. Hundreds of them, it seemed to Shelby, gazing back at her with blue eyes and brown eyes, china baby dolls whose painted-on eyes were closed in contented slumber, exotic oriental ladies in kimonos and Kabuki makeup.

Enchanted, Shelby drifted closer, admiring the bride doll with her puffy illusion veil, the collection of vintage Raggedy Anns, Bo Peep and Mary and her lamb from storyland, regal Madame Alexander princesses, Bye-Lo babies, even Scarlett O'Hara dressed in Miss Sue Ellen's green velvet portieres, right down to the gold tassels.

The collection was a little girl's delight, a big girl's pride, and it had obviously been acquired over a period of time with an eye to both investment and enjoyment and a real sense of humor. Sitting next to an exquisite antique French porcelain baby in a christening dress trimmed with convent-made laces was a naked Kewpie with bowed lips. A first-issue Barbie with pouffed bangs and ponytail stood on her tiny high heels beside a faceless cornhusk baby with dried corn silk braids. A true-to-life Shirley Temple with golden corkscrew curls held court over a trio of Hummel boys dressed in green suede *Liederhosen*. Very expensive collector's-edition porcelain sat next to five-and-dime plastic. And while some of the collection stood in pristine, just-out-of-the-box splendor, others showed the ravages of many years of loving hugs from countless little girls.

Shelby felt a smile tug at her lips and grow into a grin. What a truly wonderful and magical surprise to find tucked away in the cowboy's ranch house. From what Zach had shared about his twin, she knew the collection had to have belonged to Jake's adoptive mother, who'd passed away from heart problems some years back. Shelby knew instantly that she would have liked Mrs. Lattimer.

A lot, she decided, with a small intake of breath, because there...*there,* nestled beside a Mrs. Santa with cherry cheeks, was a blue-eyed baby with yellow curls just like the one Shelby herself had once loved a very long time ago.

"Barbara Ann," Shelby breathed, her palm pressed against the glass pane, "how did you get here?"

There was no answer from the Cupid's-bow mouth, and, of course, this wasn't her original Barbara Ann, but Shelby had no control over the wave of nostalgia that swept through her. *Her* Barbara Ann had been the recipient of countless whispered secrets, the witness to floods of fearful tears, the only stable friend in a world that kept changing too rapidly for a little lost girl to keep up with. She'd heard Shelby's nightly prayers for her real mom and dad to come and find her, and had been the confidant who'd known all Shelby's hopes and dreams. But even that had been taken from Shelby when a resentful foster brother fed the poor baby to the yard dogs out of spite, then pitched Barbara Ann's chewed-up remains into a burning trash barrel.

Shelby probed the still-tender memory of that unhealed

wound. She'd learned to grieve and that trusting wasn't safe and that tears were useless at the tender age of six. In fact, she could count on one hand the times she'd cried since then. Of course, she hadn't let Barbara Ann's murder go unpunished, and the disappearing homework, sand in the sheets and laxative tablets in the culprit's oatmeal had finally resulted in yet another transfer to yet another indifferent foster care family. It had been a price she'd gladly paid, but she'd never owned or loved another doll after that.

Gazing at this other Barbara Ann, Shelby smiled to herself, knowing it was silly, but feeling rather comforted all the same to think that just maybe her best friend had found her way into this doll heaven. The thought buoyed her spirits, and she turned to retrieve the tray in a better state of mind.

A framed picture sat on the table, and Shelby hesitated, then picked it up. A tall, beaming man with a broad-brimmed Stetson and string tie stood with his arm around the waist of a slender, sweet-faced woman in a flowered frock. They smiled proudly at a wiry dark-haired boy of about seven running to show them an overflowing Easter basket.

Shelby examined the merriment in young Jake's dark eyes, wondering at the process that had turned this exuberant child into the forceful, deliberate man he was today. What secrets hid behind this snapshot of a happy family? And what had Jake Lattimer felt when he'd come face-to-face with not only a twin brother, but the fact that he'd been given away by his birth mother to adoptive parents? Shelby's mouth twisted ruefully as she put down the picture and took up the tray again. She only hoped Jake wasn't too stupid to realize how truly lucky he'd been.

Shelby carried the tray downstairs to the deserted, pristine kitchen. A plate of buttermilk biscuits sat on the bar next to containers of homemade plum and crab apple jelly and a carafe of coffee. Shelby helped herself, then noticed through the banks of French doors that Rosalita and her daughter were outside at the pool in the midst of what appeared to be a swimming lesson. Mouth suddenly dry, Shelby washed the last bit of biscuit down with a final swallow of coffee, straightened her shoulders and went to do what was right.

Shelby arrived at the poolside steps just as Leza bobbed to the surface like a young Esther Williams in a spray of water and pink polka dots. The air was already warm with the promise of intense summer heat, and faintly scented with chlorination. Rosalita, wearing a screeching crimson two-piece that showed off luscious curves and golden tanned skin, caught her daughter under the arms with a smile and a generous serving of praise.

"That's my girl. What a great torpedo. You'll be swimming in the Olympics if you keep this up."

"Good morning." Shelby squatted on the concrete apron of the pool, her heart sinking when Leza took one look, then clutched her mother's neck. "Ah—" Shelby cleared her throat. "I believe I owe you both an apology for last night. I didn't mean to knock you down or scare you, Leza. I'm truly sorry."

The little girl's eyes were very wide and solemn. "Mama 'splained. You thought the boogeyman caught you, huh?"

Catching Rosalita's eye, Shelby gave a soft huff of laughter as the color mounted in her cheeks. "That's about the size of it, kiddo. I hope you'll forgive me."

"That's okay." Dimpling, Leza tugged on her mother's braid. "It happens to me all the time, huh, Mama?"

"You'll grow out of it," Rosalita said easily. "But Shelby should know you were only supposed to knock on her door. If missy hadn't been so nosy—" She poked a tickling finger in her daughter's midsection, evoking a flurry of giggles.

"Still, I don't usually make a habit of mugging little girls, I assure you. It won't happen again, Mrs. Perez."

"Call me Rosie." The housekeeper smiled, her dark eyes friendly again as she assessed Shelby's appearance. "You need some sun, honey. Vitamin D is great for whatever ails you. Why don't you join us?"

Shelby looked longingly at the blue water. She swam regularly at the "Y" and found the exercise a great stress reliever. A few hard laps would probably do her a world of good. "I didn't bring a suit—"

"There's a selection in the pool house for guests," Rosalita said, indicating the spacious, awning-hung building at the far end of the terrace. Next to the pool house, forming the fourth side of the courtyard that enclosed the pool, was a modest apartment attached to the rear wing by a breezeway, which, from the assortment of tricycles, riding toys, and pint-size table and chairs sitting at its front door, was where the Perezes lived. "It's time for a juice break, anyway, and I'll wager you haven't had much breakfast."

"One of those delicious biscuits of yours," Shelby admitted.

"Oh, that's not enough." Clucking like a mother hen, Rosalita led Leza up the steps out of the water. "We have to fatten you up while you're here. Why don't you change while we fetch some goodies?"

Shelby couldn't resist, nor could she think of a reason why she should. She grinned. "You're on."

Within short order, Shelby had slipped on a royal blue

maillot and was cleaving the cool water with her unspectacular but efficient crawl stroke. Rosalita and Leza returned bearing a plate of fruit and sweet rolls and a frosty pitcher of orange juice, then joined her in the water. After a while Shelby was gratified when Leza allowed her to catch her as she "torpedoed" between the two women. The weight of the little girl perched on her hip was a surprisingly pleasant burden.

"Look who's watching us," Leza piped suddenly.

Shelby's heart jerked in a spurt of involuntary apprehension, but when she turned to follow Leza's pointed finger, expecting to find her host, it was only to discover they were being inspected by two pairs of feline eyes from beneath a variegated pittosporum shrub. She gave herself a mental kick in the pants at the twinge of disappointment.

"Those darn cats." Rosalita frowned. "Your papa is going to skin them for sure if they dig up his bedding plants again, Leza. Go chase them out of—what in the world have they got?"

"Betsy!" Leza dog-paddled to the step, climbed out, then, trailing water, marched in high indignation toward the pittosporum. Dropping to her knees, her polka-dotted bottom wiggled as she grappled beneath the bush. "Let her go, you!"

The guilty pair bolted in two different directions, and Leza dragged a very old, very dirty, and very bedraggled cloth doll into the brilliant sunlight. "Mama, look what they did!"

"Leza Antoinette Perez! You're the one who left Betsy outside months ago," Rosalita said, climbing from the pool and reaching for towels.

Leza wailed, "But, Mama—"

"Come on, *chica,* we'll throw her in the washer and

see what happens. It's time to get out, anyway. You've had enough sun and I've got a big exam tomorrow.''

Squeezing the moisture from her hair, Shelby climbed from the pool, grabbed a towel and a glass of juice and plopped down in a lounge chair. "You're in school?"

Toweling Leza down, Rosalita nodded. "Getting my degree in history one course at a time. Jake's helping me through Medieval Literature this summer, Lord bless him.''

"He is?" Shelby's eyebrows lifted in surprise.

"The man's practically a walking encyclopedia. Reads all the time. He got that from his mother, Ben says. Anyway, Jake's the closest thing to a Renaissance Man I'll ever meet.''

Shelby casually straightened the towel over her chair cushions. "Where is he?"

"Good question." Rosalita picked up Betsy between two fingers, her nose wrinkling. "He gets up with the sun, talks with Don, the cow boss, puts in some time with whatever's going on—hay baling today, I think—and then heads back to the office to deal with the rest of what needs doing. He said something about having to go into Ft. Worth later, I believe." Rosalita lowered her voice to a confidential hush. "I think he's keeping himself extrabusy because of the way the wedding was called off and all."

"He must have been crushed," Shelby murmured.

"You'd think so, wouldn't you?" Rosalita's smile turned enigmatic. She patted her daughter's bottom. "Scoot, *chica.*"

"'Bye, Shelby." Leza danced over to Shelby's chair, surprised her with a spontaneous hug, then headed for home. "See you later!"

"Sure thing." Touched, Shelby had to swallow hard with the proof that she'd been unequivocally forgiven. An idea occurred to her, the thought of a little something that would seal their new friendship. "She's a real sweetheart, Rosie."

"You think so, huh? I'll let you baby-sit while you're here," Rosalita replied cheerfully, wrapping a towel around herself. "You'll change your mind in a hurry."

Shelby laughed. "I doubt it. I'm smitten. And I'd be glad to, anytime."

"It's a deal." She tossed Shelby a tube of sunscreen. "Here, you'll need this. Enjoy the sun. I'm thinking of something cool, like a chef's salad, for lunch, and then you can have another long siesta."

Shelby grimaced. "I'm not accustomed to inactivity."

"It'll do you good. Put some roses back in your cheeks," Rosalita said heartily. "Frankly, you look as though you could use a little pampering."

"I'll become a slug. I mean, I'm not the 'Life of Riley' type. What do people do out here in the middle of no-where, anyway? How do you keep from going stir-crazy?"

Rosalita grinned. "There's always plenty to do around this place. You'd better be careful what you wish for."

"When do I start?"

Rosalita raised a restraining hand. "Oh, no, you don't. Jake would have my hide. He gave orders you're not to lift a finger. So just soak up a few rays and relax and enjoy being a guest."

"Easy for you to say," Shelby grumbled, but dutifully began rubbing in sunscreen.

"Atta girl." Rosalita grinned and headed for her apartment. "I'll call you when lunch is ready."

Shelby lay back on the lounger. "I guess you can't fight city hall."

She had to admit that the sun felt wonderful on her pale

skin, and her muscles were pleasantly tired from her exertions. Behind her closed lids, she could see golden spangles. She wished briefly for her sunglasses, then decided it was too much trouble to go inside to her room to retrieve them. She gave a sigh of pure enjoyment. Maybe masquerading as a guest wasn't going to be such a tough assignment, after all.

"You'd better watch out, city girl."

Shelby jerked from a light doze at the husky words, opening her startled eyes to run headlong into Jake's chocolate brown gaze. There was something wicked dancing in them, some secret amusement that twisted his shapely mouth beneath its seductively soft brush of mustache. His gaze dropped, roamed over her sun-warmed limbs and tight maillot, and she felt it with a jolt, just as assuredly as though he'd actually touched her, caressed her curves with his callused palms, stroked her skin with his strong fingers.

"Watch out for what?" she asked in a voice that was barely a whisper.

His dark eyes gleamed. "Didn't anyone ever tell you that you could get burned?"

Chapter Four

"It's happened before, cowboy. But not this time."

Jake watched the softness leave Shelby's eyes, change from a gentle, drowsy green to the crystalline impenetrability of topaz. The sudden loss was like a kick in the gut.

He hooked a thumb in his jeans belt loop. "How can you be so certain?"

Reaching for a tube of sunscreen, Shelby's tone was offhand, her smile mocking, daring him to contradict her. "I'm as well armored as an armadillo in his shell, and don't you forget it."

There it was again. The gauntlet flung at his feet by this mere wisp of a woman, and despite everything he'd promised himself lying in a restless bed the night before, all that was male within him leaped to the challenge.

Jake caught a slender ankle within the circle of his fingers and pushed her legs over on the lounger so he could sit down. The brim of his hat shaded his eyes, making it easier to judge her expression as he rubbed the pad of his thumb against the notch of delicate bone. "Overconfidence has been the downfall of many a well-laid plan."

Her defensive hackles rose with the arch of her eyebrows, and he knew that he'd pushed a button somehow.

"I don't make the same mistake twice," she snapped, raising her knee to free herself from his touch.

They weren't talking about sunburn, and they both knew it. He'd seen something last night that she hadn't wanted to reveal, had shared secrets and recognized a vulnerability within her that touched him despite his best intentions. Hell, his mother's delicate health had trained him from an early age to protect his womenfolk, to slay their dragons and dry their tears. How was he supposed to react when instincts and practice kicked in like that? When Shelby had fit into his arms as if she were born just for him, when her trust and acceptance for those brief moments had made him feel ten feet tall?

Well, he was smart enough to know that he'd been emotionally battered lately, too, and that maybe his reaction to Shelby's nearness had been a result of his being too susceptible to being wanted and needed by damsels in distress. Lying there awake, remembering the weight of her in his hands and the scent of her skin, he'd reminded himself she'd already made it clear she didn't believe in chivalry. And he wasn't the kind of cowpoke who'd waltz up to a mustang just to see if he could get his teeth kicked in. There just wasn't any profit in it.

So he'd decided to keep his distance, play the part of congenial host, then wave her merrily on her way when her stay was done. Only, on his way to change before going into town, he'd seen her out here by the pool and made an instant detour. And instead of the few courteous, innocuous remarks he'd planned, he'd ticked her off—big time.

Well, Hoss, wasn't this what you wanted? After a night of wrestling with his instincts, he'd have thought using Shelby's hostility to derail any further fancy on his part was the easy way out of a sticky situation, but now he wasn't so sure.

Reclining on the lounger, her curves encased by the damp bathing suit, she was slender and delicate, her skin creamy and silken, an utterly feminine creature whose thick lashes threw mysterious shadows across her sun-rosy cheekbones. Her wet hair was beginning to dry in the sun, tendrils brushing her square jaw, following the line Jake's fingers itched to trace. Her tough cockiness, the "to hell with you" attitude of a born street fighter was a thousand times more intriguing to him than the sweet flirtatiousness he was accustomed to in the country girls he'd always squired about. And if Georgia had been all sweetness and sugar to him, Shelby was spice, singeing tongue and fiery psyche that filled him with a craving to savor more and explore further.

Of course, Jake thought with a wry twist of his lips, that's probably what Lucretia Borgia's victims thought as they swallowed her poison.

"What are you laughing at?" Shelby demanded, her lush mouth compressing suspiciously.

"The absurdity of the human condition, ma'am. My own, especially."

"A student of existentialism, are you, cowboy?"

"Only when the moon is full." Grinning, he rose to his feet. "And while I'd love to sit here jawin' philosophy with a half-naked mermaid, I've got to change and fuel up the chopper if I'm going to make my one o'clock appointment with our Ft. Worth banker."

Her eyes widened. "You fly your own helicopter?"

"Sure. Have for years."

"Why?"

Jake swiped a finger over his mustache and shrugged. "I hate fighting traffic almost as much as I hate cities."

Shelby swung her feet over the side of the lounger. "Just as I thought. The family's richer than God and you're the overindulged only son. As they say, 'nice work if you can get it.'"

The barb struck a sore spot, and a knot jumped in Jake's jaw. Bending, he caught her chin in his palm, lifting her face so that they glared at each other eye to eye. "You don't have the first notion of what my life is like, angel. I don't take credit for the gifts that have come my way, but I sure as hell take my stewardship of them seriously."

She had the grace to look abashed, and the color rose to her cheeks. "You're right. That was uncalled for. I'm sorry."

"Just remember you can't know the demons that ride another's soul." He dropped his hand and straightened with an inward curse. Yep, his own best instincts had been right on the money. He had more sense than to cuddle up with a female with more prickles than a cactus and a tongue as thorny as a dewberry vine. It was damned dangerous to feel sympathy for a woman who'd just as soon cut you off at the knees as look at you.

"I'm going to town now," he bit out. "Anything you need while I'm there?"

"Uh..." Shelby chewed at her lip.

Jake released an impatient huff of breath. "Just spill it, will you? I've got to go."

"Well, if it wouldn't be too much trouble..."

"What?"

"A doll."

Jake's jaw dropped at the unexpected request. "A doll?"

"For Leza," Shelby said hastily. "We made up, but I thought maybe a little present would really set things right."

Jake nodded. "One doll. Can do."

Shelby stood eagerly, her smile lighting up her face, erasing the telltale signs of stress, and practically knocking Jake's socks off in the process. "Make sure it's a baby doll. You know, an infant, not a toddler. I'll get my purse—"

"Ah…" He gave a little shake of his head to clear it, then waved her off as he made a strategic retreat. "Don't bother with that now," he said gruffly. "We'll settle up later, okay?"

"Yes. Thanks. And, Jake?"

His boots paused on the concrete pool surround. "Yeah?"

"Try to get her one with yellow hair."

Jake touched the brim of his hat and headed for the French doors. "Will do."

"Look at a big department store," she called after him.

Hand on the knob, he glanced back over his shoulder and was caught by the wistful expression on her face. His tone gentled. "My mother collected dolls. Don't worry, I know all the best stores."

"Curls. Make sure she has curls."

"Curls it is."

"Jake!" Shelby wrapped a towel around herself, then hurried after him. "Blue eyes. She has to have blue eyes. Real ones that open and close. With lashes."

He was certain that she had no idea of the unguarded earnestness on her expressive face. Had she once been a little girl who had loved—or wanted to love—such a baby

doll? With a sudden clarity of sight, Jake knew that somehow a broken heart had been involved. Dammit! He didn't
want to feel anything, didn't want his heartstrings tugged
by the vision of a tiny towheaded girl with a dirty face
and skinned knee who desperately needed someone to
love her. He swallowed.

"I can see that it's very important. I won't forget."

Shelby was beside him now, half in and half out of the
doorway, her hand on his arm. "Make sure she has a pink
dress. With ruffles, if possible. Oh, and a bonnet—"

Jake caught her upper arms. "Look, I'll take care of it.
Don't you trust me?"

"With something as important as this?" she asked, one
eyebrow arched skeptically. "About as far as I can throw
you, cowboy."

Jake laughed, and skinned a knuckle down her cheek.
"Smart girl."

Struggling to hold on to her towel, she slapped his hand
away. "I'm not a girl. I'm a full-grown woman."

Jake let his grin take on an element of lasciviousness.
"Yup. That's pretty hard to miss."

She made a sound of disgust and stepped around him
into the corridor. "Oh, grow up, cowboy."

"Sound advice from the woman who's so concerned
about a certain toy doll."

"It's for Leza." Antagonism turned her eyes to emerald. "Aw, just forget it." She stomped toward the stairway.

"I said I'd take care of it, and I will."

"Never mind. I'd rather be beholden to a rattlesnake,"
she said. At the base of the stairs, she paused and sent
him a searing glare. "And for your information, cowboy,
I am *not* half-naked."

Jake swept off his hat and gave her a deep bow.

"Ma'am, as your host, it'd be my pleasure to help arrange whatever stage of undress you desire."

Her mouth gaped open, then snapped shut. "I take it back. You're more like your brother than I thought."

With that, she turned and stalked up the stairs. Staring after her, Jake wondered whether that parting shot was a compliment or an insult.

By the time supper had come and gone that evening, Shelby was beginning to feel the day would never end. Exchanging a hospital room for this glorified prison wasn't exactly the bargain Zach had led her to believe it would be.

After crossing swords with Jake, the day had taken a definite downward turn. Neither books nor television held her interest, and she'd had enough sun. A nap didn't refresh her, and a walk down the neat, board-fenced lane gave her a glimpse of horses she didn't care to ride and disinterested Angus cattle who couldn't be bothered to turn their attention from chewing their cuds to the blond intruder scowling at them over the fence. To her disgust, she found herself listening for the beat of helicopter blades, and as her restlessness grew, the tension in her neck muscles returned.

She'd shared the evening meal with the Perezes. Earnesto, Rosie's handsome Texican husband, had a voice like Ricardo Montalban and a penchant for laughter and teasing. He'd talked about planting geraniums and phlox and sweet William, but since flowers were a subject with which Shelby had little experience, his enthusiastic conversation flew over her head like salvos that left her cowering in the foxhole of her ignorance. And then Rosie wouldn't even let her help wash the supper dishes.

Now she prowled the living room like a tiger in a cage,

picking up a magazine, then discarding it, touching a family picture here, running her hand over the oriental vase there on the mantel. It was too early to seek her bed, and she felt fidgety, at loose ends, detached from her own life in a way that was faintly alarming.

She wondered what had detained Jake, then chastised herself for her interest, insisting inwardly that she was only concerned with whether or not, despite their altercation, he'd picked up the doll for Leza. Rosie had indicated his not showing up for the evening meal was nothing unusual, that sometimes he even stayed in town overnight if business demanded. For a man who loved wide-open spaces and disliked the city so intensely, it seemed a curious thing. But perhaps he'd met a lady friend for dinner, someone more than willing to help the wealthy rancher forget his troubles. Or maybe he'd decided it was time to see Georgia?

Shelby frowned, feeling more disturbed than was warranted at the thought. Heck, he was practically a stranger, so what did she care about the state of his emotions? But she knew to her sorrow the effort and time it took to recover from a lost love. And she had to admit her behavior had been pretty hard on a man who was nursing a broken heart. Maybe she ought to cut him some slack. Of course, he could be a little nicer, too.

Flopping down on the leather sofa, she blew out an impatient breath and pulled a hand through her hair. This being the "ideal guest" business was definitely grating on her nerves. She was accustomed to the demands of her job, the routine of the station house, the paperwork, joking around and being one of the boys. There were other cases she'd been following, and a seminar on counseling juvenile offenders she'd meant to attend, not to mention mail to read, bills to pay—and here she sat like a lump on a log while Salvatore was out there somewhere planning her demise.

For the first time Shelby allowed that thought to sink in. A shiver rippled over her skin, and she rubbed her arms as though she'd felt a winter's chill. With most offenders you knew that it was circumstances or greed or drugs that brought them low, but Gus Salvatore was the first criminal she'd encountered who enjoyed inflicting suffering, as though it were some sort of sport reserved just for psychopaths.

Memory resurrected a vision of steel-colored eyes, as flat and pitiless and deadly as a cobra's. Shelby's breathing became choppy. She hated hiding out like a coward, waiting for the snake to strike, as terrorized as a mouse trapped in the serpent's den. But to face him again, to pit her will to survive against his desire for her death—she shuddered, her heart freezing with fear, not only fear of Salvatore, but fear of her own inability to protect herself. Oh, she talked a good game, but could she really have gone home to her solitary apartment? Could she meet a stranger on the street now with the same confidence as before? She didn't know. She'd grown up tough to survive, but she'd never doubted her capacity for courage until now. She wondered bleakly if she'd ever feel safe again.

The shrill peal of a telephone somewhere close made her jump. She pressed her hand to her thumping heart, only to find that her shirt was damp with sweat, and she cursed softly to herself as the phone broke off in midring. She stood abruptly, wiping the dampness from her upper lip with fingers that shook.

"Shelby?"

She whirled at Rosalita's quiet voice. "Yes!"

"Oh, I'm sorry, did I startle you?" The housekeeper's brown eyes were contrite.

"No, that's all right," Shelby denied with a shaky laugh. "I'm still a little edgy, I guess."

"B vitamins, that's what you need for nerves," Rosalita said sagely. "And red lipstick. Nothing like red lipstick for giving a woman confidence. It'll really perk you up. I'll get you some first thing tomorrow."

"Oh, no, really. I'm fine." Shelby shook her hair back with a wry grimace. "I'm not big on makeup, as you can see."

"Sweetie, with that face, you don't need it, but it never hurts a girl to enhance what Mother Nature's bestowed on her." Rosalita folded her arms and examined Shelby with an arched eyebrow. "A little mascara and liner, a pair of diamond drops and a slinky black dress and...my, my, my, you'll have all the ranch hands panting for sure."

Shelby laughed. "Believe me, that's not high on my list of priorities."

"Got yourself a fella somewhere?"

"Uh, no, but—"

Rosalita winked. "I have it on good authority that the 'young master' of this here estate is available again."

Shelby went crimson. "Rosie, for goodness sake."

"Well, when the opportunity's staring you right in the face..."

"Believe me, I've got better things to do than run after a jilted cowboy," Shelby said.

"He's a great guy."

"He's a jerk."

"You could do a lot worse."

"I barely know the man."

"You're best friends with his brother. That's a head start."

Shelby knew she was red from throat to scalp. "So? He hates his brother. That makes me about as popular as a polecat on a Sunday school picnic with Jake. Besides, we have nothing in common."

"Opposites attract."

"No, no, no." Shelby shook her head adamantly. "I am *not* interested in the man. In *any* man. I'm here strictly under duress, and you're a woman with a wild imagination. End of discussion. I mean it, Rosie. Not another word or I'll start packing."

Rosalita pursed her lips. "Touchy, aren't we?"

"I've got reason to be, remember?" Shelby muttered.

Rosalita's face sobered. "So you have. Sorry, Shelby. Don't pay any attention to me. I like to tease as much as Earnesto sometimes."

"That's okay. Forget it."

"Sure. Anyway, the telephone's for you."

Shelby looked up, surprised. "Me?"

Rosalita nodded and pointed to the hallway leading from the living room into the side wing of the house. "You can take it through there in Jake's office."

"Hello?" Shelby said, unsure who was calling.

"Hey, partner, how's it going?"

A moment later Shelby let go a sigh of relief at the familiar sound of Zach's voice. "You gotta spring me from this joint, Mugsy."

"Not that bad already?"

Shelby scanned the well-appointed office with its built-in file cabinets and shelves cluttered with books of all descriptions, from encyclopedias to the latest best-seller, cattle-breeding awards, Aledo High School and UT football trophies, and a scale model of an oil derrick. The computer and fax machine had produced a ticker tape parade of accordion-folded messages. An eight-foot pair of longhorns hung over the doorway, and what appeared to be an original Remington oil painting hung behind the mahogany desk. This was the all-male nerve center of a Texas empire, and she was definitely an intruder.

Shelby plopped herself into the huge, leather, swivel chair, her tone sour. "Do you know what 'fish out of water' means, partner?"

On the other end of the phone, Zach's wry chuckle lacked what Shelby considered suitable sympathy. "I'd say that if Jake hasn't kicked you out on your cute fanny for being so obnoxious, then we're doing pretty good."

"You 'dis-ing' me, bro?" Shelby asked in the vernacular of the streets.

"Let's just say that I'm only giving this experiment even chances."

"Well, all bets are off. I'm going to carry out this assignment just to spite you."

"Good, because you're right where you need to be."

The hairs on the back of Shelby's neck prickled. "You've heard something."

"Nothing but rumor. Salvatore may have flown the coop, which is not exactly a loss for the great state of Texas, but let's not take any chances. I'm not even going to call regularly, and only from a secure phone. In the meantime, you stay put, and don't talk to anyone, you hear me? Not your girlfriends or the doc or even Harve."

"What kind of dummy do you take me for?" Shelby demanded. "I know better than anyone what Salvatore's capable of. So save your lectures."

"Sorry, Shelby. I don't mean to second-guess you, but I'm worried. Look, you need something, you tell Jake. He'll get in touch with me."

"He hasn't been by?" she asked before she could help herself.

"No. Why, was he supposed to?"

"Uh, he went into Ft. Worth this afternoon, and I thought maybe...nothing." Chagrined that she'd inadvertently revealed any interest in the cowboy's movements, she twirled the phone cord around her finger. "Forget it, my mistake."

Zach's deep sigh gusted over the line. "I wish he would show up. Then maybe he and Georgia could settle things. She's not going to be truly happy until that happens. He's such a damned stubborn, ornery galoot!"

"When you get hurt that bad, ornery is about all you allow yourself to feel."

"Then you two really have a lot in common right now."

"Yeah." She shook her head, her lips twisting. "How very gentlemanly of you to rub my nose in it, Zach. We'll be lucky if we don't kill each other, right? Maybe I should take my chances with Salvatore after all."

"Don't talk stupid. You're going to be all right if you behave yourself."

"Me? I'm a model prisoner—oops, guest."

"With a smart mouth that won't let up," Zach said, laughing. "Just hang in there. One other thing. Tell Jake Laura Ramirez wants to make an appointment to come out and talk about his adoption as soon as Ben gets back from vacation. She's got some suggestions that may help us track down our biological father."

Zach had confided his discovery about Dwayne Rawlings on their drive out the previous day. She bit her lip. "You sure you want to open that can of worms, Zach?"

"You know I can't stand a mystery."

"I understand. So, can I talk to Laura when she comes? Or do I have to go hide out in the barn?"

"She's never revealed a source yet. I think we can trust her to keep mum."

While not close personal friends, Shelby had spent some time with Laura Ramirez on a couple of cases and still met for drinks or lunch on occasion. "It'll be good to see a friendly face."

"Jeez, Shel! You make the Lazy L sound like *Stalag 13!*"

"So I exaggerate." She couldn't prevent her voice from wobbling. "I'll just be glad when the Grand Jury convenes and I can reclaim my life."

"I know, I know," Zach soothed. "But it's going to be all right. Trust me. Jake'll take good care of you."

Zach's parting words echoed in Shelby's head as she made her way upstairs, but although she'd appreciated his call, his reassurances did little to assuage her restlessness. The four-poster bed looked lonely, not inviting, and after a moment, she turned on her heel. She found refuge in Retha's sitting room, curling up in one of the green velvet wing chairs and settling into the warm circle of light cast by a dainty brass reading lamp. Under the watchful eyes of a hundred dolls, she picked up a well-thumbed copy of *Little Women*. She was into chapter three when Jake found her.

"Evening, ma'am."

Shelby jumped. How did he *do* that? He'd surprised her again, his stealth incongruous in a man his size. Engrossed in the antics of Jo and Amy, she hadn't heard the helicopter, or the sound of his boots on the stairway. Either she was totally losing her touch, or else something about the little room had made her relax her guard to an unnatural extent. Either explanation was equally unsettling. Flushing, she snapped the book shut and rose guiltily.

"I'm sorry. I didn't mean to intrude, I should have asked—"

Jake stepped into the room, waving her back to the chair. He wore a Western jacket, dress shirt and string tie, and he carried a big sack with the name of a large department store chain emblazoned across it. His voice was gruff. "You're welcome anywhere in the house."

She hesitated, then sat again. "That's very kind of you, Jake."

"This room was my mother's retreat. We spent a lot of time here together. I used to read out loud to her when she wasn't feeling well. *Little Women* was one of her favorites." He sat down in the matching wing chair and thrust a sack at her. "Is this what you wanted?"

Shelby opened the plastic bag, then gave a small gasp of delight. Reaching inside, she lifted out a baby doll, yellow curls peeking out of a pink, lace-trimmed bonnet and matching dress. She had delicate features, chubby, dimpled fists and big blue eyes that opened and closed.

"She's perfect." Shelby smoothed the ruffled hem of the doll's dress with a tentative finger.

"They had a bigger one, but Leza's pretty little, so—"

"She'll love her." Shelby beamed at him. "Thank you. It's awfully good of you to take the trouble, especially after the way I snarled at you this morning."

He shrugged off her half apology. "It's for Leza. And since I snarled back pretty good, the rest's for you."

"What?" Shelby dug into the sack once more, feeling her face heat again with surprise and pleasure as she discovered a couple of pastel-colored T-shirts, an assortment of toiletries and scented body lotions, and a soft white batiste nightgown with a cluster of hand-embroidered pink roses dotting its simple V neck. "My goodness."

"You're traveling light, so I thought..." He shrugged

again while tugging at the end of his string tie and unbuttoning his top button. A dark fluff of chest hair curled in the opening of his shirt.

Shelby traced the outline of an embroidered rose. She wasn't accustomed to frilly, feminine nightwear, settling for an old cotton shirt or nothing at all, but the softness of the sheer fabric beneath her fingertips gave her a shiver of secret delight. She looked up, warmed despite herself by his kindness. "It's very thoughtful. I—I'll pay you back…"

"Don't worry about it tonight." Jake scrubbed his jaw with his palm and rotated his neck to relieve a kink. "I'm too beat to think."

"Your meeting didn't go well?"

"I'd just as soon string ten miles of barbed wire as deal with those city slickers."

Shelby examined him closely. Somehow, she wasn't taken in a bit. "I have a feeling you're a fraud, cowboy."

He lifted one dark eyebrow. "Who, me?"

"Hiding all that savvy under a lazy drawl and a Stetson. Bet you really put 'em off their guard before you go in for the kill."

The crease in his jaw turned into a dimple that mesmerized her with its charm. "It's been known to happen a time or two," he admitted.

"I knew it." She carefully put the baby doll back in the sack with her other surprises. "We could use your type undercover."

"Maybe you can tell me more about your work sometime. I'm a true crime fan, and I often wonder how close to reality those books are."

Shelby grimaced inwardly at the idea of revealing anything else about her life to Jake Lattimer. He'd already seen the aftereffects of her latest assignment. To confess her mistakes to him would only add to her mortification.

"I'm visiting here at Club Med, remember?" she said lightly. "Who wants to think about work while they're on vacation? What's interesting though, is how yours and Zach's interests parallel that way. Who knows, if you weren't a Lattimer, you might be in law enforcement like Zach."

"Yeah, who knows?" His expression clouded.

"He called earlier." She recounted the conversation regarding Laura Ramirez's desire to interview both Jake and his father.

Jake cursed under his breath. "Dammit, I've had enough of his interference!"

Shelby bit her lip. "I know it must be hard, but aren't you curious—"

"No." He rose and began to pace. "Sometimes it's best to let sleeping dogs lie."

"You may be right, at least in that respect. But as hard as it's been, as hard as those questions are, you still have no idea how lucky you are, do you?"

"Lucky?" Jake's tone was scathing. "If this is good luck, I'd hate to see a run of bad."

"You've been given a gift, something very special." Her throat constricted with an unusual emotion. "I never knew my parents. I don't have any siblings. Zach's a good man, one of the best. I'm proud to be his friend. I'd be prouder still to call him brother."

Jake shot her a sharp look, his dark eyes going hard. "Is that all?"

She was taken aback by his sudden fierceness. "What do you mean?"

"Maybe I'm not the only one smarting over Zach's and

Georgia's elopement. You and Zach were lovers, weren't you?''

The question astounded her, then made her furious. She surged to her feet, flinging the sack at him. ''That's none of your business, one way or the other!''

He dodged the package, then caught her arm as she tried to brush past him. ''So it's true.''

''Believe what you like,'' she spat, her eyes molten with dislike.

''What do you think, Shelby? Did Zach bring you to me for protection, or as a swap for Georgia?''

''That's despicable, even for you, cowboy.''

Jake caught a fistful of her hair in his free hand, using the leverage to tilt her face toward his. His breath was warm as it drifted across her cheeks, her lips. ''What about it, angel? Want to see if one brother's as good as the other?''

The sudden vision of herself locked in Jake's arms, his hard male mouth ravaging hers, sent a frisson of fear and longing rushing through her system. Repulsed at her own reaction, her rage exploded.

''Try it and you'll have two fat lips instead of one.'' Her voice was ice, her gaze hot enough to melt steel. ''Let me go. *Now.*''

''What's the matter?'' he mocked softly. ''The fearless cop afraid of a little one-on-one?''

''Fear has nothing to do with it. Taste does.'' She flung a desperate barb. ''And I don't settle for cheap imitations. Now get your hands off me.''

The muscle in his jaw worked, then he smiled. ''Yes, ma'am. Whatever you say.'' Releasing her, he picked up the sack and shoved it into her hands. ''I wonder who you'll be thinking of when you wear this.''

''Certainly not you.'' Her heart pounded in her ears,

and her breath shuddered painfully. "Get out," she said between her teeth.

"Good night, Shelby." Jake paused at the door, and his smiled turned wolfish. "But just for the record, I want you to know I think you're a liar."

Shelby struggled to calm herself long after he'd disappeared down the stairs, but even after her blood stopped racing and her breathing slowed, she seethed like a volcano on the verge of an eruption. *Jake'll take good care of you.* Zach's promise echoed in her mind, a mockery. Because Jake hadn't taken care of her. Indeed, he'd done the unforgivable, for he'd looked deep within her, seen her fear—and forced her to look, too.

"What the hell do you mean she's gone?"

The Baccarat tumbler Gus Salvatore held in a pudgy manicured hand exploded against the exclusive Aspen condo's native-stone fireplace in a deadly shower of glittering crystal shrapnel.

"Shoes says there's some other woman in her hospital room now." The bespectacled flunky unfortunate enough to take the call now held the phone in one hand and wiped the sweat from his balding pate with the other. His gaze met his boss's warily. "He doesn't know how they switched her—"

"I don't want excuses." Salvatore's voice was calm, eerily unemotional after his outburst of violence.

The nervous sycophant gulped and blotted faster. "No, sir."

"And I don't care what Shoes has to do. *Find her.*"

Chapter Five

"What the hell do you mean she's gone?"

Rosalita turned off the kitchen tap and faced Jake with a worried frown. "I mean, I thought Shelby was sleeping late this morning, but around ten I took her up some coffee, and she's not in her room."

"That's ridiculous. She's got to be here."

"I've looked everywhere. No one's seen her. From the looks of it, I think she may have lit out for parts unknown." Her dark eyes narrowed accusingly. "What did you do, Jake?"

"Hellfire and damnation!"

Conscience stabbing him, Jake pivoted and started for the staircase. He'd been in the hayfield fighting a balky hay baler all this sun-drenched morning, and he was sticky with sweat, fine black grass seeds clinging to his damp skin wherever his chambray work shirt stopped. He was in no mood to deal with a female temper tantrum!

Face it, Hoss, you brought it on yourself.

Breathing hard, he barged into Shelby's room, searching for signs that Rosalita's suspicions were off base. The bed was neatly made. The department store sack he'd given Shelby last night sat abandoned on the dresser top, the baby doll propped next to it. An envelope tied to the doll's wrist was marked prominently with Leza's name, as if the gift giver wanted to make certain it would make it to the proper party whether she was around to present it herself or not.

Jake jerked open the closet, but there was no sign of Shelby's duffle or purse, and the dresser drawers were equally empty. The bathroom vanity held only the toiletries they kept on hand for all guests.

Standing, feet braced, in the middle of the room, he wiped his damp mustache with the back of his hand and mouthed a string of expletives that would have made his mother wash his mouth out with soap. Then he headed back downstairs.

"I'll make a run up to the main highway and see if I can spot her," he told Rosalita grimly, scooping truck keys from the pegboard by the kitchen door. "She can't have gone far on foot."

"Unless she hitched a ride," Rosalita said.

"She's not that stupid," Jake muttered, snatching his hat.

"She could have phoned someone to come pick her up," Rosalita called after him as he hit the back steps. "What did you *do?*"

Jaw set, Jake backed his black-as-a-bat-out-of-hell pickup out of the carport, then headed up the long drive with a squeal of tires that effectively announced his state of mind to the world. Regret slashed at him like knives. All right, so he'd been out of line, even downright nasty

last night. It was just that Shelby's obvious devotion to
his brother had really gotten his goat, ticked him off with
a sharp pang of something that was suspiciously close to
green-eyed jealousy.

Shelby and Georgia, too. What was it about his twin
that elicited such feminine adoration? He'd already decided that as Shelby had said, her relationship—past or
present—with Zach really wasn't any of his business. He
knew he owed her an apology, but what in heaven's name
was she thinking, taking off without a word? The woman
didn't have a lick of sense. Why, anything could happen!

Speeding down the narrow blacktop toward the main
highway, Jake scanned the shoulders of the road and the
fenced pastures dotted with cattle for signs of a blond
head, his anxiety steadily mounting with each passing
mile. What if his hurtful words precipitated a disaster?
Shelby had left because of him, placed herself in immi-
nent danger again, when he was supposed to be keeping
her safe from harm. What kind of no-account lowlife did
that make him? And what dire consequences might befall
her if she found her way back to the city only to be spotted by Salvatore or his minions?

The thought made his mouth go as dry as the hot wind
licking at him through the open windows. Zach would
split more than his lip if he knew about this, and with
perfect justification, too. Knuckles white on the steering
wheel, Jake gunned a little more speed out of the truck.
He'd find Shelby if he had to cover every inch of ground
between here and Ft. Worth.

Topping a gentle rise, Jake shot a glance down a gravel
farm lane to his right that led into several tree-dotted pastures centered on a windmill-fed "tank" or farm pond.
He hoped Shelby hadn't made it to the main highway,
still some miles ahead, because if she had, any number of

friendly Texas truckers would be more than glad to offer a ride to a leggy blonde who—

Jake slammed on his brakes, then fought the wheel to control a fishtail skid while he struggled to make sense of the snapshot picture in his mind's eye. There had been something about the farm lane that didn't compute...but what? Then it hit him—a flash of shimmering gold, bobbing rhythmically as it disappeared behind the rise.

Reversing, he backed up, then spewed gravel as he charged up the hill like a Rough Rider at full tilt, his heart in his throat. And there she was, jogging steadily as she followed the grassy, twin-rutted lane around the silver mirror of the pond, her scraggly ponytail bobbing, the rounded contours of her bottom contracting against the red nylon of a minuscule pair of jogging shorts. A matador's cape couldn't have provoked any greater reaction than those red shorts.

With a growl of fury, Jake drove after her, passing her with a blast that made her jump sideways onto the soggy, hoof-churned bank. He skidded to a halt catty-cornered across the gravel lane, front bumper nearly in the water, then piled out of the truck and stalked toward her, relief and rage and resentment pouring out of him in a roar.

"What the *hell* do you think you're doing?"

Her white singlet clung to her curves with sweat. She wore her blue bandanna knotted at her neck, and her eyes were shielded by her sunglasses. Grimacing at the mud sucking at her jogging shoes, her breathing ragged, she struggled back up onto the gravel and gave him a baleful scowl. "Roadwork."

"Are you crazy?"

"Me? You're the one who's nuts, trying to run me down."

"Damn you, Shelby. You didn't let anyone know

where you were going. You scared the liver out of me—us!''

''No one told me I was under house arrest, Warden.'' Her chin squared defiantly. ''Anyway, I have to do something to keep me busy out here in the back of beyond, or I'll go stir-crazy from sheer boredom.''

''Of all the childish, inconsiderate—anything could have happened.''

Her eyes flashed. ''I told you, I can take care of myself.''

He ground his teeth, barely holding on to his temper. ''We both know you can't, so just get in the damn truck.''

That stopped her cold. Bending at the waist, she planted her hands on her knees, sucking in air, her eyes blazing with loathing. ''Go to hell.''

He lost it then. It wasn't bad enough that he'd envisioned all sorts of dire and deadly consequences of her folly, she had to throw his concern back in his teeth as if it were totally worthless. Well, she was going to do as she was told for once, if he had to rope and hog-tie her like a wild heifer at a roundup. With a snarl, Jake dove at her.

The flat edge of her hand caught him by total surprise in his midsection. Almost before he ''whuffed'' out a breath from the astonishing force of the strike, she'd spun, kicked him in the back of the knee, then shoved him, off balance and flailing air, straight into the pond.

Jake hit the surface in a resounding belly flop. Half-stunned and furious, he levered himself up out of the shallow water, hatless and soaked through, spitting rotting grass and muddy scum and swear words. Through a red veil of rage, he saw Shelby open the driver's door of the truck, throw her sunglasses onto the dashboard and climb in. Dadgum if the infuriating woman wasn't going to strand him out here.

In an instant Jake splashed ashore, jerked open the passenger door just as Shelby touched the ignition key, then he dragged her, shrieking and clawing at him, across the seat and out of the truck. Only the advantage of his size kept her from wrestling free. Using his bulk, he pressed her back against the rear fender, capturing her wrists in one hand, wrapping the other around her nape and roughly pushing his thumb under the angle of the square jaw that so fascinated him, to tilt her face to his.

"I ought to whale the tar out of you for that stunt," he growled down at her through clenched teeth. Water seeped from his hair, dripped from his mustache to land brackish against his tongue. "If you ever—"

The threat died in his throat.

Shelby's eyes were glazed and blank, their usual golden-green reduced to a dead putty color, her gaze turned inward to some dark and terrible place. Her skin had gone clammy and cold, her lips blue and bloodless. She'd stopped fighting him, but now she quivered in every molecule, like a blade of Johnson grass caught in a Blue Norther gale. She seemed hardly able to draw breath.

"Damn." The starkness of her expression chilled his blood. He released his hands, reaching to touch her chalk white cheek. "Shelby, you know I didn't mean—"

"Oh, please." She clawed at his hands, pushing them from her, her whisper raw with terror and desperation. "Dear God, no..."

Shock made him recoil, release her completely, then grab her again about the shoulders and shake her hard.

"Shelby!" He knew without question that she was reliving her assault, nothing less could account for her deathly paleness, the purest distillation of fear that seeped from her pores as she battled a demon he could only guess at. Somehow his anger and aggression and the touch of his hard hands on her throat had sent her back to hell. His gut twisted. "I'm not him. Dammit, Shelby, listen to me—*I'm not him!*"

A flicker of remote recognition flashed behind her eyes, and she drew a deep, shuddering breath.

"Angel, you're all right," Jake urged. "You're safe. I've got you."

Moaning softly, she covered her face with her hands, collapsing in slow motion as if all her bones had turned to jelly. She sat on the gravel beside the truck's back wheel, bent over her upraised knees, face buried in her arms, rocking herself like a whipped child. It was almost more than Jake could bear.

He knelt beside her, his hand on her heaving shoulder. "Tell me. Tell me what you saw."

She shook her head, her answer muffled against her knees. "No. I can't...."

"You've got to get it out or it'll eat you alive."

"I—I'm afraid." The admission seemed ripped from her soul.

"I'm here. Nothing can hurt you. Tell me," he commanded.

"I was asleep." Her breath caught.

"It's OK, Shelby. Where were you asleep?"

"My room over the lounge." A muffled laugh. "It was a dive of the worst sort. But the room was part of the barmaid's pay, a perfect setup because I had an excuse for always being around somewhere while the latest score went down. But then we picked up Salvatore's brother, and Gus somehow found out I was informing on them—I don't know how—and he came while I was sleeping. He came himself, instead of sending one of his killers, that's how bad he wanted me. He was on top of me, and I couldn't...couldn't..."

Jake swallowed hard. "Did he rape you?"

She lifted her head then, her mouth trembling, her eyes wide and tortured. "I thought he would, but then...then he had his hands around my throat, and I knew that it was death that excited him more."

Jake's hands tightened on her bent shoulders, and he pulled her unresistingly against his sodden shirtfront.

"There wasn't a white light, but I knew I was dying. It was my time..."

He pressed his lips against the top of her head. "No, thank God, it wasn't."

"It should have been." Her breasts heaved with her harsh gasping breaths. "I wasn't smart, or tough enough, and I couldn't make him let go."

"It wasn't your fault."

Shelby's voice wobbled, and with her cheek pressed against his damp chest, she spoke faster, in a rush of confession. "He was so heavy, and it hurt. I couldn't breathe, I couldn't...make him stop."

"It's all over. Your partners—Zach said they got to you in time. You're okay. You did fine."

"He's still out there." She shuddered. "I won't be able to stop him next time, either."

"Stop that," he said firmly, caressing her cheek, lifting her face so that she could see his determination. "It's not going to happen. I promise."

A single crystal tear formed on her lashes and trickled silently from the corner of her eye. "But if I can't do my job, what have I got left?"

That lone tear affected him more deeply than a flood, for he knew that she wasn't the type to weep lightly, if ever. His throat constricting, he caught the moisture on the pads of his fingertips. "Ah, angel," he whispered, his voice thick, "there's more out there than we mere mortals can know. Trust me. It's just waiting for you."

Then, before he had time to weigh the rights or wrongs, or even the perils or pleasures, he lowered his head to offer peace and reassurance to her trembling lips, and found his own deliverance.

Soft. That was Shelby's first sensation. How could a man this hard feel so soft? There was solace and comfort and safety here, and an unbearable, nearly inconceivable tenderness. She caught her breath and tasted heaven.

His work-hardened palm cupped her cheek, gently, as though she were something precious, something to be cherished. The brush of his mustache was softer than black velvet as his mouth melded against hers, not demanding, a simple offering of human understanding and compassion. The vision of her own death faded, replaced by an affirmation of life, and she shivered, not from fear, but from the deep inner certainty that she'd never been touched like this before.

Her hand slid up the hard muscularity of his chest, and she clung to his neck, lifting her face like a flower to the sun, incapable of any thought, any action but to savor and seek more of this magic. His arm tightened around her, and the dampness of his clothes was a cool and delicious shock against her overheated body.

Soft. The kiss was like a cloud bank, and she was drifting, dreaming, the hard contours of his lips slanting over hers a perfection of sweetness, as light and rare as divinity candy at Christmastide. When the tip of his tongue tasted the seam of her lips, it seemed the most natural thing in the world to open for him, and her soul expanded at his gentle exploration, lifting her beyond the realm of her meager experience. She was melting, floating, engulfed by the flavor of him, heady and masculine and powerful.

And the softness evoked an ache, a smoldering burn of need that blossomed deep within her, made her move restlessly. His fingers slid into her hair, tilting her back into the crook of his arm so that he had full access to her mouth, and he drank deeply of her, his tongue stroking more forcefully now, darting and exploring every nuance of her while she lay helpless and dazed and...wanting.

She froze. It was a trap. A velvet snare with the pretense of softness and caring as its bait, and the devastating deceit of passion as its dubious reward. Her fingers curled into the wet strands of hair at his nape, and she fought her way upward, struggling to free her mind, her body from the clinging, suffocating clouds of need.

He felt the change come over her and drew back, his eyes smoky, his lips glistening with her moisture. It seemed for the duration of the potent kiss, neither of them had remembered to breathe, but now they sought air in great, revealing gulps.

"You okay now?" he asked, his voice gruff.

"Yeah," she lied. She forced her fingers open, letting go of the thick silkiness of his hair with shameful reluctance, then pulled away, feeling bereft as his arms dropped from around her. She couldn't meet his eyes. "I—yeah, fine."

"I got you all wet," he said, rising to his feet and pulling her up by the hand. "Sorry."

Heat rose in her cheeks. It wasn't the dampness of her clothes, but the shameless dewing between her legs that filled her with mortification. It was bad enough that an uncontrollable flash of *déjà vu* had reduced her to a limp and spineless jellyfish right before the cowboy's astonished eyes, but then to fall into his arms like some kind of swooning maiden—it wasn't to be borne. He'd merely been trying yet again to calm her, showing her the kindness that seemed to be such an innate part of his character. And she'd responded with a flare of sexual craving—how embarrassing.

Yet he'd been the one to initiate the kiss. Maybe it was something more nefarious. Shelby shot him a sharp look. He'd already accused her of being Zach's lover. That told her clearly what kind of woman he judged her to be. Maybe this had been some sort of male rite of vengeance, to take at least in part something that had once been Zach's—or so he thought—just as Zach had taken Georgia.

Confusion and chagrin and suspicion filled her. Again she'd revealed too much, let this man see her vulnerable and wounded. He could use that knowledge as a weapon in the cruelest sense if he cared to. And as far as her eager response to his kiss, what man wouldn't be tempted to press his advantage of that weakness?

If she let him.

Her defenses against Jake Lattimer lay in tattered shreds, all but demolished. If she hoped to survive her stay at the Lazy L, she had to rebuild them, this time stronger by a hundredfold. Maybe they'd crossed a line with that blazing kiss, but she'd be damned if she'd acknowledge it and put herself at any further disadvantage where this overgrown Texan was concerned. Let him draw whatever conclusions he liked.

"I won't melt, cowboy." She tilted her chin. "I guess I got what I deserved for pitching you into the drink."

"That's a hell of a one-two punch you got there, lady." He shrugged, not looking at her, dragged his soaking shirttail from the waistband of his jeans, and briefly revealed a slash of hard, hair-dusted belly. "But I reckon I needed cooling off."

She swallowed, willing away the involuntary leap of her blood at his unconsciously sexy movement. They were as awkward as two kids forced by the school principal to apologize, but it was simpler to ignore that crossed line than to deal with the ramifications of a passion that had nearly flared out of control. And he had even conceded she could defend herself, at least in a small way. If he could be magnanimous, then so could she.

"We'll forget it, okay? And I apologize for not letting someone know I was leaving for a jog."

"Sorry I overreacted," he muttered. "I thought you'd taken off."

"But why?"

"Well, I couldn't find your duffle—"

"I took some dirty things to the laundry room in it."

"—and no purse."

"Under the mattress." She saw his affronted look and shrugged. "Habit. No offense intended."

He retrieved his hat from the water, shook it out. "And we'd had words last night—"

She had no intention of getting into that. She cut in hastily. "I promise it won't happen again, Jake. It just never occurred to me..."

Jake's disbelieving look pierced her. "What? That someone would worry about you?"

She forced her lips into a semblance of a smile. "I—I haven't had much practice at that."

"That's about the saddest thing I ever heard." Jake gestured her toward the truck.

Shelby bristled. "I don't want your pity, cowboy."

Grabbing her by the waist, he swung her onto the passenger seat, his dark gaze pinning her in place. "Is it so hard for you to accept that someone might care what happens to you?"

"I suppose it is," she admitted, defiance giving her mouth a mulish twist. "What of it?"

"Get over it, Shelby. That might be the way things are in the city, but out here, we take care of our folks, and as long as you're on Lattimer land that's what you can expect, too."

Jake slammed the door and went around to climb in on the driver's side. Shelby stared out the window, biting the inside of her lip hard to control the emotion constricting her tight throat. For the picture Jake's words painted were too enticing, too seductive. She was not so foolish as to fall into that trap, for her stay in Jake's domain was only temporary, and to allow herself to come to depend on his caring—on him—in any way was the ultimate in folly.

She could take care of herself. She had to. And now, more than ever, that meant keeping her distance from Jake Lattimer.

He'd made a mistake. Hell, more than one.

Boots propped on the corner of his desk, Jake rubbed his mustache with a forefinger and ignored the fax machine softly spewing paper behind him. There were some leases Ben would need to see when he got back, and a decision to be made regarding whether they wanted to baby the old baler through another season, but those were minor irritants. He could handle anything the Lazy L threw at him. What he couldn't accept was that here he'd put in a full day's work, and at five o'clock he should be ready for another try at a bourbon, a swim and a steak, but all he was able to think about was that he'd lost control with Shelby Hartman that day, not once, but twice.

It was mortifying to a man who prided himself on his

even temperament to realize that he went off like Mount Vesuvius every time he came in contact with the mouthy broad. She pushed buttons he didn't even know he had. She was certainly a woman with a mind of her own, a critter more provoking than a shirt full of fleas. One tilt of that stubborn chin of hers, and he went flying off the handle. But while losing his temper was one thing, totally abandoning his self-control was something else entirely.

Stifling a groan of frustration, Jake jammed a hand through his hair and rose restlessly to his feet. What had possessed him to kiss her? His brain must be made of taffy candy. Okay, so she'd looked so achingly lost and fragile reliving the trauma of her assault that every male instinct cried out to comfort and protect her, but he should have had more sense than to play with fire.

Fire. That's exactly what her mouth had tasted like, a fiery sweetness that enticed and inflamed, leaving a man helpless. Sweat broke out under his arms, and his groin tightened. She'd been so incredibly soft, her mouth like satin and spice, her body fitting perfectly against his. His sex stirred, and he cursed under his breath.

Huge mistake to kiss her. Enormous.

He strode out of the office, heading into his room next door. The familiar bedroom, with its heavy oak furniture, well-filled bookshelves, and Sahara-colored tailored spread on the king-size bed was not the serene oasis he usually found it. By the time he was halfway across the room, he was already out of his boots, shirt and jeans and reaching for his swimsuit. Maybe a cool dip would control this blazing surge of pure male lust.

Frowning, Jake pulled on his utilitarian swim trunks, then retrieved a towel out of his bath and draped it around his naked shoulders. It had also obviously been a mistake to treat Shelby with kid gloves and try to force her into the role of pampered guest. She needed diversions, activity to keep her demons at bay, or she was liable to pull some new stunt—and this time it might not be something as innocuous as a jog through the countryside.

It was his responsibility to safeguard her well-being while on Lattimer turf, so he'd just have to see that she was included in the ranch activities as much as possible, and if she were stubbornly disinclined to follow his suggestions, he'd simply have to drag her along—by a hank of her blond hair, if necessary—for her own good.

The only problem was, he'd already proved he could be a damned fool where she was concerned. Would this proximity provide too much of a temptation to sample her kisses again? From what he'd learned about Shelby herself in their brief acquaintance, she'd certainly look upon any offers of company or distraction with total suspicion. After what had transpired between them today, she might think he was after something.

Jake gave a snort of self-contempt. *Hell, she just might be right.*

For all his stiff-upper-lip posturing, he certainly hadn't acted like a man with a broken heart when he held her in his arms. Did that make him as faithless as Georgia?

"Hell, no, you're just a man, dammit," he muttered.

He'd been chaste as a monk during the two years of his and Georgia's engagement—out of respect for her, he told himself—and a man could only stand so much celibacy. Maybe he and Georgia hadn't shot sparks off every time they touched, but there'd always been the knowledge that they would consummate the relationship all in good time. But that was finished, and she was another man's wife. Was it any wonder, now that he was a free man—albeit involuntarily released from his promises—that the first sexy dame to cross his path would set off all his bells and whistles with a vengeance?

And he knew it wasn't all one-sided, either. Not the way Shelby had melted against him, opened for him without a demur, then trembled in his arms. The chemistry was bubbling, no doubt about it. It would be interesting to see what they could cook up together.

Jake hoped he was smart enough to know that a rebound relationship had little hope of succeeding, but this was only a temporary situation. Shelby would go back to the city and her police work in short order, and he'd continue his life on the Lazy L. Georgia had accused him of being too predictable, too boring to take chances. Well, here was an opportunity to prove her wrong. He wasn't a user, but what the heck—if he and Shelby both wanted it, needed it, what was the problem with a brief, fiery love affair? Shelby was a woman of the world, who'd probably scratched this particular itch with Zach already. Maybe a hot, sexy fling with Zach's twin brother would cauterize both his and Shelby's wounded spirits. At least it would sure as hell ease the ache between Jake's legs.

Mouth set, he headed for the pool, only to find Shelby in front of the Perezes' apartment. She wore the peach T-shirt he'd gotten for her with her jeans, and her freshly washed hair lay in soft gold swirls about her nape. Sitting in a pint-size chair opposite Leza, she held a pink plastic cup and saucer with as much grave dignity as if she were having tea with the queen, who in this instance just happened to be a yellow-haired baby doll.

Leza bounded up at Jake's approach, her cherubic face wreathed in a smile as big as Christmas. "Jake, look what Shelby got me!"

Needing to keep his distance, both emotionally and physically, from a woman who both stirred and disturbed him and concerning whom he'd yet to come to any real decision, yet reluctant to disappoint the little girl, Jake forced a smile. He threw his towel down in a lounge chair, then went down on one knee to inspect the newest addition to "Mama" Leza's family.

"My, isn't she a beauty. Does she have a name?"

"I'm going to call her Barbara Ann, just like Shelby's baby when she was a little girl like me," Leza said proudly.

Jake shot a glance at Shelby, noting the fine pink color that rose to her cheeks at this revelation. He was suddenly very thankful that he'd taken such care finding this particular doll, going to not one but three different shops until he'd located the single doll perfect in each detail Shelby had named.

"I know you'll take very good care of someone this special," Jake told Leza.

"We're having apple juice and graham crackers, 'cause Mama said it won't spoil my supper," Leza confided. "Want some?"

He tugged a dark curl playfully. "Thanks, punkin. Maybe after my swim."

Leza nodded, then jogged back over to join Shelby again, who immediately took up her part in the playacting, pouring tea and discussing "girl matters" such as the fineness of the lace adorning Barbara Ann's dress and whether or not Leza's friend Buddy would phone tonight. She was completely serious and attentive, listening and responding to Leza's prattle as if it were the most important thing in the world.

It struck Jake as he went around to the deep end of the pool that this was just how his own mother had related to him, with nary a hint of impatience no matter how busy she was, as if his thoughts and comments were of utmost interest and value. He remembered it made him feel special and cherished, had given him the confidence to approach kids and adults alike with assurance and an innate knowledge of his self-worth. And Shelby seemed to have the same intuitive parenting skills that Retha had possessed.

Leza cradled Barbara Ann in her arms, cooing down at her with a new mother's love, and, poised on the diving board, Jake smiled, shifting his gaze to catch Shelby's reaction—and caught his breath. Because there in Shelby's face was the same longing and adoration shining in Leza's, only magnified by a mature woman's maternal urges into something mystic and eternal. Here clearly was a woman who, for all her outward toughness, longed for a family of her own, and who'd actually have the love and the patience and the dedication to be a wonderful mother, helpmeet, and mate for some lucky man.

And Jake, low rutting animal that he was, just wanted to jump her bones.

His dive sliced the water, the cool liquid slapping him to his senses. He might be sexually frustrated and more turned on than he had been in a long time, but he had more honor than to go after a woman simply to assuage his own desire, with no thought of the emotional consequences to her. Yes, he could probably woo and seduce Shelby, but after the disaster with Georgia, he wasn't in the mood to forge new ties with anyone, much less a woman as wounded and vulnerable as Shelby was right now. She needed someone who could give her more than a quick toss in the hay, maybe even had someone back in Ft. Worth, for all he knew. To act on his hunger would only cause complications neither of them could use right now. No, there were better ways to handle this, starting with about ten thousand laps of American crawl.

The blur of blue and white bubbles was hypnotic, the undersea silence soothing as he pulled through the water, turned at the end, repeated the maneuver over and over. Finally, when he thought his lungs would burst and his muscles were burning with fatigue, he came up for breath for the last time. Hanging on to the edge with both forearms, he dragged in gulps of air, and as his vision cleared, he found himself staring at a pair of shapely ankles and sandal-clad feet.

"Do you always work so hard at everything?" Shelby asked.

"Secret of my success." Leza, Barbara Ann and the tea set had disappeared, and they were alone on the patio. Breathing hard, Jake licked water droplets from the edge of his mustache. "Something I can do for you, ma'am?"

She dropped to her haunches in front of him so that they were more on eye level, her mouth compressing with irritation. "Quit calling me that, for one. It makes me feel—"

"Respected? Deserving of courtesy?"

"Old. Antique. Like your sainted mother or something," she muttered.

Jake wrapped his lean fingers around her ankle. "Not even close."

Her eyes flashed golden with ire. "Look, I just wanted to thank you again for getting the doll for Leza, so can the potshots, will you? I know what you think of me, so if pulling me into the pool is going to make us even for this morning, then go ahead."

His vow of moments before forgotten, he rubbed his wet fingers up her leg, sliding beneath the denim hem of her jeans. He felt gooseflesh rise on her skin, and his voice was silky. "And what do I think of you?"

"That I slept with Zach." Her jaw grew taut, her eyes defiant. "Well, I didn't."

There was no mistaking the truthfulness in her expression, and he felt the jolt of that realization low in his belly, a burn of raw male satisfaction. His fingers tightened possessively on the silken flesh of her calf.

"Ours was never that kind of relationship," she continued haughtily. "We're *friends*, get it? So don't think you can make me the bone of contention in whatever kind of sibling rivalry is going on between you, because it won't work. I'm not Georgia."

Jake hoisted himself from the pool into a seated position beside her, suddenly feeling almost cheerful. "Believe me, I'd never make that mistake."

She reacted with a slight wince and a further firming of her shapely mouth, as if she thought that distinction was a criticism. Her gaze slid across the damp expanse of his hair-dusted chest, then away, and she stood up hastily. "Just so long as we're clear."

Jake rolled to his feet, catching her hand. "Wait a minute, is that why you think I kissed you? As a substitute for Georgia?"

"Well, why did you?"

"Because you needed it."

Her breath hissed in an outraged exhalation. "Good God! You are the most arrogant, self-important, bigheaded...*cowpuncher!* And if you think—"

"Easy, Shelby. Maybe I needed it, too."

The wind went out of her, as if he'd been the one to land a punch in the gut. "Oh."

Jake touched her cheek. "Lot of emotion flying around about then. Hard on both of us. Just a natural reaction, nothing to make a big fuss about."

Something behind her eyes flickered, but her chin lifted. "Exactly."

"Glad we got that straight."

"Yeah," she agreed. "Me, too."

He rubbed his thumb over the back of her hand, then released her, satisfied that they were back on some kind of even keel that hopefully would keep complications like kisses and lustful thoughts—such as taking her down on the lounger and making love with her right now in broad daylight—at bay.

"I expect not having much to do but sit around and wait is pretty hard," he said kindly, "so what say I try to find you a few chores or something to keep you a little better occupied? Might help."

Her look was partly dubious, partly grateful. "Yes, it might."

"I'll see what we can come up with." He grabbed his towel and rubbed his hair and chest vigorously. "Meanwhile, I'm hungry enough to eat an elephant. What do you suppose Rosie's got for supper?"

"A casserole of some sort. She had to go into town to take that exam."

"Damn."

Shelby laughed out loud at his disgruntled expression. "My sentiments exactly. You know what I really wish I had?"

"No, what?"

Her expression turned wistful. "A great big juicy steak. T-bone. Rare."

Jake looked at her with new respect. A woman with such simple yet elegant tastes couldn't be all bad. It wasn't much of a request, as requests went, and, after all, he was playing the role of host. For once in his life, he let impulse rule. Grinning, he grabbed her hand and hauled her toward the house.

"Come on, lady. I know where to find just what you're looking for."

Chapter Six

"Tulsa? You're taking me all the way to Tulsa for a piece of meat?"

Jake glanced at Shelby out of the corner of his eye. "Best place I know for T-bones."

He wore a billed baseball cap with the Lazy L logo and a headset that matched hers. Through the Plexiglas expanse of the helicopter's cockpit, the Texas plains rushed past, the odd dot of a kitchen light or a security lamp flickering on as dusk turned the land below them to purple. Shelby hadn't been too certain about the situation when he'd railroaded her into this flying contraption, but now she was sure he'd lost his mind.

"Would you mind giving me a reason?" she asked carefully.

An ironical twist lifted the corner of his mouth. "Let's just say I'm trying to change my image."

Now she really didn't know what to make of his strange

mood. What was there about the cowboy's image he'd want to change? Booted, burly, with a drawl that caressed you like velvet and a mind well read and as sharp as the proverbial steel trap, not to mention a family fortune or the way he filled out a pair of Wranglers—heck, he was any cowgirl's dream.

Not that she was just any cowgirl, Shelby hastened to remind herself. Just because he'd bamboozled her into coming with him by bribing her with the promise of a steak didn't mean that she'd reconsidered about keeping her distance. It was just that somehow he'd been so friendly and forceful and matter-of-fact there didn't seem much purpose in resisting something as innocent as a dinner invitation. Only she'd forgotten that a rancher like Jake Lattimer might tend to do things in a big Texas way.

"You're sure about this, are you?" she asked.

"No, but we'll see how it turns out."

"I'm not sure what Zach will have to say about my leaving the premises."

"I wouldn't jeopardize your safety, honey. Besides, what could happen? No one even knows your where-abouts, or where we're going, much less that we'll land in Tulsa for a bite to eat and be back before daylight. So you might as well relax and enjoy the flight."

There wasn't much else she could do, Shelby thought sourly. "Okay, cowboy, it's your rodeo."

He shot her a quick grin that reminded her of the picture in his mother's sitting room and made her heart trip over rebelliously. Then he spent the remainder of the flight giving her a running commentary of the geology of the region, the economic forecasts for the beef industry for the next six months, and his feelings concerning The Mavericks' newest country release.

To her surprise, Shelby found herself relaxing, joining

in the conversation, feeling safe enough inside this cowboy's clattering whirligig to have a little...*fun?* Zach was right, she decided, she'd been on the streets too long. When she got through all this, she was definitely going to reclaim her life, learn to socialize again.

It was only when the taxi Jake hired to take them from the small private Tulsa airstrip pulled up in front of what looked to be a five-star establishment that Shelby balked.

"Oh, no, you don't." Looking down at the worn blue jean jacket she'd tossed over her T-shirt and jeans, she shook her head. "I'm not dressed for a ritzy joint like this."

"And I am?" He gestured at his own jeans and striped Western shirt. "You forget this is Oklahoma."

"But—"

Jake plucked her sunglasses out of her breast pocket and plunked them down on her nose. "There. You're as pretty as a movie star anyhow, and now you look like a celebrity. So forget about dress codes. Let's eat."

Ignoring the way her face flamed at his compliment, he took her arm and waltzed her into the elegant restaurant, through a crowd gathered for some posh social/political event. He hailed an acquaintance or two, got caught in a newspaper photographer's flash shaking hands with the mayor, then was greeted with pleasure by the maître d', who whisked them to a secluded, romantic table for two.

In short order they were plied with magnificent slabs of rare beef, Duchess potatoes and julienne carrots. Jake insisted she have a glass of wine, while he stuck with iced tea because he was "driving." The New York cheesecake had to have been made in Manhattan that morning.

"That was the best steak I've ever had," Shelby admitted, feeling replete and pampered, and yes, even a little in awe at being with a man whose mere presence resulted in such deferential treatment from the waitstaff. It was a little like being Cinderella on the arm of the prince.

Jake wiped a droplet of steak sauce from his mustache and sat back in his chair, looking as satisfied as Elizabeth with a bellyful of cream. "They only serve Lazy L beef here."

Shelby gaped, then laughed incredulously. "You brought us all the way up here for some of your own beef?"

"I know how to raise the finest cattle in the state of Texas, ma'am." His lips quirked. "But I never said I could cook."

On their way back to the airstrip, Jake surprised her again by stopping off at a disreputable-looking roadhouse called the Derrick Club. A loud country-western band wailed from the bandstand, and couples in jeans and cowboy hats circled the smoke-filled room to the clink of long-neck bottles and shrill feminine laughter. Cowboys and wildcatters and truckers mingled with hairdressers and secretaries and rodeo buckle bunnies.

Jake kept a protective arm around Shelby's waist as they pushed through the roisterous crowd to the brass-railed bar. His solicitous attitude warmed her heart even as it made her smile secretly. She was more at home among these working-class revelers than he was, could pick out of this milieu with a cop's easy expertise the troublemakers and the hookers and the good ole boys just out for a high time. She might even be handier in a brawl than Jake, and from the look of the Derrick Club, that kind of entertainment happened on a nightly basis.

"Jake, you dirty son of a gun!" The brawny bartender looked to be a mixture of all-pro linebacker and Hell's Angel, from shoulders as big as boulders to a flowing head of sable hair caught back Indian-style with a leather thong. He stuck out a hand the size of an iron skillet. "How the hell are you, man?"

"Can't complain, Bart." They wrung hands. "You keeping busy?"

"Naw, business is slow these days. Only had to bust three heads last night." Bart noticed Shelby, and his gaze gleamed with masculine appreciation. "Damn! Is this that pretty little bride of yours? Why—"

"I'm Shelby." She stuck out her hand to ease the awkward situation, trying not to notice how Jake had gone stiff at her side. "Just a friend. Jake's showing me some of Tulsa's high spots."

"Wedding's off," Jake informed Bart gruffly. "Didn't work out."

"Sorry. But I see you ain't letting grass grow under your boots, are you, partner?" Still holding her hand, Bart grinned and leaned toward Shelby with a conspiratorial air. "You watch out for lover boy, Shelby. He had himself a new girlfriend every week when we were playing football back at UT."

"And you're as full of it as you ever were, Bartholomew," Jake said with a scowl. Untangling Shelby's hand from Bart's big paw, he draped a proprietorial arm over her shoulders. "Don't let his act fool you, Shelby. Bart's a Ph.D. in Romance languages, teaches at State when he's not running this joint."

Bemused, Shelby smiled. "It's nice to meet you, Bart."

Straightening, Jake let his dark gaze roam the crowded honky-tonk. "Say, Russ around here tonight? I know how much he enjoys keeping low company."

"Nope. Haven't seen him or Baby Sister for a couple of weeks. Heard they were running a rig down Lubbock way, hit a gusher. That damn Campbell luck is somethin', ain't it?"

Jake laughed. "Never known it to fail. Is Bliss still flying the company planes?"

"Yup. And raising hell with the menfolk every time she shows her pretty tail around here." Bart gave a low, appreciative whistle. "Let me tell you, boy, Baby Sister Bliss Abernathy is hell on wheels."

"Glad to know some things never change," Jake said wryly. "Give 'em my best next time they're in, okay? Come on, angel. Long as we're here, we might as well try out the dance floor."

Ignoring Shelby's protests that she didn't know a two-step from a schottische, he pulled her into the circling dancers.

"I don't even like country music." Shelby's steps were awkward, her cheeks flushed with embarrassment.

Jake spun her expertly, caught her close, then for some inexplicable reason, their steps meshed and the motion of the dance flowed naturally. "It may not be the Rolling Stones, but if you listen close, you'll find out where rock 'n' roll has been hiding out lately."

"How did you know I like Jagger?" she asked suspiciously. His big hand lay warm beneath her jacket in the small of her back, and his woodsy scent tickled her nose.

"I'm not the only one who could be called predictable," he chuckled against her ear, and the brush of his mustache made goose bumps jump to attention along her spine.

As Jake whirled her around the floor, hands clasped, thighs brushing, somehow in Shelby's mind the country tune was replaced by "Satisfaction," and it was difficult not to add her groan to Mick's sexy-hungry growl that she "ain't got no," either. Despite her best intentions, she was vibrating with awareness, but she knew it was some sort of artificially induced sensitivity, brought on by tension and loneliness and the sheer pleasure of being with a handsome man who handled you gently, with consideration.

So she did her best to ignore that her mouth went dry when Jake smiled at her, and her heart kicked into overdrive at the casual touch of his hand on her elbow. He seemed oblivious to any undercurrent between them, and by golly, she was not so callow and careless that she couldn't control herself where a dadgum man was concerned.

To spare the more temperamental livestock, the Lazy L's 'copter pad was located behind the machinery shed across from the barn. The eastern horizon was limned with the first rays of gold when they landed again. Shelby and Jake had been quiet on the return flight, scarcely passing a dozen words between them, but it had been an easy silence, friendly, neither of them feeling the need to fill it with inanities. Even after missing a night's sleep, Shelby felt wakeful. After all, darkness was her element, the realm in which she'd moved and worked for so long the heartbeat of the nighttime city was like a clock within her, pounding out the rhythm of her life. She wondered idly if that would ever change.

As the chopper blades beat to a halt and Jake helped her down, the sky changed from gray to blue to orchid and peach. Walking toward the lane leading from the barn corrals to the house, she gave Jake a quizzical smile.

"What a ride. Remind me to ask for details before I agree to tag along with you next time, cowboy."

"Would you have come if I had?"

She bit her lip, then was honest. "Probably not."

"Took your mind off things for a while, at least. It wasn't that bad, was it?"

Shelby shook her head. "No. It was good, Jake. Thank you."

"It's nice to get away sometimes." He paused for a minute in the middle of the lane, watching the sun slowly illuminate the sleeping ranch. "This is the best, though."

She turned to share his regard, seeing through his eyes the well-tended barn and outbuildings, the sleek cattle stirring inside the lush pastures, the years of pride and care than had made the Lazy L a showplace, but more than that, a home.

"You're a very fortunate man," she said softly.

Jake turned a dark, speculative gaze toward her, nodding. "It's good to be reminded of that now and again. I'm going to check on Lucy. Want to come?"

If she'd had any sense at all, she'd have refused, but it hadn't been a night for making sense, so she found herself nodding, following him to the barn, watching him open Lucy's stall and rub his hands over the mare's gravid belly. Lucy nickered quietly, stomping and shivering as if impatient for the blessed event to begin. The scent of hay and horse and life mingled in a primordial mix that called to Shelby with a primitive, instinctual message mere words could not translate.

"Won't be long now," he said. "She's bagging up already."

"What?" Shelby blinked, mesmerized by the sight of Jake's strong hands stroking the mare's chestnut hide. What would it be like to be touched with such sensitivity?

"Getting ready to produce milk for the foal. Here, feel this." Jake caught her hands and guided them to the bulge of Lucy's stomach, then laughed softly when the foal moved inside its mother and Shelby jumped. "Quite a miracle, huh? I never get tired of nature's glory."

"You really love all this, don't you?" A note of wonder colored the question, but he stiffened and dropped her hands.

"Guess you find that hard to believe." He jammed his hands into his back pockets, shoulders hunched defensively, his mouth flattening into a thin line. "Nothing to get all excited about out here in Dullsville. No cops and robbers, outlaw days and Indian raids are all gone, only an occasional coyote or rattler to—"

"Jake."

But he was on a roll, the words grinding out of him.

"—nothing but dull old life and death, birth and renewal, the change of the seasons, and here I sit, but I wouldn't change it and—"

Shelby reached up to place her palm against his lips, stemming the tide of words. His breath was moist against her skin, the tickle of his mustache whisper soft. "Jake, don't. Maybe I don't completely understand, and it's not a life I'd choose, but you don't have to justify anything."

She saw a flicker of something, perhaps disappointment, in his eyes, and dropped her hand. He rubbed a finger over his mustache, then looked away. "Yeah, I guess you're right."

And for some reason, Shelby felt as though she'd just lost something precious. Fatigue crashed down on her like a thousand-pound weight. "I—I think I'm ready to turn in now."

He was instantly solicitous, seeing her out of the stall and back to the morning-quiet house with muttered apologies for keeping her up.

"Stop it, will you?" She paused on the second step of the staircase, still not quite eye level with his superior height, her lips trembling in a tired smile. "I enjoyed it, Jake. You did make me forget…things."

"You'd better get some rest," he said, his voice suddenly gruff with concern. "It was thoughtless of me to—"

She blew out an impatient puff of air. "Can it, cowboy. I'm a big girl, and I'm glad I went. Although I know now what Cinderella felt like after the ball." She shrugged, her lips curving in a grin. "I think we'd both agree, a few bags under the eyes is a small price to pay."

"OK. Good." Looking relieved, he squeezed her arm, then released her. "But you'd better hit the sack now."

"I think you're right. Good night." She climbed the stairs, then cast him a glance over her shoulder. "Just one thing."

Jake looked up at her, his tanned hand perched on the knob of the bannister. "What's that?"

"Personally, I don't think you should do a damn thing about your image."

Like an itch that couldn't be ignored, Shelby's words produced a rash of aggravation over the next few days for Jake. He couldn't decide what to make of them. Had there been a thread of grudging approval from the city girl, or was she merely dismissing him as a hopeless case of dull, rural predictability?

With a snort of disgust at himself and his persistent thoughts, Jake parked his truck in the circle drive and went inside the ranch house. A mid-afternoon quiet hovered in the foyer. Jake removed his hat, ran a forearm over the sweat dewing his brow, and breathed a sigh of pleasure at the contrast of air-conditioned coolness to the eighty-degree temperatures outside.

Not that things had been that dull around the Lazy L. In fact, they'd been working their butts off rounding up the yearling calves to haul to the feeder lots in Ft. Worth. The prices were still lower than he liked, but the quality and weight of the stock was going to make up for that, and just as soon as his ranch hands could finish the hay baling and hauling, they might even be able to take a well-earned breather for a day or two.

They'd been so rushed, every cowboy working from daylight to long after dark, that Jake had even missed every one of his dad's calls from Florida. Rosalita, who'd taken them, reported that the elder Lattimer's golf game was improving, that he spoke highly of a certain Ms. Stringfield he'd met on the links, and that he'd be home on schedule.

Grabbing the day's pile of mail from the basket on the foyer console, Jake headed to the kitchen for a glass of iced tea to ease his parched throat. He hadn't seen any reason to complicate his dad's vacation with news that they were hiding a female cop friend of Zach's with a price on her head on the ranch. Explanations would come soon enough.

While Ben had been equally offended and incensed by Georgia and Zach's elopement, Jake knew his father had mixed feelings about discovering his son was a twin, feeling a natural and understandable empathy for Zach as a son who'd been unjustly denied him. Ben had even expressed regret that he and Retha hadn't had a chance to raise the brothers together.

Jake grimaced, admitting to himself that Ben's emotional response to Zach had thrown him for a loop. He didn't quite know how to react to Ben's wanting another son. He'd always been the crown prince of the Lazy L, and having a usurper in their midst was at the very least unsettling. Jake snorted. Hell, that barely scratched the surface of his rivalry and jealousy of his newfound brother. Such feelings weren't honorable, and they made Jake feel selfish, petty, and guilty as hell.

It was still a mystery why he and Zach had been sep-
arated, especially since Ben had discovered not even Tom
Barnette, the lawyer who'd handled the adoption, had
known there was a set of twins involved. There was no
love lost between the Lattimers and Barnette due to a
business deal arranged by the attorney that had gone sour
and cost not only the Lattimers but Campbell Drilling a
pile of money, but there was no reason to believe Barnette
was lying about this.

Jake shook his head. They might never know the truth
of what Abby had done, or guess her twisted reasoning.
But then, what the hell difference would it make?

Shifting his thoughts away from that painful reverie,
Jake wondered if his father's new lady friend might turn
into something special. Ben Lattimer was still in his
prime, a handsome, silver-haired specimen of a man who
could still turn the ladies' heads. But he'd been a widower
ten years now, and Jake knew that while his dad missed
Retha, there were times when he was lonely. Jake didn't
think his mother would have wanted Ben to be alone, but
so far, even though he'd squired around an armful of
handsome fillies, Ben hadn't given any indication of re-
marrying. Jake supposed that being a one-woman man ran
in the Lattimer family whether he and his dad shared
genes or not.

A feminine shout of annoyance caught Jake's attention.
He looked through the patio doors just in time to see
Shelby hurl a potted red geranium at a certain black-as-
Hades cat. The plastic pot hit the cement at the tom's
heels, exploding in a crash of green plastic and black pot-
ting soil. With a yowl, the feline culprit exited the scene
at light speed. Jake bit his lip to keep from guffawing out
loud.

Dressed in cutoffs, tank top, floppy straw hat and gardening gloves, Shelby shook her fist at the retreating animal and mouthed a few choice epithets Jake was almost sure he was glad he couldn't hear through the French doors. Then she turned back to the flower bed she was filling for Earnesto, inspecting the chewed and bedraggled bedding plants Attila had evidently attacked behind her back. Picking up her trowel, she knelt down and went back to work.

Jake blinked, then tore his gaze away from an extremely provocative view of her shapely tush. He suddenly felt hot again. Spreading the mail out on the kitchen cabinet, he retrieved the tea pitcher from the refrigerator and poured himself a tall drink, studiously ignoring any further activity outside on the patio.

True to his word, Jake had done his best to keep Shelby occupied, interested, and too busy to dwell on her predicament. The strategy seemed to be paying off. Even though he still caught her occasionally gazing off into space, her inner sight focused on that dark terrible place only she could journey to, all in all, he believed she'd begun to find some peace.

He had to admit, for a city girl, she'd jumped in with unusual goodwill, even when it was clear she was at a total loss. She hadn't been that keen on getting on a horse—saying that while a Harley might throw you, at least it didn't *buck*—but she had a natural seat and athletic posture that served her well as they'd driven calves in from the hollows and gullies. She'd painted a fence, cleaned tack, baby-sat Leza, ridden into Aledo with him to pick up feed and fertilizer, then had the unique courage to tackle an Elaine's special burger dripping with chili and cheese and jalapeños they got "to go" from the Bearcat Café. She'd beaten him at poker and even fried chicken—badly—for supper one night.

Her skin glowed golden with a newly acquired tan. Her hair had gotten lighter, and the bruises around her neck had faded until now they were nothing more than shadowy reminders of her brush with death. With the lessening of her inner tension, they'd even managed to avoid any more all-out confrontations, verbal or physical. He'd heard her laugh more than once, enjoying her company as well as admiring her courage and determination. One thing was for sure, Shelby Hartman wasn't afraid to tackle anything new.

Which brought him right back around again to that niggling, itching sting of self-doubt. He swallowed half the glass of tea in a single swig, then stood frowning at the dew condensing on the cold glass. Was he really too conservative and set in his ways? Unimaginative and closed to new experiences? When had being solid and dependable come to be equated with being a stick-in-the-mud?

Muttering a curse, Jake reached for the mail, reminding himself that his self-esteem had just taken a battering that would have driven lesser men to their knees. Hell, he liked the way he'd turned out. And if Georgia didn't have better sense than to—

He went still, his fingers frozen on a padded envelope addressed to him in Georgia's feminine hand. His jaw clenched at the instinctive knowledge of what he held. He almost set it aside unopened, but then anger reasserted itself. He'd be damned if he'd let her make a coward of him.

Ripping into the package, he pulled out a pink, floral-scented envelope and a black velvet box. The note was mercifully brief: I'm sorry.

He knew his scowl was black as thunder, but he resolutely thumbed open the little hinged box, then stood staring at the gaudy marquis-cut diamond that had graced

Georgia's slender finger for two full years. He was suddenly very glad that at the last moment he'd opted for a new stone rather than offer Georgia his mother's modest engagement ring set. At least the sentiment attached to that still remained untainted.

"Jake!" Shelby burst through the French doors in a flustered rush. Her cheeks were pink with heat and frustration. "You've got to do something about Attila! I—"

Jake looked up. "He's not *my* cat."

"That's what Zach always says." With a spurt of laughter, she swept off her straw hat, blinking to adjust her eyesight from the bright sunshine to the more subdued indoor lighting. "That devil—"

She broke off abruptly, taking in his expression. Her gaze dropped to the tiny box just as he snapped it shut. Forcing his tone to normalcy, Jake shoved the incriminating object back into the padded envelope.

"Was there something you wanted, Shelby?"

"No, I'll take care of it," she said hastily, taking a step back. She licked her lips, and her eyes darted again to the package in his hand, then away.

In embarrassment, or worse, pity, Jake thought. His scowl deepened.

"I've taken all I'm going to from that ratty feline," she said in a rush. "Where's the broom? Just look what he did when I turned my back."

She turned to show Jake the side of her shapely calf, now marred by parallel rows of bloody claw marks. Ducking into the laundry room, she grabbed a broom from the wall holder, and headed for the doors, still babbling inanely.

"Damned rabid beast took vengeance on me for aiming a flowerpot at his scheming head, then skedaddled into the storage room behind the pool house. But if he thinks

I'm going to stand still for this, he's got another think coming."

"Have at him," Jake said darkly. "The bloody booger's got it coming and then some."

"Yes, well..." She hesitated, searching his face. "Yes, I will."

Then she hurried out, broom in hand, to seek satisfaction.

Jake's hand closed around the envelope, crushing it. He knew then how Shelby had felt when the demons came rushing at her and she had lain there in his arms—exposed, wounded, naked.

As feelings went, they weren't worth a damn.

"Damn you, cat!"

Shelby kicked through the clutter of the stifling storage room. If she could just locate Attila, he was going to be one flattened feline.

Dust motes danced in the light pouring through a dirty window and cobwebs drifted from the rafters. Behind a pile of dusty boxes, old paint cans and stacked-up furniture, a pair of evil yellow eyes gleamed in the shadows.

"I see you." Shelby thrust the broom into the crevice, rocking cans and dumping sacks that jingled with nails to the dusty concrete floor. With a hiss, Attila bolted, and Shelby lunged after him, too late. All she saw was a blur of ebony vanishing out the door.

Puffing, she leaned against the broom handle. "You sorry, moth-eaten, tuna-breathed beast—I hope you rot!"

The scratches on her calf stung and she bent to inspect the damage. They weren't deep, and she had to admit to herself she wasn't really so much mad at the cat as chagrined by what she'd accidently seen on Jake's face as he held what could only be Georgia's diamond engagement ring. It wasn't right to look into another's soul and see such anguish.

He must really love her.

The thought made something twist in Shelby's chest. Resolutely she ignored the sensation, turning her gaze to take in the mess cluttering the dim storeroom. Now here was a project.

According to Jake's prescription, she'd been fighting her demons by staying almost manically busy. Engaged in chores all day and too tired to even dream at night, sometimes she even forgot there was someone out there who wanted her dead. She had to feel some gratitude toward Jake Lattimer for that small mercy. And actually, the cowboy's company hadn't been half-bad.

Shelby rolled her eyes. Who was she trying to kid? Jake Lattimer was a man totally outside her experience, a mysterious masculine critter who fascinated and bemused. He found ways to bring something worthwhile to the most mundane activity, and while he wasn't given to idle chatter, his wealth of knowledge about a wide variety of subjects peppered whatever laconic conversation he did make with subtle insight and surprising humor. A cowboy with the intellect of an Einstein. A hayseed with the wit of Will Rogers. A hard man, with a core of kindness and love of nature that would shame St. Francis himself. If ever there was an enigma, Jake was one.

With a shake of her head, Shelby knew it was almost certain she'd never be able to figure out Jake Lattimer, which made her glad she wasn't a permanent fixture on the Lazy L. But while she was a guest, she could at least continue to make herself useful.

Since Attila had ruined all hope of finishing Earnesto's flower bed this afternoon, Shelby decided she might as well tackle the storeroom. Knock down a few spiderwebs, throw away the trash, straighten up the clutter, and then there'd be a lot more room to maneuver in here. Rosalita ought to be tickled pink.

And in the back of her mind, Shelby knew it would keep her out of Jake's way until he'd had a chance to recover himself. She'd seen something raw and painful in the cowboy's dark eyes, and she didn't want to repeat the experience.

By the time she'd restacked a dozen folding chairs, sorted out a giant garbage bag full of old boxes, yellow newspapers and assorted broken garden tools, then lined up paint cans on a rickety wooden shelf and sorted through at least twenty-five different kinds of nails and tacks, Shelby had worked up a sweat. If she could just stack the rest of the boxes and shift a few pieces of discarded furniture to the back wall, then she could give the place a good sweeping and call it done.

A large canvas-covered bundle proved stubborn, and she tugged impatiently at the tarp to find a handhold—only to have the cover slide free, revealing a very plain, very old pine cradle, a pioneer Texas Hill Country piece. Shelby caught her breath and smoothed her palm across the time-worn wood. It felt warm to the touch, almost alive, and she could almost smell the pungent hint of resin that still breathed from the pores of the lumber.

What was something this special doing abandoned in a storeroom? Surely generations of Lattimers had slept in this bed, probably even Jake himself. Judging from what she'd gleaned about Jake's mother, Retha herself would probably have a conniption to find this precious heirloom in this corner, dusty and forgotten. It ought to be ensconced in a place of honor, at the foot of the master bed, awaiting the next addition to the family tree.

Sinking to her knees, Shelby touched the peak of the

bonnet with trembling fingers. She could almost see the
well-beloved child who'd sleep here next, a lusty babe
with hair as black as midnight. In her mind's eye, she saw
Jake bending over the cradle, proud and tender as only a
new father could be. He'd never reject or abandon his
offspring, never leave it alone to fend for itself in a harsh
world. No, if she was certain of only one thing in this
life, she knew that Jake Lattimer would protect his own,
build a haven of safety and commitment and dependability
for the ones he loved that would never fail, never yield,
even to death itself.

Hands clenching on the edge of the cradle, Shelby
closed her eyes, overcome by a yearning so piercing she
nearly cried aloud. Her skin was hot, yet she felt cold and
shivery. What wouldn't she give to be the woman he
loved, the mother of this phantom child?

Shelby's eyes flew open, and she pressed her fingers to
her lips in horror. From what secret, insane bubble in her
brain had that come from? It was Georgia Jake Lattimer
loved, and from the intimate glimpse she'd just seen, it
would take him a long time to recover from losing her.
Maybe he never would. It wouldn't pay for Shelby to get
involved with the rancher, not even if she were already
halfway in love with him.

"No, I'm not." Shelby lunged to her feet, her breathing
suddenly erratic. It was ridiculous, absurd. Just because
she'd enjoyed being with Jake these past days, just because since that night in Tulsa, things had been on an
even keel with them, just because she'd worn a stupid
gown embroidered with roses to bed every night, that was
no reason to go off the deep end.

She drew another ragged breath, striving for calm. So
she was a little infatuated. She'd admit that much, but in
love? No way! She was bruised and vulnerable by her

assault, so of course any man who showed her some kindness, even if sometimes it was of the tough-love variety, would necessarily garner her favor. But the Lazy L wasn't the real world. She couldn't expect anything but trouble to bloom and grow in this rarefied atmosphere. They were oil and water, city girl and country boy—no, there were just too many obstacles. And if this was where her troubled emotions were leading her, well, she'd better cut her losses and run.

Abandoning the cradle and her broom, Shelby headed for the door, muttering. "You heard me, sister. It's time to get the hell out of Dodge."

Chapter Seven

It was a torrid embrace, a clench worthy of the hottest romance book cover or the sexiest James Bond movie, and it was taking place right at the Lazy L's kitchen sink.

"Oh, excuse me." Shelby rocked to a flustered halt, her feet skidding on the cool, apricot tile.

The couple broke reluctantly apart, Earnesto looking dazed and hungry as his wife's fingers lingered in his black hair, Rosalita's lush mouth well kissed, her dark eyes sultry with the innate knowledge of her feminine power.

"Oh, hi, Shelby." Rosalita's voice was low and throaty, her slow smile as smug as a cat's. "Ernie was just congratulating me on the *A* I got on my test."

Her face aflame, Shelby backed hastily away. "That's great, Rosie. The phone—I—" She took a deep breath. "I'll go use the one in Jake's office."

Then she fled, wishing she could cover her ears to

drown out the sounds of low laughter and heartfelt sighs. And wishing that her deepest core hadn't leaped in jealous response to the happy couple's obvious passion and love for each other. Some people made it together. Some people found their destinies in marriage and child rearing and growing old together. If only—

Shelby shied away from the next thought. Swiping her hair out of her hot face, she crossed the living room to the corridor leading to the office. God, she was losing it! Hadn't she learned anything from her experience with Gary? When a street-smart girl like her started daydreaming about white lace, orange blossoms, honeymoon peignoirs and fairy-tale "happily ever afters" in rose-covered cottages, then something was seriously out of kilter. Boredom, cabin fever, something in the water—whatever the reason—the sooner she got back to her own world, the better.

Reaching across the desk in Jake's—thankfully deserted—office, she punched Zach's number into the phone, waiting impatiently as the phone jangled on the other end. He had to be in. She needed him to fix this—now. So what if he was out chasing bad guys? She'd call him at home. Georgia would know where he was and—

Someone picked up the receiver. "Rawlings."

"Zach. It's me. When can I blow this joint?"

"Shel? What the—"

"I mean it, Zach. I'm desperate."

"Get serious, partner. What do you want me to do?"

"Have the court date moved up."

Zach heaved a sigh that gusted through the wire. "Even if that was possible—which it isn't, I've got to escort a prisoner out of state in less than an hour."

Shelby propped a hip on the front of the desk, her bare legs sticking slightly to the polished surface as she twirled the cord between her fingers. "Not if the sanity of the key witness is at stake. Talk to the judge, will you?"

"Shelby, I can't believe it's that bad. What's Jake done now? Beat you?"

"No..."

"Called you names?"

"No."

"Oh, the old 'fate worse than death' then," he suggested with heavy sarcasm. When she didn't answer right away, the tenor of his voice changed. "You don't mean...? Shelby, what's going on?"

What could she say? That she had the hots for his twin brother? That her heart when pitty-pat and her insides melted and she felt safe when Jake held her in his big, strong arms? That she was intrigued and fascinated and fast losing all grip on reality? *Yeah, right.* There wasn't any explanation that wouldn't make her look like a damn fool. A damned fool *female,* which, in her line of work, was even worse.

"Just get me out of here, okay?" Her voice was harsh to her own ears. "I told you I'd be bored senseless inside a week, and I was right. I've tried to play by the rules, but either you find a way to let me get back to the real world, or else Salvatore won't be the only one who's in the wind."

"Look, I'll speak to Jake. Dammit, if he's messing with you—"

Her stomach lurched. "No, there's no need for you to talk to Jake. I can take care of it—"

Jake's deep voice cut across her protest. "If he's got something to say to me, maybe I better hear it."

Shelby jumped, looking up to find Jake poised in the office doorway, a soft T-shirt stretched over one arm, his chest breathtakingly bare, his hair damp from the shower.

Oh, God! Had he been privy to her whole conversation with Zach?

In one stride he crossed to the desk, jerked the phone from her grasp, barked into it. "Yeah?"

Shelby shrank back from the fury etched on his countenance, the rage that turned his eyes from chocolate brown to black marble. He slapped the shirt down, his bulk on one side and the phone cord on the other trapping her against the desk. As he listened to Zach's diatribe, his knuckles went white around the receiver.

"Anytime, Rawlings," he snarled after a moment, cutting into the tinny shouts coming from the other side of the conversation. "So come get her, she's a real pain in the butt, anyway." He listened again, his expression going dark as a thundercloud. "Oh, yeah? You and which army? Well, *brother*, now you know how it feels."

He smashed the receiver home, the movement crowding her so closely the soft curls matting his chest brushed the tips of her breasts beneath the grimy tank top. Repressing a shudder of pure sexual awareness, she lifted her chin. She would not be cowed by this man's anger nor her own unaccountable susceptibility.

"You are one real piece of work, you know that, lady?" he growled. "Going to take off without a word, were you? Just like that."

Just like Georgia. The unspoken words hung in the air between them like an invisible, impenetrable wall.

"Not just like that. If I had been, you wouldn't be seeing me now," she countered hotly.

He grimaced. "So your timing's a little off. I have to give you credit, you sure had me hornswoggled. I really thought you were beginning to fit in around here."

"Don't make me laugh." She'd be damned if she'd admit she'd felt the same way. Prevarication was preferable to admitting such a foolish weakness. "You didn't really think I'd adjust to having cow manure between my toes, did you? It was an act, cowboy, just another assignment. I'm a chameleon, you know. I can blend in here just as well as I did at Salvatore's hideout, but that doesn't mean I like either one. And I've certainly had my fill of country life."

She could tell her barb pricked him, but his eyes only got darker. "And I guess I was wrong to expect simple courtesy from a guttersnipe."

His return jab made her catch a sharp, angry breath, and her mouth compressed.

"At least I admit my blood isn't blue. My pretensions aren't in that direction, not like some people's."

He caught her shoulders. "You calling me a bastard?"

"If the shoe fits."

Eyes narrowing, he nodded. "Yeah, you might be right. Being a gentleman sure hasn't paid off."

Dipping his head, he startled a squeal out of her by nuzzling the curve of her neck, licking the salt from her skin with his tongue. Shocked, frantic, she pressed her hands against his chest.

"Stop it! What do you think you're doing?"

"Zach thinks I've already taken advantage of you, and I'll be damned if I'll take the blame for something I haven't done...."

Panting, she slid her hands up to the tops of his shoulders, then dug in her nails—nails that for the first time in her life had actually grown out instead of being nibbled off. With a grunt, he jerked back, the sharp movement nearly snapping her neck.

Nose to nose, they glared at each other, brown eyes delving into greeny gold, breaths mingling in rapid gasps, as if they'd both run a great distance to meet at this place.

She saw something primitive and hungry lurking behind those chocolate orbs, felt the same restless, reckless stirring within herself, and with her look dared him to take what they both wanted.

His dark eyes burned. Then he tilted his head to one side, bending closer by slow, excruciating degrees. Hypnotized, Shelby held her breath, feeling as though she'd stepped off a sheer drop into midair.

A measured "harrumph" from the doorway froze them both, snapped their heads in the direction of the tall, trim, silver-haired man in the aqua golf shirt who stood watching them with a wry gleam in his eyes. Jake blinked once, then straightened like a man roused from a sleepwalk.

"Hello, Dad."

"Curiosity killed the cat, Dad."

Ben Lattimer chuckled and swirled the last of his bourbon in the bottom of a cut-glass tumbler. His ostrich-skin boots rested on an overstuffed ottoman, and he had the rumpled appearance of a man glad to be back in his own home. "Does that mean Attila has met his maker at last?"

Jake slouched on the leather sofa, his long legs stretched out in front, his expression morose. Hours earlier, supper had been an awkward meal radiating with Shelby's embarrassed hostility, but now the house creaked with a late-night stupor and all was quiet. The brass lamp at Ben's elbow was the only illumination in the living room, and it cast a well of golden light that enfolded father and son in a circle of well-established intimacy and friendship as they caught up on the news and what Dwayne Rawlings had told Zach. Jake frowned down into his own glass, then tossed back the dregs.

"No, Zach's black-hearted devil is still intact, blast the luck. I just mean that letting a nosy reporter like Laura

Ramirez poke around in things that are better left alone is asking for trouble.''

''Son, we've got nothing to hide,'' Ben said. ''It seems logical that your birth mother—that Abby—must have had a good reason for separating you and Zach. Someday that reason might be important to know.''

''What can Ms. Ramirez dig up that Tom Barnette hasn't already told you?''

''We'll never know unless we let her try.''

Jake chewed the edge of his mustache. ''I'm still not convinced it's worth the trouble.''

''Both you and Zach deserve to know the truth. It didn't take those blood tests to prove you were brothers.''

''Don't remind me. But just because we were conceived together doesn't mean I have an obligation to be friends—especially after this business with Georgia.''

''Then why did you agree to help out Zach's partner?''

Jake hesitated. Even now he wasn't sure. Shelby had seemed so tough on the outside, so wounded on the inside, he didn't really feel he'd had much choice but to let her—even help force her—to stay on the Lazy L. That just went to show you how wrong a man could be.

He pulled a finger over his mustache. ''It seemed the right thing to do at the time, I reckon.''

Ben's mouth twitched. ''I'll bet.''

Jake bristled. ''Meaning?''

''Meaning your old man isn't so old or so blind that he can't see what's going on between you and Miss Shelby.''

''Nothing's going on.''

Ben nodded, his head tilted at a skeptical angle. ''That right? In that case, as your father, I'll have to ask you just what your intentions are toward that young woman.''

Jake lurched to his feet. "I don't know what you're talking about."

"Don't play the game unless you mean it, son."

Shoving his hands into his pockets, Jake gave Ben a look that was both helpless and resigned. "Dad, I'm not even in the stadium."

"We found her, boss." The balding subordinate couldn't keep the note of triumph from his voice.

The newspaper, folded open to the *Tulsa World* society page, hit the Italian marble coffee table in front of the steely eyed man on the leather couch. Outside, virtually ignored by the chalet's occupants, the breathtaking, vivid green vista of the Rocky Mountains spilled in all directions.

Carefully, with the tip of one slim finger, the seated man turned the paper to a better angle. Hatred projected from him like an aura of evil.

"That's her for sure," the henchman said eagerly. "Shoes made the ID."

"Who's the man?" Salvatore asked.

"Her old partner, Rawlings. He's with the Rangers now. They must be doing the protective custody bit, but they sure screwed up, big time."

"That they have. Call Jenkins. Tell him I want to be in Oklahoma by midnight."

"If you're trying to hitch a ride, you'd have better luck out on the main highway."

Startled by the tall figure who'd materialized out of the midnight dark, Shelby jumped, her jean-clad bottom nearly slipping off the top rail of the lane fence. She caught herself just in time, then cursed under her breath.

How did Jake Lattimer *do* that? She shot the rancher a look of annoyance.

"Just trying to find a little peace and quiet, cowboy."

"Couldn't sleep?"

How could she admit that she was so unsettled she hadn't been able to so much as lay her head on the pillow? That a stilted supper with Jake's admittedly very cordial father hadn't done anything to soothe the ache of restlessness in the pit of her stomach? She couldn't. Not to this man, whose raw masculinity was the cause of that ache, and whose hostility and disdain prevented her from doing anything about it. So she shook her head, gazing up at the starlit sky, foisting off an excuse. Any excuse.

"Too noisy. Damn grasshoppers—"

"Crickets."

"—and wolves—"

"Coyotes."

She huffed an aggravated breath. "So I prefer a lullaby of diesel motors and ambulance sirens to all this back-to-nature stuff. What about you? I thought all you cowboys went to bed with the chickens."

"Except in foaling season."

Interest piqued, Shelby slid from the rail, her tennis shoes raising small puffs of dust as she hit the ground. "Is it Lucy?"

Nodding, Jake turned toward the barn. "Yup. Night watchman sent for me. Looks like this is it."

Despite everything, she couldn't disguise her eagerness. "May I come?"

His back stiffened, but he stopped and turned slowly back to her. Under the pale lavender illumination of a mercury vapor security light set on a pole by the gate, the planes of his lean face took on an extra measure of harshness. "Why?"

She shrugged, unwilling to reveal a fascination with the miracle of birth and so settling for nonchalance. "Why not? There's nothing else happening around here."

He seemed to consider. "All right, then. If you think you've got the stomach for it."

Indignation squared her shoulders. "I've delivered babies before, and in places not as pleasant as a nice, dry stall, either."

"Then come on. I don't suppose it hurts to have another midwife in attendance, even if she is a city slicker."

Jake's words proved prophetic, because in short order Shelby found herself inside the large, hay-strewn stall, positioned at the straining mare's head, holding Lucy's halter and trying to calm a mother-to-be who was obviously in trouble.

"How long has she been like this, Alonzo?" Jake barked to the grizzled ranch hand kneeling beside him in the straw. The mare's heaving flanks were wet with sweat.

"Swear to God, she was OK just a minute ago, boss."

"Damn, I'd hate to lose the baby and the mama, too." Jake examined the mare, a worried frown on his face. "Wait. Here's the bubble. Maybe..."

Shelby craned her neck to see the first presenting edge of the amniotic sac. Although she didn't know squat about equine birth, that seemed a good sign.

"There's a hoof," Alonzo began eagerly, then his face fell. "Hellfire! Only one!"

Cursing a blue streak, Jake was already stripping out of his shirt. He caught Shelby's eye. "Keep her as still as you can, angel. Got a hoof going the wrong way. Got to push the baby back and turn it or..."

"Yes." Eyes wide, Shelby gulped and nodded, then turned all of her skills to calming the laboring mother, stroking the mare's pretty forelock, crooning to her in a low voice, promising all sorts of nonsense if only Lucy would just do her part.

Meanwhile, Jake struggled with all his strength to fight the mighty contractions trying to expel the foal into the world. Grimacing, his arm inserted in the birth canal, he pressed the foal back with all his strength. The sweat popped out on his brow, and the muscles in his chest and arm bulged with effort. Alonzo added his weight to his boss's back for leverage, but it was Jake who fought on and on....

It seemed a lifetime. An eternity.

Perspiration drenched Shelby's clothes, and she felt totally exhausted. But it was nothing compared to the effort Jake put forth over and over.

"Boss, we have to pull 'er," Alonzo gasped at last. "Let me get the tackle."

"Dammit, no!" Jake grunted. His face grew almost purple with effort. Shelby had never seen such determination. "If I can just—got it!"

Jake fell back with a groan of relief, his chest heaving as he gasped for air. Alonzo looked up at Shelby.

"Hold on to her, miss. There's both hooves, and lookahere, there's the nose!"

Jake scrambled back into position at the mare's tail, he and Alonzo quickly peeling remnants of the amniotic sac from the foal's nose.

"Come on, Lucille, you can do it," Jake urged. "Give 'im a hard push, squeeze all the juice out of those lungs!"

As if on command, the mare shuddered in a final great spasm and delivered a soaking wet bundle of hide and bones into the straw.

"Don't let her get up yet, Shelby," Jake ordered. "It's best if the blood continues to flow through the umbilical cord as long as possible."

In awe, Shelby nodded, stroking Lucy's velvety ears and whispering praise. The little awkward bundle shivered, drew its first breath, shivered again.

"A filly, boss!" Alonzo crowed. "Red like her mama."

"There, she broke the cord. Burn it with iodine and get the enema ready," Jake ordered.

They busied themselves with the various duties of birthing. After a few minutes Jake nodded to Shelby and she released the anxious mother. After a couple of tries, Lucy stood up, immediately turning to nose and lick her new daughter. Mesmerized with wonder, Shelby stepped back out of the way and watched with envy the immediate, unconditional outpouring of love. She felt humbled, elated, privileged to have witnessed such a wonderful miracle.

"Is she really okay?" she asked Jake hoarsely.

He stepped to her side, grinning like a proud papa handing out cigars. "Perfect. Watch this."

They watched as the newborn, only minutes old, attempted to stand. Half an hour later, with vaccinations and cleanup complete, the little filly had actually taken her first steps—right to her mother's teat.

"She's a prizewinner, boss," Alonzo said, storing away medicinals. "Look at how straight her legs are. What you going to call her?"

"Not Ethel." The protest popped out of Shelby's mouth without conscious volition.

Jake chuckled. "So you *were* listening."

"She needs a prettier name than that," Shelby amended, flushing.

"We'll think of something," Jake said easily. "I'm going to wash up in the tack room."

"I'll stow this stuff away, but then I'm hitting the hay, okay, boss?" Alonzo asked.

"Sure." Jake rubbed the bridge of his nose between two fingers. "Past my bedtime, too."

Shelby could hardly take her eyes off the new baby. "Would it be all right if I watch for a while longer?"

He shrugged. "Suit yourself. Just don't make any sudden moves and spook them."

"Don't worry. I'm a whiz at stakeouts." Her grin was a trifle lopsided as she settled into a corner of the stall. "See? Totally inconspicuous."

After Jake and Alonzo left, Shelby got more comfortable, resting her back against the stall wall, her eyes avid on the new mother and her offspring. The mare whickered softly at her baby, nudging her closer. The baby's eyes, just moments before so bright and puzzled and interested in this new world she was seeing for the first time, now looked heavy with weariness. Shelby smiled to herself as the little filly finally succumbed, half-sliding to her knees, then collapsing in a pile of long legs and awkward angles to nap. After all, being born was serious, tiring work.

As well as being nothing short of absolutely miraculous. Stifling a yawn of her own, Shelby rested the side of her head on her fist, letting her musings meander. Despite all of its complications, life was something to be cherished. Maybe surviving Salvatore's attack had given her a new perspective on that. Perhaps when she got back to the force, she'd look into that family intervention program, maybe work on her family counseling degree again. After all, she knew the problems foster kids faced better than most, and if she were realistic enough to understand that her work and her luck with men narrowed the odds of her having babies of her own, then the least she could do was help nurture some "throwaway kids" nobody wanted.

"Hey, Sleeping Beauty. If this is the kind of work you do on a stakeout, remind me to commit my crimes on your watch."

Shelby blinked, turning to find herself face-to-face with Jake, who was down on one knee beside her in the hay, gently touching her arm. He smelled of soap, and his hand was cool from the water he'd used. He'd donned his shirt again, but it hung open, revealing a swarthy swatch of hard male chest.

"I wasn't asleep," she said in a whisper.

His lean cheek creased, showing a dimple. "Yeah, yeah."

She straightened. "I wasn't—"

"Shh. Nobody's criticizing." His hand strayed up her arm, found the angle of her jawbone and lingered there.

"With you I never know."

She looked down, swallowing, loving the warmth of his fingertips against her skin, hating the fact that she hadn't the strength to break the contact. But something had to be done, before she made a fool of herself. She gave herself a mental shake, forced herself to meet his eyes with a smile.

"Look, thanks for letting me share this, Lucy and all. It was very...special." Amazed at her own temerity, she leaned forward and gave him a quick peck on the corner of his mouth, then started to scramble up. "I'd better go—"

"Too late." The words were low, a husky drawl, but his hand was swift, cupping her nape, using her own momentum to tumble her hard against his chest. "You're driving me insane, you know that?"

"Jake." Her fingers splayed against his chest for balance, but then stayed, curling into the thatch of curly hairs, brushing the bronze nipples. Her touch evoked a shudder from both Jake and herself, and she gave a moan of pure helplessness. "Oh, damn…"

He was equally dismayed, but furious, too, at his own powerlessness. "Just shut the hell up, will you?"

Then his mouth slammed down on hers, rawly hungry, devouring her, the force of his need taking all resistance from her so that she threaded her fingers into his dark hair, holding him fiercely, her thirst for him equal to his hunger. His tongue was rapacious, delving deeply into her mouth, stealing her secrets, making her quiver through every extremity. Every shiver lodged low in her belly to ignite a white-hot heat. She met his exploration with enthusiasm, responding with eager, demanding thrusts of her own tongue.

Shelby felt the world tilt, and then she was on her back in the fragrant hay, Jake's long leg thrown over hers, his hand working upward from the hem of her T-shirt. She'd worn no bra, and when his large, work-callused palm cupped her breast, the perfect rightness of it made her cry out against his mouth and lift herself more fully as an offering.

"Ah, Shelby, you're sweet." His words were a rasp, like whiskey and smoke.

Shoving up her shirt, he laved the satiny mounds of her bosom with his tongue, making her squirm and pant and hold the back of his head tightly, for fear that he'd stop. When he took one turgid nipple into his mouth and suckled gently, the velvet brush of his mustache combined with the tugging in a sensual symphony, plucking chords that vibrated into the core of her womanhood, melting her to liquid heat, molten need.

On fire for him, she wanted nothing in the universe

more than to touch him. When he came back to her mouth, she pushed at his shirt with frantic fingers until he shoved it completely off. Exploring his ribs, the slightly concave dip of his navel, the hard planes of his hips beneath his denim jeans, she reveled in their differences, thinking that never had anything in her life fit so well, hardness to softness, angles to curves. The bulge in his jeans pressed against her thigh, undeniable proof of passion run rampant.

His breathing was gusty against her neck, his hands everywhere, massaging her breasts, teasing her nipples, curling down to explore the indention of her waist. Then he popped the snap at her jeans fly and slid his fingertips beneath the waistband into the soft, dark nest at the juncture of her thighs.

Shelby nearly came apart then, her breath sobbing in her throat in panic. This mindless need, this blatant sexual hunger—with a man she hardly knew! She caught his wrist, her eyes flying open.

"Jake, no."

He drew back, staring at her with eyes that burned with ebony flames. His fingers moved against her most secret folds, drawing a shuddering breath from her. "I have to."

Her voice was strangled with desire and humiliation. "Why? Because of what Zach did with Georgia?"

If possible, his eyes got even darker. "This has nothing to do with Zach and Georgia." He dragged her hand to the bulge at his crotch, pressing himself against her. "*That's* what this is about."

"That's all?"

"What else could it be?"

What else indeed? Bitterness spurted within her, soured her mouth and the taste of him still lingering there. What else would a man like him, a prince with every privilege, want with a street urchin like her? *Fool! Did you think he was going to love you?*

Her teeth chattering, she pushed him away, her voice husky with some emotion she dared not name. "Despite what you've been led to believe, I'm not that kind of girl, cowboy."

"Shelby, dammit!" He pulled her back, covering her with his body, holding her hands beside her ears. "That's not what I mean. I mean, I feel—"

"You're not in any state to know *what* you feel," Shelby said, too calmly, in the reasonable voice she used for psychos and drunks. "I can understand that. You're on the rebound. I'm lonely, too, and tempted, I'll admit. But we've both got enough complications in our lives to know this isn't a good thing, no matter how good it feels right now. So back off, cowboy. We'll just both have to agree that things got a bit out of hand."

Jake bit out a string of curses that surely had Miss Retha spinning in her grave. "You are the most hardheaded female I've ever seen. Why, I ought to—"

"Please, dear, we shouldn't fight. Not in front of the children."

"Huh?" Jake blinked, then looked up.

Lucy stood over them, inhaling softly, her big horsey eyes inspecting them with almost human disapproval where they lay sprawled in the hay.

Jake clenched his jaw. With another oath, he released Shelby, rolling to his feet and pulling her up in one swift movement that had Lucy shying back with a snort and bits of hay and chaff flying through the dusty air. "You're right. To hell with it."

Knees shaking, Shelby agreed. To hell with the Lazy L. To hell with Jake Lattimer. And to hell with this ache for him that even now urged her to throw herself back into his arms and damn the consequences. But her survival instincts were screaming alarms, and she knew that sometimes discretion was, as they said, the better part of valor. She lifted her chin.

"You said it, cowboy. This isn't working. First thing in the morning, I'm clearing out."

Turning her back, she stalked out of the horse stall, found herself running—like a coward, she thought disdainfully—for the haven of the house and her room...with its lock on the door.

Not to keep Jake out. Gentleman cowboy that he was, he'd never force his way into her bed. No, it was to keep herself from succumbing to the lure of his arms, because she'd seen the kind of man he was, strong and tender and passionate; and turning away from the magic of his lovemaking was the hardest thing she'd ever had to do.

Shelby reached her bedroom door with the sure knowledge that she had to leave the Lazy L...before she made the mistake of starting to believe that maybe she could stay.

Chapter Eight

Jake clawed his way upward, coming to the surface of consciousness with his heart pounding and sweat dripping from every pore. He jackknifed to the edge of the king-size bed and buried his face in his hands. A spectral pre-dawn light peeked through the drapes at his bedroom window, but all he could see was the darkness inside his head.

He pulled a hand down his stubbled jaw. Damn, what a dream! He'd been maybe three or four again, gathering Easter eggs like in the picture in his mother's room, but someone else had been there, too. Another little boy or maybe Hoss, the imaginary playmate he'd had when he was little....

Jake stood abruptly. No, it had been Zach. Zach, who'd taken a bite of egg and started choking, turning blue right in front of Jake's horrified eyes while all the adults around them pretended not to see. A black foreboding filled Jake, constricted his throat, choking him as surely as the egg had his dream twin.

"This is crazy."

Jake took a pace toward the window, breathing hard, oppressed by a sense of impending disaster. Pulling on his jeans, he succumbed to the compulsion beating at his brain, striding from the room into his own office, flipping through the Rolodex until he found the number he'd never thought to use, then punching the buttons in an agony of impatience.

"Hello?" The voice was breathy, wary.

"Georgia, this is—"

"Zach!" Her voice caught, dissolved into sobs. "Thank goodness you called back. I couldn't bear it...where are you?"

Dismayed, his gut sinking, Jake broke in. "Georgia! Sugar, this is Jake. What's happened? Georgia—"

"Jake? Oh, God, Jake! Somebody shot at him!"

Jake sat down hard in his desk chair, his breath leaving him in a "whoosh." He fought to keep the panic out of his voice. "Tell me. Is he—?"

"No, no! He's all right. The shooter missed."

Jake's forehead dropped into his palm. "Thank God."

Georgia's watery snorts subsided a bit as she took a breath. "I didn't mean to scare you, Jake. I'm just not good at this yet. But if anything happened to him..."

"I know, sugar, I know," Jake soothed, and somehow he did.

Only a woman who truly loved her man could face what Georgia Lee Rawlings had to every day, especially since her own grandfather had been killed in the line of duty. For the first time, Jake acknowledged that Georgia had never felt that depth of commitment and devotion toward him, or he toward her. And what a waste of both their lives if they had bound themselves together without a true bond of love. He'd never really thought about how courageous Georgia had been in her decision, how much courage she'd still need to stand by her lawman husband through just such crises as this one. If Jake was anything close to the man he liked to think he was, he ought to be grateful for the heartache she'd saved them both.

"Can you tell me what happened?" he asked quietly.

"Zach was transferring a female prisoner for the Feds. It happened when they were leaving the Tulsa airport. Blasted out the whole back window of the sedan, he said, but other than a few glass cuts, they're both okay."

Jake blew out a breath between his teeth.

"Jake?"

"Yeah, sugar?"

Georgia hesitated on the other end of the phone line, then spoke in a rush. "Is that why you called? Had you heard?"

"No. I just had a bad feeling. Hell, it's hard to explain."

"They say twins know these things sometimes," she offered.

"Never put much stock in stuff like that, myself," he said, then gave a wry smile. "May have to rethink that attitude. Anyway, are you okay now? Do you need someone to come stay with you? I'll come if you say the word, or I'm sure Rosie—"

She sniffled a little, then gave a weak laugh. "I swear, Jake Lattimer, you are the kindest soul I know. I just wish…"

He interrupted gently. "Now's not the time, sugar. We'll talk later, okay? I just want to know if you're all right."

"Yes, fine, now that I know Zach's safe. He's going to call again as soon as they clear up some details."

"You need anything, you let us know?"

"Yes. I'm sure Zach will be calling you, too."

"How's that?"

Again she hesitated. "The prisoner was a blonde. Zach thinks someone might have thought it was Shelby."

Jake felt the blood leave his face, and he bit out an oath.

"Yeah, I know," Georgia said, her low laugh a broken sound. "It's a dangerous world out there. You keep her there, Jake. You keep her safe."

"I will. And you can tell Zach I said so."

Jake hung up the phone, scrubbing his mustache with a forefinger that still trembled ever so slightly. He'd nearly lost his brother, and the feeling didn't sit well at all. And here was proof positive that Shelby was still a target herself. It made him mad as hell. He wanted to strap on a six-shooter and call in the cavalry. Two people he cared about, and their very existence threatened...

He stopped. Swallowed hard. Despite everything that had happened, there was a bond between him and Zach he couldn't deny. Maybe it had happened in utero, maybe the first time he'd seen his own reflection in his twin's eyes, maybe when they'd tried to pound each other into pulp—it didn't matter. Whatever rocky trek still lay ahead of them in their relationship, Jake wanted to know his brother. Whatever Abby's motives in separating them, they'd found each other, and that was an immeasurable gift. It was hard to accept such a notion when your pride was wounded, but Jake wasn't a man who could never own up to a mistake. It was time to make their peace, and when this was all over, he was going to make it his first priority. As for Shelby...

Jake stood abruptly, turned to stare out the front window at the fenced lane leading up to the house, the contented cattle just beginning to stir in pastures glazed with first light. Yes, he cared about her. She was so touchingly fragile under all that bluster, so valiant and brave, and he wanted her more fiercely than any woman he'd ever known. They burned like torches for each other, igniting with a touch, a look.

But what would their necessarily brief affair accomplish other than ease the ache in his loins? Just because she'd seemed to fit in around the Lazy L lately didn't mean they had enough in common to plan a future together. Just because she'd been so genuinely moved by the foal's birth he'd believed for a moment she could grow to love the land and the life here as much as he did, that didn't mean it was anything other than a lonely cowboy's crazy pipe dream.

Shelby was walking wounded, he'd known that from the start. How could he justify taking anything else from her to satisfy his own selfish needs? He'd always been collected, balanced, ever-reasonable in his relationship with Georgia, but Shelby stripped away all semblance of his control with her sassy mouth and challenging attitude. However, acting on his impulses, the way he had been recently, had her running scared, threatening to clear out. And if she left because of him now, she would be putting herself back in the gravest danger.

He couldn't allow that to happen. And if he had to eat crow to keep her from bolting, then so what? Her pretty hide was worth protecting, even if he was the last man on earth who had the right. Mouth twisting, he left the office.

He knocked on the door to Shelby's guest room a few moments later.

The minute she heard the sound, she came awake, lunging to her elbow, poised and ready...for disaster? She shook her head. Would she ever again be able to sleep with assurance? Her dreams were circumscribed by a fear that made her feel unsafe in her own bed. And worse, Jake himself had compounded that fear with the previous night's close encounter.

"Who is it?" she asked.

"Me."

Jake. "What do you want?"

"Relax, Shelby," he called through the oak-paneled door, surprised at the harshness of his own voice. "This isn't a social call."

"What a relief." She swung her feet to the floor, shoved fingers through her straight gold locks and went to unlock the door. "It's not another OB case, is it?" she asked, swinging the door wide. "Mainly 'cause, 'Miss Scarlett, I don't know nuthin' about birthin' no babies.'"

For a moment Jake could do nothing but stare at her, an undeniable hunger in his eyes. "You did all right last night," he said at last. "Better than most the first time out."

Avoiding the sight of his bare chest and the flutter of her heart, she shrugged off the compliment. "A fluke. So what brings you to milady's bedchamber so early in the morning?"

"Zach." Briefly, he related what Georgia had told him, watching her blanch as he had earlier at the shocking news.

"He's really all right?" she asked finally.

"So Georgia says. But any harebrained notion you've got about skedaddling today has got to be scotched right here and now."

Shelby shook her head. "Forget it. Zach overreacts.

He's just assuming someone mistook his prisoner for me. The incidents probably aren't related at all."

"Can you afford to take that chance?"

Shelby hesitated, then bit out a single, explosive expletive and looked away. "This takes the cake, doesn't it?"

He wanted to go to her, take her in his arms and chase that scared light out of her eyes with his kisses, but he knew she would not welcome his comfort so he stayed with the small of his back pressed against the doorknob. Even as he watched, she squared her shoulders, drew herself up, so valorous and alone it nearly broke his heart.

"I'm sorry to have imposed on your hospitality this long. There are alternatives. I'll talk to Zach about the safe house and—"

"That's not necessary." He cleared his throat. "Uh, about last night—I apologize. Clearly, it was a mistake—"

"You can say that again!" she muttered, a flush stealing over her cheeks to counteract her earlier pallor.

"—and it won't happen again."

She slid to her feet, wrapping the sheet toga-style with a flourish. "You can bet the ranch on that, cowboy!"

He didn't know why her vehemence wounded him, but he clenched his jaw, keeping his features impassive. She was twitchy, and it would serve no purpose to raise her ire. "Look, there's no reason why we can't make peace for the duration. Deal?"

Her look became haughty. "A cease-fire?"

"More a cessation of hostilities."

"That's what got us into trouble last night."

Exasperated, Jake shoved a hand though his hair and glared at her. "Look, you and I both know I'd like nothing better than to take you down on that bed and make love to you until neither one of us can walk, but you made your feelings clear and that's that."

"Glad you were listening." Her cheeks glowed, but she met his gaze defiantly.

He jabbed a finger at her nose. "Just don't think I'm going to let you use female histrionics as an excuse for doing something stupid—like walking off the Lazy L straight into some killer's gun sight."

"Why, you lug-headed, bow-legged polecat!" Incensed, she took a step toward him. "I'll show you—"

"Don't bother, I've seen it all, and I'm not impressed." Opening the door, Jake paused, leveling her with a stony look. "So stay put, your virtue is safe. I'll stay out of your way. You stay out of mine. On two thousand acres, that shouldn't be too hard."

"Welcome to the Lazy L, Ms. Ramirez." Ben Lattimer stuck out his big paw, his smile one of masculine appreciation. "I must say, you don't look like any nosy reporter I ever saw."

"I get that all the time, Mr. Lattimer." Laura Ramirez laughed and shook the rancher's hand, then let him lead her into the well-appointed living room. The afternoon sun cast scalding beams through the windows, but the air-conditioning made the house a cool oasis after her hot drive from Dallas. "Let me assure you, however, I'm as nosy as they come. And call me Laura."

Laura knew she looked well in a neat fuchsia suit that showed off her dark coloring and petite, but well-rounded figure. Large gold hoops dangled at her ears. She was self-confident enough to take admiration in stride, and had found during her investigative career that her open friendliness and approachability evoked a lot more answers than an uptight business persona.

"It's kind of you to see me," she said, seating herself on the leather sofa and tucking her short skirt neatly under her trim thighs.

"On the contrary, any help you can give us about the boys is most appreciated. You've known Zach a while, haven't you?"

Laura nodded. "Since he was on the Dallas force and I was just a cub reporter. He's always shot straight with me about what I wanted to know on the crime beat. And speaking of shooting, you know what happened in Tulsa last week, don't you?"

Ben stretched his ostrich-skin boots out in front of him and scowled. "Damned nasty business. Even though I didn't know Zach existed until just a couple of months ago, I admit I can't help some paternalistic feelings for the boy. And this, well, it makes me want to take a horse-whip to somebody. Thank the Lord he wasn't hurt."

Laura smiled to herself at Ben's reference to "the boy," acknowledging Ben's warmth toward her friend with approval. Zach hadn't had very many breaks, so finding a surrogate father as well as his twin brother had to be a bit of good luck. That is, if Jake Lattimer ever got over Zach's stealing his bride out from under his nose— a situation about which Zach expressed his doubts. Made things a tad awkward around the home place, Laura guessed. Still, there had to be something going on if both twins were interested in finding out more about their birth parents and the whys and wherefores of their separation.

And it won't be bad for my career, either. With a wry inward smile, Laura envisioned the Pulitzer she'd win for the in-depth "Adoption Then and Now" piece she'd been working on for over a year. She'd interviewed adoption agencies, the Vital Statistics Bureau, foster care families, birth mothers who'd given up their babies, birth fathers who'd kept theirs, adoptive parents, nurses, doctors and social workers. But dry statistics could only go so far.

Zach had already told her how, after finding out he had a twin, he'd decided that Abby and Dwayne Rawlings must have adopted him, too, just as Jake had been adopted by the Lattimers. But then when he'd confronted the old drunk who'd been the only father he'd ever known, Zach had been doubly shocked to find that while Abby Pickett Rawlings was indeed his birth mother, Dwayne Rawlings denied any blood relation. So now there was the mystery of not only who had sired Abby's twins to solve, but why she'd chosen to give away only one of the babies.

Laura's own mother's heart swelled with empathy for the frightened teenager who'd made such a difficult decision. As hard as she knew being a single mother was sometimes, Laura couldn't imagine giving up her five-year-old hellion, J.R.—better known as Rufio among her family for his mahogany locks—to a stranger. But to give up one baby and keep the other? What outside pressures had made the mother take such a step? Yes, indeed, this was a riddle Laura Ramirez intended to solve. The Lattimer/Rawlings twins' story would add a personal, human-interest angle, the heart clincher that made the difference between just an interesting newspaper series and a real prizewinner.

"Yes, Zach was lucky," Laura agreed solemnly now. "Law enforcement is a dangerous business."

Ben's expression was wry. "So we're learning."

Laura's instincts told her there was a level of meaning beneath his words, but she filed that away for later consideration and reached for her notepad and pen. "Would you mind if I ask you some questions now?"

"Fire away."

Laura listened and took careful notes as Ben told her

about his and his wife's desire for children. Her ears perked up when he revealed that attorney Tom Barnette, now candidate for the state senate, had arranged the legal paperwork. Good, she thought, scribbling rapidly, a celebrity politician would add another level of interest to her story.

"What did Mr. Barnette say when you contacted him about there being another baby involved?" she asked.

"He was as surprised as we were. Since we first talked, he's contacted the nurse who ran a home for unwed mothers and worked at the little hospital in Brownsboro, but it was so long ago and she's so old, she didn't have any memory of it, either."

"There are ways to track these things down." Laura made another note. "I got the names of some of Abby's old classmates out of a yearbook Zach had. I'm trying to locate them now."

"Good thinking," Ben said.

"It never hurts to ask," Laura replied with another smile.

A clunk of boots and a large male figure materializing in the doorway intruded on the conversation.

"Where the hell's Shelby?"

"Watch your mouth, son. There's a lady present," Ben said.

Instantly the straw cowboy hat was doffed, and the tall man approached them with an apology. "Excuse me, ma'am. Didn't know we had company."

"Good God." Laura stared up at Jake Lattimer in sheer astonishment. "Zach told me you looked alike, but this is amazing."

Ben chuckled softly at her rapt expression. "Meet Laura Ramirez, son."

Jake Lattimer took Laura's proffered hand, and his jaw worked. "The reporter."

She beamed at him. "That's right. Nice to meet you, Jake."

"Laura's willing to poke around, see what she can come up with about you and Zach. That's okay, isn't it?" Ben asked, cocking one silver eyebrow.

"I still don't see what's the point," Jake growled, releasing her hand. "But what the heck. Sure, go for it."

Laura had run into this dichotomy of emotion from other adoptive children and sympathized. The part of them that didn't want to know the details of their birth—and what some of them thought of as abandonment—warred with an innate curiosity about who they were and where they came from. It looked as though Jake Lattimer still had to come to terms with what he might think of as a fly in the ointment of his otherwise privileged existence.

"I won't pursue anything you're not comfortable with," she assured him. "We can stop it here, no harm done."

"No." He shook his shaggy head. "It's important to Zach, and hell, whatever you uncover isn't going to change *my* life any, so we might as well find out the facts and get—what's the psychobabble word for it?—*closure* on the issue once and for all."

"A commendable attitude," Laura agreed cheerfully. "I don't think you'll be sorry."

"Yeah, that's what they all say—" A delicate slap of leather sandals on the hardwood floor swung him toward the doorway, his words changing to a growl of demand. "Where the devil have you been?"

The blonde in the doorway whipped her fingers through her wet hair, tucking the strands behind her ears, and tilted her chin to scowl back at him. "Lucille's stall. Helping

Earnesto change the fan belt on the mower. Leza's swimming lesson. Staying out of the head honcho's way, as per orders. By the way, did you know that under all that feline fluff, Elizabeth the Fourth is pregnant? Very, very pregnant."

Jake bit out an oath. "Attila!"

"I know this animal." Laura began to laugh. "All together now—"

As one, each person in the room ground out, with various degrees of enthusiasm, "He's not *my* cat!"

Lips twitching, Shelby flicked a glance in Laura's direction. "*Cómo estás,* Laura?"

"*Muy bien,* Shel." Puzzled, still chuckling, Laura rose to greet her friend with a warm hug.

With a quirk of feminine envy, Laura wondered not for the first time at the ability nature had given Shelby to look like a million sexy bucks, even damp-haired, *sans* makeup, and in a worn denim jacket, T-shirt and sprigged knit skirt that had probably come from Goodwill. But she could have been pure Paris haute couture, at home at the White House or the mean streets with equal ease, and she wore the look with such utter chic and unselfconsciousness a girl couldn't even really be jealous. Shelby just didn't know what she had. But the look on Jake Lattimer's face said he obviously did.

Oh, ho. Laura's intuitive feminine antennae caught the signals of friction and sexual awareness sparking between the two of them. Zach's rancher brother and the lady cop? Very interesting. Very interesting indeed.

"So this is where you've been keeping yourself lately." Laura kept her expression innocent. "Vacation? How nice."

"In a manner of speaking." Shelby's smile was a tad too bright. "Always hankered to spend a spell on a dude ranch, you know."

Laura snorted. "Yeah, right. City girl like you."

"Just don't go off again without letting someone know," Jake said between clenched teeth. He slammed his hat back onto his head and addressed his father. "I'm going to run the south line. Tell Rosie not to wait supper." He tipped his hat. "Ladies."

As the rancher vanished through the doorway, Laura felt as though a tornado had erupted, then blown out of the room in the blink of a eye. Whatever burr was under Jake's saddle blanket, it sure was making him ornery. And Laura had a sneaking suspicion Jake's particular burr had pine green eyes and a mouth designed to drive men wild. She wondered what Zach thought about the situation.

Ben rose to his feet, clearing his throat. "Uh, why don't I see if I can get Rosie to rustle us up some coffee and some of those little lemon tea cakes she makes? Could you stay for supper, Laura?"

Laura glanced at her watch, then smiled regretfully. "I've got time for coffee, but my little boy's at my mother's and he wasn't feeling quite up to par when I left. Much as I'd like to, I'd best beg off. I think we've got enough to get started with, don't you?"

"Sure, and you can call any time something comes up," Ben agreed. "You ladies have a visit while I scrounge our grub."

As Ben disappeared toward the rear of the house, Laura grabbed Shelby's wrist and tugged her down on the sofa with a hiss. "Okay, spill it. What gives?"

Shelby dragged a hand through her hair and shrugged. "This is Zach's idea of a good, safe time."

"Ah. That Salvatore stuff?"

"You know about that?"

Laura pressed Shelby's hand. "Enough to know you

handled yourself like a trooper. And don't worry, your secret's safe with me. I never saw you.''

Shelby blew out a breath. "Well, Zach's kept me incommunicado out here until I'm about to lose my mind.''

"Not surprising, with that other tall, dark Texan looking thunderclouds at you. Or as if he'd like to eat you for dessert.''

"You have a vivid imagination.''

Laura grinned. "My powers of observation are beyond keen.''

"Not this time. And I've had it with Zach's overprotectiveness. Can you give me a lift back to town when you go?''

"Well, sure…''

"I can stand the safe house until the court date. It's only a few more days, anyway.''

"That doesn't sound nearly as nice as the setup you've got here,'' Laura told her.

Shelby shrugged again. "Like you said. I'm a city girl, and I'm bored out of my skull by all this country bumpkin stuff. I mean, the Lattimers have been very kind, and they sure put on a mean Fourth of July barbecue for all the hands day before yesterday, but I've had all the fun I can stand. It won't take me two shakes to pack my stuff and say my goodbyes. Can I count on you?''

"Of course.'' Laura gave Shelby a quick, bewildered stare just as Ben returned with Rosie and the coffee tray.

Biting into a lemon tea cake, Laura considered. Things must be a little more complicated on the Lazy L than Shelby was willing to let on. Shelby Hartman had never run away from anything. But then, she'd never been known to tell a bald-faced lie, either.

* * *

All right, so she was a coward. And a liar. So what?

Shelby tossed the last balled-up T-shirt into her scruffy duffle and zipped it closed. All she knew was that if she had to walk on eggshells around Jake Lattimer one more minute—one more *second,* she was going to go stark, raving bonkers. Laura Ramirez's arrival was a heaven-sent opportunity, and she didn't intend to blow it.

"'Keep out of my way'—ha." She jerked the handles on the bag and headed for the bedroom door. A week of staying out of Jake's way had just meant finding him in her thoughts twenty-four hours a day, when he wasn't actually in her face "checking" on her to make sure she stayed out of trouble—like some kind of truant schoolgirl.

And the worst part, the *absolute* worst part, Shelby knew as she paused in the upstairs hall and found her feet drifting toward Retha's sitting room, was that none of her ire or irritation had stopped her from wanting Jake Lattimer with every fiber of her being. She leaned her head on the door casing with a little groan. A hundred dolls looked back at her with sympathetic eyes.

What's the matter with me? The yearning that swelled in her throat threatened to undo her completely. So she was infatuated with a fat-headed cowboy who made her blood boil and her senses spin. Who made her so mad she could spit and then turned her inside out with tenderness and a glimmer of his own vulnerability that she could vaguely sense but still not touch. Was that love? Was it?

Yes, a voice whispered. *Yes.*

"No. Impossible." Shelby pushed away from the door, clattering down the stairs as if the devil himself pursued her. There was no possible life for her here, and she knew it.

The problem of her skewed perception was simply

caused by the rarefied atmosphere of the Lazy L, she told herself, coupled with the proximity of an attractive, fascinating man and the fact that she was still somewhat soul wounded by her near-death encounter, that was all. Just as soon as she got back to her normal environment, things would fall into place again and she'd laugh at this emotional aberration.

But even the idea of returning to work gave her a chill. She was shocked to realize the excitement of police work had lost its luster compared to the peace of country life. Hitting the streets again, even for the good of humanity, produced a flurry of butterflies in her stomach. Shelby clamped down hard on those feelings. So she was still a little gun-shy. Fear was something she could, *must* overcome. She wasn't about to throw away a perfectly good career, the only thing in her life that was really her own. She'd face her demons and win, and the sooner she got started, the better.

Shelby dropped the duffle at the base of the stairs. The murmur of Ben and Laura's conversation drifted from the living room, punctuated by Rosie's throaty laugh and a plethora of Spanish. While they finished up, she'd tend to the one thing she knew she had to do.

She wasn't Georgia, and she wasn't going to leave Jake—and whatever there was between them—without a word. She owed him that much. Hell, he *deserved* that much.

Minutes later, she looked at Alonzo with dismay. ''But I've got to talk to him!''

Alonzo spat a stream of tobacco juice in the hay he was sweeping out of Lucille's stall and squinted at Shelby through the late-evening glare. ''Well, miss, didn't say you can't talk to the boss, just that you gotta catch up with him if you want to do it tonight, or else wait till he comes in tomorrow morning. Took a bedroll and intends to run the south range tomorrow. He likes to do that sometimes. 'Only' kids grow up solitary, you know.''

"But—" Shelby clenched her jaw, stymied, then her eyes narrowed into the grim look she reserved for the direst perpetrators. Her latest partner, Harve, had always called it her "ten-gallon glare."

"I'll be damned if that cowboy's going to get his way again," she muttered darkly, then met the grizzled cowhand's puzzled gaze. "All right, Alonzo. Which way is south?"

Ben Lattimer set his empty coffee cup on the service tray, his attention caught by the ragged roar of a vehicle blasting down the long drive. He paused at the front window, a frown tugging at his brow. "Well, I'll be damned..."

Laura Ramirez, gathering up her purse and notebook while she chatted with Rosie, looked up, her reporter's senses alert. "Trouble, Ben?"

"You could say that." Chuckling, he shook his head as the two women gathered close behind him to peruse the dust-boiling departure of a ramshackle green pickup. "Alonzo's truck, and Shelby's behind the wheel."

Laura looked at her wristwatch in dismay. "But she wanted me to give her a ride into town."

Ben lifted his silver eyebrows. "That so? Seems she has something else on her mind."

Rosie rolled her eyes. "*¡Madre de Dios!* At last! Me, I'm getting real tired of those two tippy-toeing around. What they both need is a swift boot in the butt."

"Now, Rosie," Ben said gently. "They have to work things out together—or not. It's not up to us."

Muttering darkly in Spanish that made Laura grin, Rosie turned and began to gather up the coffee things.

Ben turned a kind smile at Laura. "Everything considered, maybe you'd better not plan on waiting for Shelby. I'll drive her in myself if she wants, but somehow, under the circumstances..."

Nodding, Laura returned the older man's understanding smile with a mischievous glint of her own. "Ben, I think maybe you're right."

The door of the warehouse office located within earshot of Dallas's Love Field closed behind a slender man nervously twitching his JCPenney polyester tie. The man called Shoes shifted from one foot to the other, squinting at the figure silhouetted by the single-bulbed desk lamp and swallowed audibly.

"I know you're sore at me, but I swear Tulsa wasn't my fault—"

"You made the ID. You missed the mark. Now I've got every Texas Ranger in the state breathing down my neck. I'm not pleased."

"Just give me another chance." Desperation made Shoes's voice squeak. "She's bound to surface soon."

"We're running out of time."

"I'll find her."

"You'd better."

Chapter Nine

"Hellfire and damnation! What now?"

Jake tossed the dregs of his coffee into his rock-circled campfire and scowled at the chugging, yellow-eyed apparition jouncing across the inky pasture toward him like a juggernaut. All hell must have broken loose back at the ranch for Alonzo to pitch across the dark fields with such reckless disregard of terrain, vehicle chassis, cattle and assorted wildlife. Even the crickets beside the stream, trickling through the little stand of live oaks, hushed at the approaching ruckus.

Jake sighed. So much for his peaceful night alone under the summer stars.

The whirlwind that exploded out of the battered truck before it even bounced to a stop in the grassy clearing was a surprise, though.

"Just where the *hell* have you been hiding, cowboy?"

Hair flying, slim legs flashing white through the unbuttoned opening of her skirt, Shelby rounded on him, every line of her luscious body radiating fury. And a frustration that matched his own. She was magnificent, stunning in her anger, and Jake felt her presence like a punch in the gut. Shaking his head to clear it, he frowned.

"I'm not hiding. What's happened? What's the problem, Shelby?"

"You." She was on him then, punching him in the chest with a forefinger. The truck lights turned her face into a golden relief, showing cheeks suffused with temper. "You're the problem. I can't take a breath without you counting them for a full week, but the minute I need you, there you go, hightailing it off, just like a man."

A muscle jerked in Jake's jaw. "Now wait a minute..."

"Ride the south range—what the hell does that mean? I've been traipsing up hill and down dale for hours and—"

"What?" Jake's eyes narrowed as he began to get a glimmer.

"Yes, hours!" she cried.

"You were lost." Jake laughed. "Why don't you just admit it?"

"I told you there was too much wide-open space around here," she snapped. "But I was not lost—exactly. At least you had the good sense to build a signal fire. Why don't you carry a cellular phone, anyway, Mr. High-Tech Rancher?"

"I was trying to find a little solitude, for reasons we've been over before."

"Typical macho baloney. Only now, thanks to you, I'm sure Laura's already left, so there goes my ride, and my behind's sore from bouncing in that torture machine of a truck, the mosquitoes are eating me alive, and if you'd had the least speck of consideration—"

Jake clamped a hand around her wrist before she could punch him again. "Hold it right there. You were going to up and leave with Laura, just like that?"

"To save anyone further headache, yes."

"A headache is not exactly what I'd call you, sister."

Her eyes flashed emerald in the uncertain light of campfire and truck headlights. "I know what you think of me, cowboy. I've had enough of you and this damned wilderness. And even though I didn't have a society mama to teach me the niceties, I was trying to be courteous. I told you before, I wouldn't leave without a word, not like Georgia."

"Forget Georgia," he said roughly. "She did me a favor. I ought to send her flowers. Hell, I'll send her a whole houseful of them when I get back."

"Now you're not making sense. But what else can I expect from a loco mule? This is what I get for trying to say goodbye, trying to say..."

She stopped, and Jake saw the convulsive quiver of her throat as she swallowed. The skin of her wrist was like heated satin, the pulse jumping erratically beneath his fingertips. The look on her face cracked what was left of his self-control.

"To say what, Shelby?" he asked, his voice a raw whisper. Thumbing the cords of her wrist, he tugged her closer.

Her eyes were as dark and turbulent as a forest whipped by a midnight tempest. Her lips moved, but nothing came out as she searched his face. But she must not have found what she was looking for, or else she lacked the words, or maybe the courage, because, with a shudder, she dropped her gaze and turned away. Jake felt such a piercing surge of hopelessness and hunger that it took his breath.

"Nothing," she muttered. "Forget it. I—"

"Not this time." With a jerk, Jake pulled her hard against his chest, holding her wrist pressed against his breastbone, his other arm wrapped tightly around her waist. She was slender and fragile and trembled against him, driving him mad, taking him past the point of temptation and leaving him helpless. He growled down into her startled face. "Didn't I tell you to keep your distance? Didn't I warn you what could happen?"

She wet her lips, and her voice shook, but she was all defiance. "I'm not afraid of you, cowboy."

"Well, lady, that's where we're different, because you scare the hell out of me."

Shelby's eyes widened. "I do?"

"Spitless. But I can't do it anymore. I can't hide from this." He shifted his weight, letting her feel the hard bulge pressing against his denims, grimacing at her soft gasp and the way her lids fluttered. "Can you?"

Slowly she shook her head. "No. I can't, either."

Then she was raising on her tiptoes, sliding her free arm around his neck, pulling him down to capture his mouth in a kiss so wild and needy it completely undid him. Groaning, he melded his lips to hers, tasting her as a thirsty man at an oasis of ambrosia. She was heat and heaven and so responsive his body surged and red mist clouded his brain.

He'd never felt such desire, pure and fiery and eternal, all wrapped up in the slender flame combusting in his arms. Her tongue licked at him, an enticement, and she pressed her curves against his chest as if she couldn't get close enough. And they weren't. Yet.

Jake pushed her denim jacket from her shoulders, shoved his hands under the hem of her shirt and cupped the rounded mounds of her bare breasts. When he thumbed the pebbled tips, she squirmed and shivered, pressing closer, her hands now busy with the snaps on his shirt. Then he was the one shivering as she raked her nails through his chest hair, scored the flat male nipples and traversed the corded planes of his belly down to the place where his jeans snapped. Jake was afraid the top of his head was going to blow off.

With another groan he pulled her down to her knees on his unfurled bedroll, stripping off her shirt, unbuttoning her skirt and letting it drop. She was busy tugging at his shirt, and then it was gone, too. Clad in the briefest of bikini panties, her skin glowed like warm ivory, a bold contrast to the tanned skin of his trembling, workman's hands as he stroked her golden curves.

Her lips traced the cords of his throat, the top of his shoulder, biting and licking as if she'd consume his very being. Sliding her hands down the curve of his spine, she slid her palms beneath the denim at his hips, urging him closer, her rapid gasps nearly a whimper of need.

"Oh, angel..." He caught her face between his hands, his eyes scouring her flushed features and the pouty fullness of well-kissed lips.

"Why do you call me that?"

"Because you're the nearest thing to heaven this poor cowboy's ever seen. And I need you like hell."

Quivering, she reached for him, murmuring his name in wonder. "Jake..."

He rolled her to the blanket, covering her mouth with drunken, hungry kisses, inflamed past endurance as she tangled her tongue with his, giving and taking equally with him. By the time he'd kicked out of his boots and jeans, then wiggled her out of her last undergarment, he was on the edge of what little control he possessed, his breath gusting harshly, his body tensile and trembling with the rightness and splendor of joining with her in this most basic, most sublime of human acts.

There was no coyness in her, no shyness, only an insatiable need that made her arch against his hand as he tested the wetness between her thighs. Murmuring against his lips, she gave a little sigh and threaded her fingers into the thick hair at his nape, spreading her knees, opening herself to him without reservation in a gesture so giving it humbled him utterly.

And he wanted her, but more, he wanted her to feel this with him, so he bent his head and took a nipple between his teeth, teasing her to the edge as his skillful fingers stroked and stroked...

With a cry she came apart, her whole body clenching in the ancient mystery of fulfillment. She was beautiful, more precious to him than riches or knowledge, and the fact that she'd trusted him with this made his heart swell.

Gasping, she tugged petulantly at him. "You. Now, Jake."

"No rush, angel."

"I said *now*." Her fingers closed over his manhood, wringing a groan of pleasure, then she was guiding him to the secret heat of herself and he lost all capability of thought.

Hot. Wet. Tight. Jake sank himself into her willing flesh, clenching his teeth at the ultimate joy of being one with her, with his woman. For she was his, from this moment on. Like a miner staking his claim, he'd hold to this with all his will, all his tenacity, for he'd found treasure beyond price.

He could feel the whiplash of her rebounding passion, the return of tension in her slender form that urged him to move. There was no control left in him. Plunging deep, he thrust into her, praying he wouldn't hurt her, rejoicing as she rose fully, gratefully to meet him.

They rode the storm together.

And at the end, when she convulsed in his arms again, there were tears on her cheeks, this woman who so rarely wept, but as he pitched into his own oblivion, he knew they were tears of joy, the same flavor as his own.

When he could finally think again, he found her draped bonelessly against his chest. The old truck's battery had given up, leaving them bathed only in the orangy glow of the campfire's dying embers. As he settled the edge of the blanket over their nakedness, she whispered against his skin.

"Jake?"

"Hmm?"

"Are we camping out?"

"Looks that way."

"I've never been camping."

"Never?"

"Uh-uh." Her voice was drifting, a long way away. "I think I like it."

Smiling, he would have kissed her again, but she'd fallen asleep in his arms, in perfect trust, and, for the moment, that was better than a thousand kisses.

"This is what you were running away from, isn't it?"

Jake's deep voice penetrated the sensual fog swirling around Shelby's head. He'd wakened her with sweet caresses at dawn, taken her to paradise and beyond again, and now lay under the scratchy blanket, with her tucked spoon-fashion against his muscular bulk, her back to his front. Still reeling, her limbs like liquid, she could hardly think, much less deny what was patently obvious.

"You're pretty smart, cowboy." Her sigh joined the

chitter of birds and the early-morning breeze in the oaks. Somewhere in the thicket, Jake's paint pony nickered softly. She pressed her lips against the brawny forearm on which her cheek rested. "I was afraid it'd be like this."

"Yeah. Me, too." He nibbled her shoulder, the velvet of his mustache tickling her skin and making her squirm deliciously.

"Well, you don't have to sound so disappointed."

Jake rolled her to her back so that he could meet her eyes. "Is this the face of a disappointed man?"

Shelby laughed softly, then indulged herself, tracing the outline of his upper lip with a fingertip, the curve of his dark eyebrow. "You look..."

"Sappily happy? Disgustingly smug?"

"Satisfied." Shelby felt the heat rise in her cheeks. "Like me, I guess."

He gave her a hooded look, then took her finger in his mouth and nipped it gently. "So, since it appears the worst has happened, maybe there's no longer a reason for you to head back to town?"

Despite herself, her mouth drooped, making her smile tremulous. "Or all the more reason to go."

"No." He fastened his mouth on hers for a blistering moment. "Not just yet."

What could she say? There wasn't enough willpower in the universe to make her leave the solace of Jake's arms until she had to. "No," she agreed in a whisper, shaken to her depths by her need for him, "not just yet."

A subtle tension left him, and he smiled. "Just so we're clear. It was getting damned monotonous, you know. Your threatening to haul it back to some grungy safe house just to avoid the inevitable."

Shelby flushed, and she struggled to an elbow, clutching the blanket to her breasts. "Oh, is that what this was—inevitable? How very mortifying."

"If we hadn't both felt it from the first, we wouldn't have fought it so long and so hard, angel." He traced the curve of her bosom beneath the blanket hem with a stealthy fingertip, grinning when she couldn't contain a shiver. "See?"

She slapped at his hand. "Don't get cocky, you bast—"

"Uh-uh." Scooping her breast into his palm, he pulled her back against his chest, murmuring against her mouth. "Let's not get into my parentage, okay?"

"Oh, Jake, I'm sorry." She pressed her hands against his cheeks. "That's not what I meant. You and Zach—oh, hell! What does it matter at this point? You're both good, fine men. A pedigree or lack of one means nothing. But finding a brother..."

"You know, when I was little I always wished I had a sibling. Even went so far as to have an imaginary playmate for a time." He chuckled. "Drove my mother crazy talking about Hoss until she realized I wasn't referring to Dan Blocker's character on 'Bonanza,' but...what's wrong?"

Shelby felt goose bumps on the back of her neck. "Zach once told me he had an imaginary buddy, too. Called him Hoss."

Jake's eyes widened. "Uh..."

"Yeah," Shelby said, shaking her head. "Maybe you two ought to have a long talk. And about more important things than your family tree. I certainly haven't got one to brag about."

"It's who you are inside that counts, Shelby." He grinned and stroked her nipple. "So relax, I like what I see."

She caught her breath in a little gasp. "Is this all you farm boys have on your minds?"

"Living close to nature keeps us...focused."

"And insatiable."

"That, too." He touched his forehead to hers. "What I meant was, maybe I'm curious about being born a twin, among other things, but I know who my real parents are. And there was never a kid more blessed than me for having Retha and Ben as Mom and Dad."

In an instant Shelby's throat grew thick. "Do you know how lucky you are to be able to say that?"

"Yeah, I do. And God help me, Shelby, when I think about how you grew up, I'd give anything..."

No one had ever said that, and a feeling of warmth, of protection succored her world-battered spirit. It was enough.

"You know," she said softly, encouraged by his care to share an intimacy of her own, "when I was little, I used to kneel down with Barbara Ann at night, fold her little plastic hands in prayer, and we'd beg God for real parents."

"Shelby." He nuzzled her lips, his voice rough.

"I'm glad He didn't answer those prayers, Jake."

"You are?"

"If He had, yes, things might have been different. But I wouldn't be me. And I might not be here with you now."

His eyes darkened. "You keep talking like that, city girl, and you could find yourself in real big trouble."

"Oh, I'm counting on it," she purred.

"And you called me insatiable." Laughing, Jake rose to his feet, naked as the day he was born, and reached for his jeans.

Shelby curled to a seated position, enjoying the view,

but pouting slightly. "I thought that was a clear invitation, cowboy. Where are you going?"

"To fetch the pony. Truck's dead, so we have to ride in double. I'd kill for some of Rosie's coffee, and the idea of tucking you into a real bed is very appealing. I know what a softie you are, and I'll admit a night on the ground didn't do my back any good, so—"

"I don't know, Jake..." Languidly she let the blanket slide to a dangerous and strategically planned position, then lay back and kicked it free altogether, allowing the cool morning air to wash over her bare skin. Jake stood frozen with one foot in his pants, his face stupefied.

"Actually," she murmured, "this back-to-nature stuff is starting to grow on me."

Jake forgot his jeans and came to her, his voice husky, almost reverent. "Angel, I can't tell you how glad I am to hear that."

"He's going to kill her."

"She's playing with fire, all right."

"Murder, that's what it'll be, pure and simple."

"Yeah, but what a way to go."

Ben Lattimer grinned at Rosie over the rim of his afternoon coffee mug, then cut his gaze back through the expanse of breezeway glass to the couple kibitzing outside on the pool deck.

Shelby, in a plain dark maillot that made her look sleek as a seal, treaded water and sent sprays toward the blue-jeaned cowboy planted on his haunches poolside. Her pretty, exotic features were more animated than Ben had ever seen them, radiant almost, from the inside out, but it was his son's indulgent grin under his white straw cowboy hat that surprised and pleased Ben more.

The boy had fallen, and fallen hard. It was about damn time.

"He never looked at Georgia like that," Rosie commented, propping an elbow on the kitchen island to watch with Ben. In the two days since Jake's camp out—an event it was clear Shelby had attended but no one was tactless enough to comment on—the two had been virtually inseparable, as giddy as teenagers, making even the most mundane of ranch activities a lark.

"That was part of his and Georgia's problem, don't you think?" Ben returned.

"Sure, but who could tell your boy that? Once he's set on a course, he doesn't go back on his word. You should know. You raised him."

Ben blew a sigh onto the hot brew in his mug, an old favorite he and Retha had picked up at a truck stop somewhere in Arizona the year they'd taken Jake to see the Grand Canyon. Even at that young age, the boy had been obedient and dependable, never stepping off the marked path to spit into the big hole and give his mother a heart attack like other kids, always considerate, always thinking of others.

"Yeah," Ben muttered, "he's done a grand job of living up to Lattimer expectations. Not that I don't admire him for being responsible and solid. But dammit, Rosie, it's about time someone taught him how to cut loose, to do something for himself—and Shelby may be just the little filly for the job."

"Or it's a rebound thing, and they'll break each other's hearts."

Ben's mouth twisted as he put on his best Humphrey Bogart imitation. "'You pays your money. You takes your chances.'"

"Uncle Ben!" Leza pounded into the kitchen in a thunder of sneakers and a bobble of curls, practically leaping into Ben's arms, a wounded expression on her piquant features.

"Hey, there, sugar," Ben crooned, balancing the little girl on his lean hip. God, he'd give anything to fill this empty house with grandchildren just like her. Which was another—if selfish—reason to hope for the best with Shelby and Jake. "What's the trouble, cowgirl?"

"'Lizabeth won't let me play with her."

"Hmm. I wonder if that means what I think it means?"

Rosie rolled her eyes. "Oh, good Lord! Kittens."

Leza's brown eyes went round with delight. "Really?"

"I wouldn't be a bit surprised if we didn't have a blessed event real soon."

"When, when? Can I have one, Mama?" Leza stretched beseeching hands to Rosie, who laughed and took her offspring from Ben.

"We'll have to talk to your papa about it, *chica.*"

"Oh, please. I'll be good. I'll—oh, look!" Leza's mouth popped open and she pointed at the pool. "Mama, Mama. Shelby pushed Jake in. That's not right. No horseplay at the pool, you said. She gets a time-out."

"Oh, my God…" Rosie clapped a hand over her mouth to forestall an incredulous laugh at the sight of Jake surfacing, the brim of his straw hat dripping, his sodden mustache drooping like a dishrag. "She's done it now. He'll kill her for sure. I'd better go—"

"Hold your horses." Ben latched a hand on Rosie's arm to stop her rescue attempt. His grin was as big as his home state, his low chuckle rich with humor and hope. "Would you look at that?"

All three watched as the pair in the water began a leisurely backstroke up the pool—Jake in his soaked hat, boots and jeans, grinning foolishly as Shelby chortled and criticized his form.

"Rosie, how'd you like the night off?" Ben asked suddenly.

"Huh?" She cast her boss a quick look, got the message and grinned. "Sure. Earnesto and I've been wanting to take Leza to that new Putt-Putt miniature golf course. Wanna go tonight, honey?"

"Gee, yeah!" Leza wiggled down and lit for the door. "Wait'll I tell Papa."

"I think I'll go to the movies," Ben said. "Bet Margery Hopkins might like to join me."

The pair in the pool huddled together in a shadowy corner, then disappeared completely under the surface. Ben caught Rosie's eye, and his smile grew even wider.

"Guess I'd better make it a double feature."

"Ms. Ramirez is here to see you, Mr. Barnette."

Tom Barnette slapped a sticky note requesting a bit more airbrushing onto his latest eight-by-ten campaign photo, dropped it back into its manila folder, then pushed the button on his intercom. "Send her in, Bethany."

Rising, Tom buttoned the jacket of his Brooks Brothers pinstripe, straightened his silk tie and smoothed the silver at his temples that threaded his fair hair. At fifty-eight, he knew he was still a fine figure of a man, lean and brown from hours in the gym and tanning booth, with just the right hint of youthful exuberance and mature dignity the home folk wanted in their candidate—he hoped.

While he sincerely despised reporters, he knew they had their uses, and since the latest rumors had the attorney general sniffing around some old business matters that didn't concern him, Tom wanted to keep the media in his corner at all costs. Maybe he shouldn't have gotten quite so greedy with that Aegean Insurance deal, but damn, it was hard not to when the pickings were so easy. Who'd have ever thought that little bit of shenanigans would come back to haunt him? It wasn't as if he'd stepped over the line of illegality, just put his toe over.

"Ms. Ramirez, welcome." Tom greeted with some pleasure the petite woman with the sultry eyes and mouth who strode confidently into his office.

"It's kind of you to see me, Mr. Barnette," Laura said.

"Call me Tom," he said, jovial.

As they shook hands, he gave her a once-over, his blue eyes lighting with approval at the sexy señorita in her royal blue coatdress and leather-strapped briefcase. Hers was the kind of lush beauty Tom had always found hard to resist, but he had better sense than to come on to her—not with the election at stake.

Besides, he had enough woman trouble as it was. His long-suffering wife, Regina, suspected there was someone else and was giving him the cold shoulder treatment except in public—and his newest mistress in a long string of lovers was beginning to whine her demands. Yes, Ashlie was being tiresome, thinking her status as a Dallas Cowboys cheerleader gave her some sort of special privilege or something. He had to admit, if there was one thing he found harder to resist than a dark-eyed Hispanic sexpot, it was the blonde bimbo rah-rah type, and if Ashlie wasn't so hot in his bed, why he'd just—

"I'm usually very good with this kind of thing, but have we ever met before?" A small, perplexed pleat marked Laura Ramirez's brow.

"Now that's something I surely wouldn't have forgotten," he said, giving her fingers an extra squeeze and showing a flash of dimple.

"My mistake." Laura gently retrieved her hand. "Er, perhaps we could get started?"

"Yes, indeed." Smiling, Tom waved her to a leather armchair. "Have a seat, Ms. Ramirez—"

"Laura will do."

He dipped his head, then found his chair at the desk again. "All right, Laura. But you're not what I was expecting, and I must say, it's a very pleasant surprise."

"Thank you." She was polite, cordial, a trifle cool, every inch of her five-foot, two-inch frame professionalism personified. "I know you're busy, so I won't take up any more of your time than necessary, so if I could start with a few questions…"

"About the totally unfounded concerns of the attorney general? I'll be glad of the opportunity to refute these malicious rumors. I have nothing to hide, but evidently my opponents are becoming desperate, and—"

Laura cleared her throat, crossed her knees and flashed him a big smile. "Actually, Tom, that's not why I'm here at all."

He blinked. "I beg your pardon?"

"While, of course, I'm following your campaign with great attention, my interest is the Lattimer adoption. I believe you've spoken with Ben Lattimer about the discovery of his adoptive son's twin brother?"

"Well, er, yes. As a matter of fact…"

"I'm working on a series about adoption and unwed mothers and how the system has changed over the past thirty years or so," she explained, "and the Lattimers have been kind enough to cooperate. They're also curious about uncovering the whys and wherefores of the twins' separation, since the DNA tests were absolutely conclusive. I know it was all a long time ago, but as the attorney who handled the Lattimer adoption, I thought you might be able to shed some light on this?''

With a feeling of relief that the reporter wasn't there to grill him about Aegean Insurance, Tom steepled his fingers in front of his mouth, then gave her a regretful look. ''As you know, it was a long time ago. I've handled hundreds of such cases in my legal career.''

''Yes, but any detail you could remember—''

Tom masked his irritation. Why wouldn't Ben Lattimer let this go? ''I'm sorry you've made a trip for nothing, Laura, but I'm bound by the law of confidentiality here. Even if I knew or remembered pertinent facts, there is the question of the birth mother's right to privacy. I'm not at liberty to disclose anything. The records on adoptions back then were sealed, and for a very good reason, I think. It doesn't do anyone any good to stir up these old tragedies.''

''Even for the children involved? Both Jake Lattimer and Zach Rawlings have indicated their desire to learn the truth of their parentage.''

Tom spread his hands in appeal. ''Even so. While I'm as mystified as anyone about how a set of twins came to be involved in what I knew to be a single adoption, I can at least assure you that I only handled the paperwork for one child at the time Ben and Retha Lattimer adopted their baby.''

''Well, as far as that goes, Zach Rawlings's father— adoptive father, that is—confirmed that his wife was indeed Zach's birth mother, and that he married her when Zach was still an infant, so one piece of the puzzle is in place.''

''My God,'' Tom said slowly. ''She kept one brother, but gave the other up? Interesting. That would indeed explain a great deal. But as far as my involvement went,

Laura, everything was strictly on the up-and-up. One set of papers for the Lattimers, as I said. As for the rest, I have to respect the law in this matter or jeopardize my own career. My hands are tied.''

"Well, I certainly respect and appreciate your position, Tom," Laura said warmly. "And there are other avenues of investigation still open. For instance, Mr. Lattimer said you'd been in contact recently with the nurse who ran an unwed mothers' home in Brownsboro. Could you give me her name? She might be able to shed some light on a few details that wouldn't necessarily violate the confidentiality requirements. There are a couple of possible scenarios that might explain what happened. I think the Lattimers would be satisfied with that much."

"Uh, Lillian's a bigger stickler for the rules than I am," Tom said slowly, his mind calculating fast. The last thing he needed was for her to uncover anything he was connected to that even remotely resembled a scandal. And the Lattimer adoption was looking worse by the day.

Would directing Laura to retired nurse Lillian Hampstead be likely to do him any damage? They'd worked closely together those early years, handled several prestigious adoptions through her home for unwed mothers.

But even though Lilli was thirteen years his senior, it hadn't been all business between them. No sir, not by a long shot. Still, Lilli wasn't a dummy. She knew when to keep her mouth shut. She'd have no reason to mention their torrid little affair, or anything else, even if the reporter did question her. Heck, there were plenty of women who could do him a lot more damage in that department, and he knew Lilli still had a soft spot for him, even after all this time. As an altruistic old broad with a big heart who'd helped place hundreds of unwanted babies, she could even make him look good with the reporter.

And every bit of positive publicity helped these days.

"Look, I'll tell you what," Tom said, flipping through his address file for the number his own private investigator had supplied him with when Ben had first called. "The nurse who ran the home in Brownsboro was a lady by the name of Lillian Hampstead. I don't know if she can help you, but be sure and tell her I sent you."

Laura reached for the number he scratched on a notepad. "Thanks. I really appreciate this, Tom."

"Don't mention it." He rose to escort her from the office. "And I hope you'll remember me at election time."

"Oh, you can depend on it," she said, smiling, but her eyes unreadable. "You're a hard man to forget."

Chapter Ten

Shameless.

That's what she was, Shelby thought. Sprawled in the huge king-size bed beside her, Jake slept the deep, undisturbed sleep of the just—or the completely sated. Moonlight drifted in the window, cutting pale, translucent panels of alabaster against the dark furniture, and from a great distance a whippoorwill called. She felt a small surge of satisfaction that she'd recognized it, thanks to Jake's tutelage. Not bad for a city girl.

Of course, the city girl had a lot to account for. Such as cavorting like an oversexed nymph with the brawny cowboy—anytime, anyplace and against her better judgment. And under Jake's father's own roof, no less.

No-class hussy.

Restless, disturbed, Shelby slid quietly from the bed. All right, so she had no doubt Ben and Rosie guessed what was going on, but she could act with discretion.

There was no reason to risk embarrassing anyone just because she and Jake were doing their best to set the house on fire with their lovemaking. She'd find her own bed, so that in the morning she could come downstairs with at least the pretense of having some sensibility.

And maybe a little distance would help her put some perspective on what was happening. Like a turtle bobbing to the surface for a gasp of air, Shelby knew she'd been dancing with the tadpoles without regard to essential things like breathing or thinking. Jake had that effect on her. His simplest touch, always tender, always passionate, cast every thought and inhibition from her mind and body. She blushed at the thought of the pile of chlorine-saturated clothing lying in the bottom of Jake's shower and how they'd gotten there. Her lack of control where he was concerned was downright frightening.

Shelby shivered in the air-conditioning, then plucked the chambray shirt Jake had worn to supper from the back of a chair and slipped it on. The woodsy scent of his cologne and the musk of his skin enveloped her, making her shudder with desire.

Dangerous. The man was definitely dangerous, and even though they were lovers now, had shared the heights and depths of the greatest intimacy known to humankind, she hadn't the foggiest notion what was going on behind those dark brown eyes.

With a last, longing look at the man breathing peacefully on the tumbled sheets, she let herself out of the room, padding down the hall in the darkness and up the stairs with complete assurance, as if she'd lived on the Lazy L all her life. She thought she was heading for her own room until her feet took her into Retha's sitting room. Flicking on the small candlestick lamp on the end table, she found the comfort of the well-worn wing chair, a spot that had become her particular thinking and hiding place since arriving. Somehow, she felt welcomed and accepted here, as if she belonged.

But that was all wrong, and if she couldn't see that, Shelby told herself fiercely, then she was hiding from herself. The fears and feelings that had been held at bay by the magic of Jake's loving washed over her in waves. With a groan she buried her face in her hands, rocking herself like a child.

"Oh, God, what am I doing?" she whispered.

She knew perfectly well. She was spoiling herself in the most selfish, shameless fashion. For a woman who'd never known many luxuries, Jake Lattimer was the ultimate indulgence, a man who made her feel feminine and cherished and wanted. And there was no way under the blue Texas sky that it could last.

She should have left while the getting was good, no matter how distasteful or dangerous her return to Dallas. She'd known better, known it would be...wonderful. And infinitely harder to give up once she'd tasted the delights with Jake. If she had a lick of sense, she'd borrow Alonzo's truck this minute and put as many miles between her and Jake Lattimer as the old jalopy could stand.

But she didn't have any sense left, not where the cowboy was concerned. There was disaster in her future, and she knew there was no way to avoid it.

Shelby jumped up, rubbing her fingers up and down her arms in agitation, pacing back and forth in front of the unblinking audience of Retha's doll collection. Her gaze snagged on a mop of blond curls. Here she was again, on the outside looking in, as always, like a little girl with her nose pressed to the candy store window. Amazed at her own temerity, Shelby slowly pulled open the glass door, reached inside and gingerly lifted out the replica of her Barbara Ann.

Shelby's throat swelled, and she clutched the baby doll to her chest in a spasm of anguish. All her life, things had been out of reach, and a life with Jake was just the same, a tempting fantasy that would disappear over the horizon in the blink of an eye. Lowering herself back into the wing chair, Shelby tucked her knees beneath her and lay the doll in her lap, tenderly stroking the pale curls and painted cheeks. She wasn't surprised when a hot tear splashed on the doll's plastic skin, and another dropped to dampen the tiny, smocked dress. This Barbara Ann wasn't hers and never could be.

Neither was Jake. And she had to understand that, forgo any false hopes or dreams.

Oh, he was hers for the moment. A man like Jake would never enter into a physical relationship lightly. But there were a thousand extenuating circumstances that made anything more impossible—the differences in their outlooks, lifestyles and upbringing, not to mention the fact that just a few short weeks ago he was ready to commit completely to Georgia. It was just a matter of proximity, and a powerful chemistry. A sensible woman understood these things. But then a sensible woman wouldn't have lost her heart.

Shelby pressed fingers to her lips, but nothing could stifle her ragged moan of pain. Foolish, foolish woman, to fall in love with a man she couldn't have, to dream of cradles and family and enduring roots. To want what Retha had.

The dead woman's presence within this homey setting seemed to mock her.

She exhaled sharply, struggling for reason. So it couldn't last, and she knew it, and prolonging her and

Jake's time together would only make the end even more painful. Still, she was only a woman, and a man like him only came along once in a lifetime. Better to have loved and lost, as they said, and she was too weak to deny herself whatever time they had left.

"But I won't hurt him, Retha," she promised on a raw whisper. "I won't."

When the time came, she'd walk away, leaving Jake to the freedom and land he loved, with no awkward demands or expectations. But this was her time out of time now, and she *would* take it, whatever the personal cost to herself later. She'd have the rest of her life to pay the price.

"I thought I'd find you here."

Jake stood in the doorway, a dark silhouette, shaggy hair, bare chest, unsnapped jeans. The angle of his shoulders was aggressive, his tone belligerent. Shelby jumped guiltily.

"I'm sorry. I—I've intruded on your mother's special place again. I don't know why I—"

He ignored her stammering. "You weren't there when I woke up. I didn't like it."

She gaped at him. "You didn't?"

"Hell, no." He strode to her chair, tilted her chin upward with his palm. "So from now on—what the devil? You've been crying."

"No, of course not. I never cry, you know that." She freed her chin from his grasp, tucking her feet more securely under her, while surreptitiously wiping her damp cheeks. "I couldn't sleep, that's all, and didn't want to disturb you. Got a lot on my mind."

He wasn't buying it. Squatting down in front of her chair, he eyed her suspiciously. "Like what?"

She shrugged, cast around for something plausible, then lied. "Getting back to work. Testifying."

"Being a target again," he said flatly.

"Once I give my testimony, I won't be. Salvatore won't have a reason to come after me then, the damage will be done."

"Unless he makes it a personal vendetta because of his brother. I don't like it, Shelby. There are too many *ifs*."

Her voice went quiet. "It's not your job to worry."

"The hell you say." His jaw throbbed angrily.

"Don't." She touched his cheek, her eyes pleading. "Not now. Don't spoil it."

His mouth worked, but he clamped down on his half-formed protest, his gaze dropping to the toy in her lap. His expression changed, softened. He flicked the bow at the doll's neckline with a broad fingertip. "Ah, is this the famous Barbara Ann?"

"Close enough." She gave a little self-deprecating laugh. "Pretty silly hang-up for a grown woman to have, huh?"

"I think you're not as tough as you'd like everyone to believe. Especially me."

That he could see her vulnerability so clearly alarmed her enormously. She wouldn't have him feeling guilty when the time came to part. She wouldn't have him acting out of some kind of mistaken sense of responsibility for her.

"You know I can take care of myself," she said, almost a warning, then made a move to stand. "I should put her back. Your mother—"

Jake captured her with both palms on the arms of her chair, making a cage. "Loved to show off her collection. She'd be delighted you appreciate it. She always wanted a daughter to share it with, seeing how her menfolk weren't much for frills and girly things."

"Snips and snails, huh?"

Jake grinned. "Bloody nose, racket to wake the dead, muddy boots all over—and that was just Dad. Me, now, I slammed doors and scratched knees and got a concussion when I was eleven trying to break a bronc. She'd have tanned my hide if I hadn't ended up in the hospital."

"She loved you."

"Yeah."

"She gave you books and a spanking when you needed it, and she let you fly." Sudden tears shimmered in Shelby's eyes. "I think I would have liked her."

"She would have loved you."

Shelby made a strangled sound, and the next thing she knew she had her arms around Jake's strong neck, Barbara Ann dangling down his back, her lips pressed into the curve of his shoulder.

She fought a surge of despair. *It's going to be harder than I thought.*

"Angel..." He scooped her up, one arm under her knees, the other around her shoulders. "What is it?"

She gave a watery snort, struggling for a bit of her old insouciance. "Don't mind me. It's the middle of the night, and I've got the blues. Isn't that something even cowgirls get?"

"Only if her cowboy doesn't know what he's doing." Jake lowered his head and kissed her hard, spinning her doubts skyward like lassos.

She melted against him, sighing her need. His tongue melded with hers in a fiery exchange, and she was clinging to him, the doll slipping from her fingers to land forgotten on the rug so that she could scour his back with her newly grown nails and sink her fingers into the lush hair at his nape.

With a groan, he turned and headed for the stairs, carrying her as if she weighed no more than a puff of Texas thistle.

"Jake?"

"Relax, Shelby. There's no room in my bed for the blues. And that's just where you belong."

"Sangria, *¿gringo?*"

"Not on your life, toots."

Laura Ramirez wrinkled her pert nose at Zach Rawlings, laughed, then handed him a long-necked Corona beer from her refrigerator. "Honestly, Georgia, how do you put up with such a plebeian?"

Leaning her jean-clad hip against the tile counter in Laura's modest ranch house kitchen, Georgia Rawlings shifted a hand through her strawberry locks and shot her new husband a look that surely made his toes curl. "Oh, he has his moments."

"I'll bet." Laura's snort made her oversize silver earrings swing against the bow of her turquoise halter top. Matching shorts and sandals completed the outfit. Pouring out the fruit-laced wine mixture into fat, green glass goblets for herself and Georgia, she added a sprig of fresh mint and shook her head, feeling just a pang of envy. "You two. So much happiness could give marriage a bad name, you know."

Zach took a pull on his beer. "I recommend the institution wholeheartedly. You should try it."

"So says the newly converted. And thanks, I think I'll pass. One ornery male in my life is quite enough." She gestured through the cozy living area toward the glass patio door. The subdued "blip-blip" of a video game emanated from the vicinity of the sofa and TV. "Let's take this out on the patio and get some air before I light the grill. I can't tell you how glad I was you decided to come over. Kinda needed to see you were okay with my own eyes, Zach.''

"Thanks, pal. But it wasn't that close a call. You know law enforcement—ninety-nine percent BS punctuated by one percent sheer terror.''

Georgia picked up her sangria, sipped, then followed Laura toward the entrance. "He got the terror part right—mine.''

"Now, sunshine…'' Zach's deep voice was cajoling, then his attention turned to the small figure prone on the sofa. "Hey, J.R., my man! What's happening, bro?''

"Hey.'' The wiry, dark-eyed five-year-old with the shock of mahogany locks didn't glance up from the screen or his manipulation of the video game controls.

"Mutilating the bad guys again?''

"Yup.''

Laura dragged her fingers through her offspring's hair, only to have him shake off her touch. It wasn't much, but her mother's instincts said something wasn't quite right. "Haven't you had enough of that, Rufio?'' she asked. "It's a pretty evening and…''

"Aw, Mom, I just reached the third level. Just a little while longer?''

"Until supper's ready,'' she agreed after a moment's consideration, then led her guests outside to the minuscule concrete patio with its baskets of potted geraniums and lush ferns. The yard was fenced, neatly tended, and sported a de rigueur swing set and a sandbox loaded with toy trucks in one corner. A pint-size bike with training wheels lay on its side in the grass.

"What's the matter with the kid?'' Zach asked as he pulled the sliding glass door shut behind them. "Seems a little off his feed.''

"I think he's picked up another bug at day care,'' Laura

said, pulling up chairs around a cast iron patio table and plunking down with a sigh. "Or maybe he's just growing again. That wears them out sometimes."

"What's the word on that TV station wooing you?" Zach asked.

Laura shrugged. "Haven't come down to money, yet."

"You'd seriously consider it?" Georgia asked. "Give up newspaper work?"

"Well, I love the printed word, but I couldn't turn down the opportunity if it's offered. I have to think about Rufio's college education. When they whisper things like 'anchorwoman' and 'big bucks,' it's hard not to get my hopes up, but I'm taking it all with a grain of salt right now. But back to the subject at hand. You really doing okay after Zach's scare, Georgia?"

"Coping." Her sweet features revealed a glimpse of both humor and courage. "I'm investing heavily in Kevlar these days—'Bulletproof Vests 'R Us.'"

They all laughed, and Zach slipped his hand to his wife's nape for a quick, encouraging squeeze.

Laura fished a slice of orange out of her drink. "After all that's happened, I guess your old partner will be first in line for a free sample. You know I saw Shelby when I went out to the Lazy L?"

"You saw the Lattimers?"

"You asked me to, didn't you? I don't let grass grow under my size fives, *gringo*. That's another reason I'm glad you're here. I want to bring you up to speed on what I've found out. And by the way, that twin of yours is an amazing sight, Zach. Now I see why Georgia was so confused when she first met you. Talk about mirror images."

Zach shifted and rubbed a haze of foam off his mustache. "Yeah, double your pleasure—"

"Double your trouble," Georgia finished wryly. "And I should know."

Zach set his forearms on the table. "Uh, Laura, about Shelby—"

"Relax. She explained about being incommunicado, and I haven't mentioned it to anyone. She was ready to hitch a ride into town with me that night, though."

"What!" Zach hissed an expletive. "She's not supposed to stir an inch until I fetch her for the Grand Jury proceedings. In fact, I've got to give her another call and set that up in the next day or two."

"That reminds me, Zach," Georgia interrupted with a snap of her fingers. "Shelby's partner. What's his name—Spaulding?"

"Yeah, Harve. What about him?"

"He's called twice today looking for you, wanting to check on Shelby. Said he knew you were in touch with her and wanted to escort her to the hearing."

"And you?"

"Shelby who? I played the dumb wife, just like you told me."

"Good girl. Harve's okay, but the fewer who know about Shelby's whereabouts the better. It's been hell convincing her to stay put on the ranch, but if she's getting so itchy she begged a ride with Laura, I'd better get her out of there pronto."

"Whoa, partner." Laura waved a hand as if to hold him in his seat. "Everything must be okay, because nothing came of it. She disappeared before I had to leave." Laura's smile became impish as she peeled the succulent orange flesh from the rind and popped it between her white teeth. "I guess she got sidetracked...."

"Meaning?"

She gave her friend an arch look. "I'd bet my bippy your brother and Shelby are playing home on the range."

"What?" he growled.

Laura dropped her lashes consideringly. "You know, until sweet Georgia came along, I always wondered if you and Shelby might not end up together."

Zach looked taken aback at the idea. "Uh-uh. It'd have been like kissing my sister."

"Well, Jake Lattimer wasn't acting at all brotherly toward her the last time I saw him."

Now Zach cursed in earnest. "You don't mean that sorry SOB is really putting the make on her? She said something, but I thought she was giving me the business for stranding her in the boonies."

"Hmm. From what I saw, something powerful's happening between them. Exactly what is anybody's guess." Laura shot an anxious glance at Georgia. "Hope that doesn't ruffle any feathers."

"Oh, no. I'm relieved." Georgia bit her lip. "Jake deserves a great lady like Shelby."

Zach's brawny paw closed around the beer bottle as if it were his brother's neck. "Not if he hurts her! Damn it all. He's a Leo on the rebound, and I led her right into the lion's den like some sort of sacrificial lamb. He may be doing this to get back at me."

"No," Georgia denied firmly. "That's not Jake's way, and you know it. The morning after Tulsa, we didn't exactly talk, but I got the feeling he was beginning to understand, and maybe Shelby's got something to do with that. If so, then I'm grateful. Maybe we can all end up friends again."

Zach ground his teeth. "If he's taking advantage of her, I'll—"

"Shelby's a big girl, Zach," Laura reminded him, then

grinned. "And from what I could see, she was giving him hell. Remember who you're dealing with here. That 'lamb' of yours has fangs. If anyone can take care of herself, it's Shelby Hartman."

Georgia clamped a hand over a sudden giggle that made Zach frown then slant an apologetic look at Laura. "Sorry. Cheap date. One drink and she's gone."

"Oh, shut up, you," Georgia told him amiably. "I was just thinking Shelby's ability to take care of herself is probably what's driving Jake slap crazy. He needs to be needed, poor thing."

"Yeah, Zach," Laura said, laughing. "Save your sympathies for the one who truly deserves them."

Zach released an exasperated breath. "Women."

Georgia blew him a pouty kiss. "And what would you do without us, flatfoot?"

"Don't say it," Laura warned, laughing again. "And men do have their uses, right, Georgia? Like lighting barbecue grills for poor helpless females. Would you do the honors, Zach, while I get the pork chops? Marinated them just the way you like."

Mollified, Zach grinned. "All right, you're on."

While Zach performed the masculine duties over the gas grill and meat and the women worked on salad and bread, Laura recounted her conversation with Ben, then went on to tell Zach about her meeting with Tom Barnette.

"Just another slick lawyer with a lot of jive and no answers, huh?" Zach commented sourly over a loaded plate a short time later.

"Well, he has a certain charm, I'll admit." Laura frowned, struck again by the an uncanny sense of familiarity she'd felt on first meeting the candidate.

Despite any recollection of it, surely she'd run into him

somewhere before. She'd seen his picture dozens of times. That had to be it. And she'd always been susceptible to men with the devil in their eyes and an incorrigible roguish charm—her own son being the worst culprit. She glanced toward J.R. who had fallen asleep on the sofa and wouldn't be roused to eat. Laura made a mental note to schedule another checkup with the pediatrician, then bit into a wedge of tomato and continued.

"I did get the name of a nurse who was working at the hospital in Brownsboro though. 'Course, just our luck, she's picked up and moved in the past few weeks and didn't even leave a forwarding address."

"Another dead end," Georgia said. "Too bad."

"I didn't say I'd given up." Laura's expression grew bland. "I have my little tricks."

"Watch out when she gets that look," Zach warned his wife. "You don't want to know."

"Now, would I bend the law or do anything underhanded in the pursuit of a story?" the reporter purred.

"I take the Fifth on that one, pal."

"You just leave things to me," Laura said.

After that, the conversation turned to general topics over Amaretto cheesecake. It wasn't very late when Zach and Georgia said their goodbyes and Laura quickly straightened the kitchen, then tucked J.R. into his own bed, barely rousing him to brush his teeth.

She stood in the doorway of his bedroom, feeling her heart swell with love and a niggling worry. There were so many things a child needed. Anything she could do to give her Rufio a head start in the world, she'd do, and that included landing the TV news job if she could.

Quietly Laura pulled the door closed, then went into her office. Her "Adoption Then and Now" story still had the key elements of a prizewinner, and it just might be the coup that pushed her over the top among the other candidates for the television position. She needed to locate Lillian Hampstead. She picked up the phone and dialed a number from her notebook. As the old saying went, there was more than one way to skin a cat.

"Just like a darn woman," Jake glowered. "What do you want me to do, line it with mink? Fill it with tuna fish?"

With a disdainful twitch of her tail, Elizabeth lumbered out of the old feed crate Jake had set up as an obstetrics ward in the barn's tack room. Secluded, cozy, hay-lined—what more could an expectant mother ask for? But Elizabeth was having none of it, for the moment, her complaining yowl like fingernails on a blackboard.

"Now, you just haven't given it a fair shake," Jake protested.

Her gravid bulk under all her Persian fluff was a handicap, and she couldn't escape as Jake scooped her up and tried to place her back in the box to familiarize her with her accommodations. With a hiss, the feline straightened all four legs and extended claws—apparently willing to resist this cat Hilton, tooth and nail. Jake, wise in the ways of cats, knew when to desist.

"All right, have it your way." He plunked a hip onto one of the tack boxes, and instantly Elizabeth calmed, coming to rest on Jake's thick thigh with an almost human sigh of relief, arching as Jake raked his hands along her distended belly. The examination made him open his eyes in wonder. "Criminy, how many babies are you going to have?"

Elizabeth dropped her chin to his kneecap, reveling in the attention, a low rumble purling from her throat. Something about her looked so weary, Jake didn't have the

heart to move her, even though he'd had a long day over-
seeing the removal of the last feeder calves, had just watered off the rest of the horses and was looking forward
to something cool—in the way of a drink and a certain
blonde.

Just thinking about sitting out in the evening air with
Shelby to talk over the day and unwind made him sigh
with pleasure. It was a homey image, and not so very
exciting, but somehow it seemed right and fitting. Something that might grow on a man, for say, the next fifty
years or so.

Beneath his fingers, Jake felt the subtle movement of
new life in Elizabeth's womb. It was an elemental truth
out here on the ranch, life and birth, the cycles beginning
again. What would it be like to make a new life, create a
child of his own with Shelby? Something primitive roiled
through Jake at the image of her swollen with his baby,
his palms pressed to the rounded flesh of her belly to feel
his son or daughter kick against his hand.

There was a chance it had already happened, of course.
Neither one of them had stopped to think about such
things that first time, even though he'd been meticulous
about protection since then, as any gentleman should.
Deep in the primal part of his soul where a male claimed
his mate, he was glad there was at least a chance she was
pregnant. It would make it harder for her to leave. And
that was the last thing Jake wanted.

Jake smoothed Elizabeth's fur, shaking his head at himself. He might as well admit it, he was head over heels
in love with the skittish filly. Flat-out loco for Shelby in
a way he'd never ever experienced with another woman,
especially not Georgia. He wanted Shelby, not just in his
bed, but in his heart and home, for all time. He wanted a
whole houseful of kids with her, maybe even some foster

ones, too, if she liked. He wanted to wake up with her head on his pillow, to love her and fight with her and kiss her sassy mouth every day of his life. And in Jake's book, the only way to do that was to put a golden band on the lady's hand and haul her home for good.

Of course, he knew he'd have a struggle on his hands at first. She'd throw up all sorts of damnable arguments just to spite him, stuff about incompatibility, different lifestyles, her career. Junk. Immaterial junk that could— *would*—be worked out to their mutual satisfaction. Because down deep, Jake knew she loved him, and that's the only thing that mattered in the long run. And he was a stubborn cuss, as Zach had pointed out. This was one time he didn't intend to take no for an answer.

The simple fact was he couldn't stand the thought of being without Shelby. Nor could he abide the idea of her facing the Grand Jury alone. So, he'd be right there for her, whether Miss High-and-Mighty I-Can-Take-Care-of-Myself Hartman welcomed him or not. She'd been alone all her life, and now, he was finding, so had he. They fit each other like two pieces of a puzzle coming together, and by damn, he'd spend the rest of his life—if she'd have him—making sure that neither one of them ever felt lonely again.

Jake frowned. She had just better be ready.

"What you looking so fierce about, son?"

At the sound of Ben's question, Elizabeth started and jumped off Jake's leg, making him grimace at the cut of her claws though his jeans. He stood, rubbing his abused flesh ruefully, eyeing the older man.

"Females."

"Yup. They can sure sour a man's stomach sometimes." They left the tack room, Ben ambling down the line of stalls with Jake at his side, stopping to peek in at Lucy's sleeping filly. "Decided on a name yet?"

"Babaloo." At his dad's raised eyebrow, Jake explained sheepishly. "One of Ricky Ricardo's Cuban songs. Shelby didn't think Ethel was a pretty enough name."

Ben's gaze was understanding. "Interesting choice, but I guess it keeps the theme. By the way, Rosie's got supper ready. And Shelby's making margaritas."

"A woman of many talents."

Ben chuckled. "Thought you'd noticed."

"Only a deaf, dumb and blind man wouldn't." Jake hesitated. "Dad…"

"Sweet thing, too," Ben said. "Got a hard-candy shell on the outside, soft as nougat inside. Warm heart, just like your mother's. Likes to sit in that little sitting room, dreaming and planning just like Retha. Women—who can figure them? Still, it's nice to have a woman curled up there again."

"You don't mind?"

"Heck, why should I?" Ben shoved his hands into his pockets, kicking up dust in the lane as they came to the house. "In fact, it occurred to me, if your mind was headed in that direction, that maybe all those dadblamed dolls might make a fine wedding gift someday. For a bride who appreciates such things, of course."

Jake felt his throat grow tight. "Shelby would."

"That's what I thought. There're your mother's rings, too, if you think that might help."

Nearly overwhelmed by his father's instinctual understanding, Jake rubbed his jaw in consternation. Yeah, it would help. It was just the kind of sentiment Shelby would find irresistible. And he was man enough to understand he'd need all the help he could get. But he'd have to find the perfect time, the perfect place—hell, it was complicated! Not the least part was explaining to Ben why he—the solid, responsible, dependable son—was acting like a calf-sick, love-starved cowpoke.

"You probably think I'm loco. I mean, just a few weeks ago I was about to stand up with Georgia, and now here I go—"

"Jacob." Ben put his hand on his son's broad shoulder. When he called his son by his full name, Jake knew he meant what he said. "What I think is that you've finally come to your senses."

Chapter Eleven

It should have been a simple thing. After all, Jake told himself, he was experienced in the proposal business. He'd asked Georgia with proper ceremony, candlelight and dinner, just like a gentleman was supposed to. No sweat. A little champagne, a little small talk, pop the question, done. Nothing to it.

Jake was beginning to understand, however, that with Shelby Hartman, nothing was ever that simple. In fact, there was a diamond burning a hole through his jeans pocket right this minute, and there wasn't a damn thing he could do about it.

Since the night before, when he'd had his talk with Ben, the skittish female critter hadn't lit long enough in one place for him to wipe his sweaty palms and take the plunge. Or the moment just didn't seem right over trimming horses' hooves. Or Alonzo or Jimmy materialized just when he was about to go on bended knee in the hay barn. Or Leza bubbled into view, claiming Shelby for herself, leaving Jake standing with his mouth hanging open and the words lodged in his throat—again. He couldn't remember when he'd been so tongue-tied.

It was downright discouraging.

Jake's boots echoed hollowly in the tile hallway. From the living room, Ben's deep laughter accompanied an "I Love Lucy" rerun. The supper dishes were done, the Perezes retired to their own abode, and there wasn't hide nor hair of Shelby to be seen. He dug down in his pocket and retrieved his mother's engagement ring—a minuscule diamond in an old-fashioned platinum setting. The gem winked at him balefully from the middle of his work-roughened palm.

With a muttered oath aimed at his own cowardice, his own fear of rejection, he shoved the innocent ring back into the confines of its denim prison. There wasn't a reason in the world he shouldn't track Shelby this minute to wherever she was hiding—probably the sitting room—and just do it, by gum. Nothing could be worse than this waiting on tenterhooks for the perfect moment.

He'd taken one step toward the stairway when Shelby appeared from the direction of his office, her fingers shoved into the back pockets of her tight jeans, her expression strangely preoccupied. She seemed to stare right through him for a chilling moment, then her green gaze snapped into focus.

"Jake."

"What is it?" His scowl was for his own sudden fear.

She shook her hair back from her face, tilting her chin at a familiar angle. "Nothing, really."

"Spill it, angel."

She straightened, channeling energy into her stance, but

her teeth nibbling her lower lip betrayed her. "I said, it's nothing. That was Zach on the phone, that's all."

"What'd he want?"

"The judge is talking about setting up the date of the Grand Jury, and he wanted me to know I might have to be out of here at a moment's notice."

"When?" Jake didn't like the strangled sound of his own voice.

She shrugged. "There's nothing definite yet. He'll let me know. I asked him to let Georgia pick up some court clothes from my apartment to bring when he comes..."

Jake felt the walls closing in, time running out. The ring in his pocket seared his thigh. "Shelby, we need to talk—"

"Later." She caught his hand. "Take me riding now. I need some air."

The request floored him. Shelby actually *choosing* to be on a horse? Unbelievable. But the practical part of him balked. "It's getting dark."

"Humbug. The moon's coming up." She smiled at him, taunting him, teasing him with her feminine wiles, an almost frenetic light in her eyes. "And I've never been on a moonlight ride. What's the matter...chicken?"

"You're crazy."

"That, cowboy, has never been in doubt. So what do you say?"

Jake couldn't read her mood. But from a great distance, he could hear Georgia's voice, begging him for more adventure, more spontaneity in their relationship. *Take me on a moonlight ride, Jake.* If he expected to keep Shelby's interest, he'd better be prepared to do the unexpected, right? He brightened. Okay, so he rode horses all day for a living, but to Shelby it was a novelty and very romantic—a perfect romantic evening for a proposal, in fact.

He squeezed her hand, felt his heart levitate and grinned. "All right, city girl, you're on."

But Jake's vision of a sedate amble atop two amiable beasts under a full moon, a few amorous kisses, and then the opportunity for him to open his heart to the woman he loved never materialized. In fact, it was all he could do to keep up with Shelby as she raced across the pastures, hell-bent for leather, as if the devil himself were after her and not the man who warmed her bed.

She was going to break her fool neck! Slapping the reins, Jake spurred his own mount after her, and they galloped like madmen, startling night birds and rabbits. He shouted at her, but she either couldn't hear or ignored him, and his anger began to build. Loco female! What was she up to? Tumbling over a rise this side of the tank, just when he thought she'd surely kill herself and her horse, he caught up with her, capturing her reins and sawing them both to a feverish stop on the grassy verge.

He was out of his saddle and dragging her down from hers before he had a conscious thought. He opened his mouth to berate her for her foolhardiness, but she surged against him, covering his lips with her own, taking hungry kisses, nudging his thighs with her knee, turning to flame in his arms.

And there was absolutely no hope that he could resist. With a moan, he pulled her into the cradle of his legs. She fit him so perfectly, flowing against him as if she were made for him alone, her mouth the ultimate sweetness, her hands busy on the snaps of his shirt.

Then they were in the grass, not yet crisp and brown in the July heat, still lush and green on the edge of the stock pond. The scent of the grass, crushed beneath their bodies, rose like a heady perfume, rich and fragrant with life. Heat exploded in the sultry air as they reached for each other, strained together, too ravenous to wait for niceties, shoving aside the barest essentials of clothing only.

Then he was inside her wet heat, plunging deep with a groan that broke from his depths. Her response was wild and sweet, everything a man could want physically, and yet even as he joined with her in the closest intimacy possible for a man and woman, he sensed a wall between them, harking back to the defenses she'd raised on their first meeting.

He'd have none of it. He wanted all of her—body, emotion, soul. Over and over, he wrung the highest triumph from her, bringing her to peak again and again, branding her with his lovemaking there in the grass under the moonlit sky. But when he finally sped to his own ultimate release, he was no closer to knowing if he'd won the battle or lost.

She rose, adjusting her clothing, while he was still struggling to right the ringing in his ears and calm his gusty breaths. "Come on, cowboy."

"Shelby? Hellfire and damnation!" Scrambling to his feet, he refastened his jeans on the run, hurrying to catch her as she mounted her horse, cursing as she turned the animal toward the barn and whipped it into a canter. The race back to the ranch was more sedate, but no less silent, and still alarm bells clanged in Jake's befuddled brain. So much for a quiet cuddle and an opportunity to show her the ring.

Back at the barn they tended the horses quickly, Shelby at her most efficient, effectively blocking anything he had to say with the mundane tasks of unsaddling and watering. And then she was ahead of him again, striding toward the house, leaving him in her wake, and the attitude rankled and his temper steamed. What did she want from him? Hell, he felt *used*.

She had to pause on the back entrance to dodge two cats clamoring to be let in, then followed the two animals, tails waving like flags, up the long glass-lined corridor toward the kitchen and their feeding dishes. The pool lights sparkled like sapphires and the moon caught and hung in silver ripples as the skimmer worked, but Jake ignored the peaceful scene on the patio for once.

Shirttail out, hat askew, he stomped along after Shelby and the cats, then lengthened his stride and caught up with her by the kitchen counter. Throwing his hat aside in unaccustomed carelessness, he grabbed her elbow and swung her around.

"What the hell's the matter with you?" he demanded.

She tossed her head, glaring down her nose at him. "Matter? What's the difference, cowboy? You've had your fun."

Jake's teeth snapped together. "Now wait a damn minute. You're the one—"

"—who's not complaining," she said, too sweetly. "Let go of me."

He jerked her closer. "Dammit, Shelby. Not until you tell me what's going on in that feeble brain of yours."

She bristled. "So now I'm stupid, too?"

"That's not what I mean and you know it."

A yowl erupted from behind them. A pitch-black alley cat somersaulted, ratty ears over chewed-up tail, in the middle of the kitchen floor, landed with an outraged screech, then scrambled for cover in a mad dash toward the front of the house. Elizabeth hissed her contempt, gave the claws she'd just bloodied on Attila's nose a disdainful lick, then slunk sullenly back into the laundry room.

"Hell's bells," Jake began, amazed.

"Every woman's entitled to her space." Shelby

dropped her eyes pointedly to the hand still wrapped around her arm. "I said let go."

"You haven't answered my question."

"It's a stupid question. Besides, I stink. I'm going to take a shower."

"Not until we get this straight, dammit."

Her expression went suddenly savage, and she pulled free with a smart judo move that took him off balance. "Lay off, cowboy. I don't owe you any explanations."

Dumbfounded, Jake raked her with his look, taking in the brittle tension in her stance, the fisted hands. Not owe him any explanations? Hell, they were lovers, weren't they? Didn't that count for anything in her book? But even a cowpoke with the brain the size of a pea could tell he wasn't going to get anywhere with her in this state.

He raised his hands in surrender. "Sorry, lady. My mistake."

Her mouth twisted, and a flicker of something like regret darkened her eyes. But then, with a slash of brittle smile, she tossed her head and made for the stairs. "Just so you don't forget it."

Wrung out, Jake slouched against the cabinet in the empty kitchen. This wasn't turning out at all the way he'd planned. Masculine doubts planted by Georgia's at-the-altar desertion birthed new suspicion. Had it all been an act on Shelby's part: the fire, the tenderness? Or was this resurgence of the tough cop brought on by the pressure of the nearing court appearance? Or maybe the role she'd played here on the ranch had been just as she'd once said—a role, and now the part in this particular play was coming to an end and she'd shed that skin just like an old rattler coming out of its hide.

With a muttered oath, Jake tried to shake the damaging visions from his head. There could be all sorts of reasons

Shelby was so moody and fractious. He'd get to the bottom of it. He had patience. But even a patient man knew when to retreat.

Retrieving a long-neck beer from the refrigerator, he carried it into the living room. Ben had disappeared for the night, but Jake didn't bother to turn on the TV again. Sinking down in the old leather armchair, he toed off his boots and planted his feet on the ottoman, sipping the beer and staring into space.

Like a sap. Like a man so head over heels in love and frightened of losing the best thing that had ever come along in his life.

A sudden movement into his lap made him start. His jaw dropped. Attila, tail dragging, yellow eyes furtive and wounded, circled delicately, with nary a claw point penetrating Jake's jeans, then dropped into a dejected lump on Jake's thighs.

Jake put out a tentative hand, then stroked the cat's back. The only response was a feline sigh. Jake echoed it with one of his own.

"I know just how you feel, buddy."

Laura Ramirez eased her old Volvo to a stop, double-checked the address in her notebook, then eyed in some surprise the entrance to the exclusive Forest Hill town house complex a few well-placed phone calls had led her. The helpful attendant in the booth answered her questions, checked her credentials, then waved her through with directions. The plush landscaping, walking paths and tennis club all bespoke affluence, not what Laura had been expecting when she'd finally tracked down the retired OB nurse.

She parked in front of a gracious, two-story attached town house that looked like something transplanted from

Henry VIII's time with its Tudor beams and old brick. A charming English garden—well watered in this dry Texas heat—foamed along the pathway to the iron strap-hinged door in a fragrant froth of Queen Anne's lace, petunias and roses. Laura pushed the doorbell with a faint sigh of envy. She'd love to move Rufio to a place like this where there were lots of green lawns and trees.

"Yes?"

Laura came to with a start as the front door opened and a pair of bright blue eyes inspected her. The elderly woman was slender, well dressed and coiffed, but her leathery skin showed the unfortunate effects of almost eighty years under the Texas sun, despite the skillful application of cosmetics.

"Yes, ma'am," Laura said, instinctually putting on the deferential persona she would have used for a respected, and very strict, schoolteacher. "I'm looking for Miss Lillian Hampstead?"

"Yes." Cautious, she trapped Laura in a sharp stare. "Who are you?"

Laura introduced herself and showed her press card. "I hate to bother you at home, Miss Hampstead, but you've been hard to locate, and Mr. Tom Barnette said you might be able to help me."

"Tom! Why, I haven't heard from him in years."

"Uh, he said he spoke with you a few weeks ago," Laura said, puzzled. "I'm looking into an adoption—a set of twins—that happened at the old Brownsboro Hospital."

"Oh, my!" She waved Laura inside with a laugh. "That's right. Oh, this ole head of mine! I'd forget to wear it if it wasn't tied on."

"Then you do remember?"

"Well, honey, it was a long time ago." She ushered

Laura into a small, tastefully appointed sitting area where a tray waited. "I was just about to have some tea and late lunch after my bridge group. My grandnephew just moved me in here, you know. Taking care of his Aunt Lilli like the little lamb he is. Didn't want to worry about security and so on. Can you imagine? Who'd bother an old woman like me?"

"I'm sure you're very comfortable."

"Hard to move out of the old place. 'Fraid I raised quite a stink," Lillian admitted, then gave a mischievous grin. "Don't you tell him it was the best thing I ever did. Can't have the boy thinking he knows completely what's best for me."

"No, I can see how that might be inconvenient," Laura agreed with a smile.

The older woman beamed approvingly. "You're a nice little thing. How about a cup of that tea? And then you can tell me what this is all about."

Laura accepted, told her about the series she was working on, then outlined what she knew of the Lattimer/Rawlings adoption. Lillian interrupted her explanation time and again with reminiscences of babies, births and new mothers—not one of which had any bearing on Jake and Zach, as far as Laura could tell.

"Those were the days, land's sakes!" Lillian said, her eyes vague from years of memories. "Didn't ever intend to run a home, but that's the way it worked out for quite a few years. Poor little darlings, mamas and kids, not knowing which way to turn. Lots of times the County Welfare folks would refer them to me. Word got around. Let me tell you, there's no better feeling in this world than to take a little throwaway baby and find the tyke a set of happy parents to love and care for it."

"Do you have any children of your own, Miss Hampstead?"

"The Lord never blessed me that way, but He more than made up for it in the joy I got from my work." She leaned back in her chair, her veined hands pressed against her bone china cup. Her face, which still bore the remnants of a great bone structure that would have made her a striking woman in her time, was etched with sentimentality. "I've got albums and albums, you know. Thank-you cards from the parents, pictures of their little ones growing up."

"And Mr. Barnette helped out with the paperwork?"

"Well, of course, there were lots of attorneys involved. Had to keep everything strictly legal, you know. But Tom did his work for free. Why he even did all the legal paperwork when his little baby-sitter got in trouble. Didn't charge her folks a penny! That's the kind of man he is, honey. Lots of folks think he's a scalawag, and Lord, he was a pretty thing back in his heyday, but there's not a mean bone in his body."

Laura decided to reserve judgment on that. It was clear the old lady's memory of the lawyer was clouded by those rose-colored glasses she apparently wore.

"About the night this set of twins was born, Miss Hampstead. Think hard. I know it was stormy, and the doctor didn't get there. Both Ben Lattimer and Mr. Barnette think you delivered the twins yourself. Surely you remember that?"

"So many babies..." Lillian shook her head, a tiny pleat creasing her wrinkled brow as she set her cup aside.

"We're positive the birth mother kept one twin, but put the other one up for adoption. The question is, why? These men are grown now, but they'd like to know that, as well as the identity of their birth father."

Lillian jumped. "Oh, no, honey. Even if I knew, I couldn't divulge that kind of information without the courts telling me to."

"Well, I don't think it'll come to that," Laura assured her, then hesitated. "Well, now that I think of it, that might be the next logical step, if they want to pursue it. But I think they'd just be satisfied knowing why the mother chose to separate them, especially since the Lattimers would have willingly taken both boys at the time."

"It must have been a hard choice for her," Lillian murmured, tapping a fingernail against a flawless set of dentures. "What was that? It all blurs together after so many years…"

"If you could just try, Miss Hampstead." Laura sat forward eagerly on the edge of her dainty Queen Anne chair. "We could probably put all this to rest once and for all."

Lillian's lips pursed and she mused. "Stormy night. Was that the night we had to use the kerosene lamp? Oh, yes, it was! That's right. It stank to high heaven, and we were so afraid it was unsanitary, but the power was out and those babies were coming so fast, and there was no doctor. Of course, how could I have forgotten that?"

"As you said, it was a long time ago. You're doing fine."

Lillian gave Laura a disgusted look. "It's hell to get old, honey. I'm going to have to ask that doctor of mine to change my medication again, I'm getting so senile."

Laura smiled. Lillian might be a little vague from old age, but it was charming. "But you do remember? A set of twin boys, probably dark haired."

"Oh, honey, I don't remember their hair color," she said with an apologetic look. "But I do recollect a poor little mother's weeping and wailing. I don't know if she's the mother you're looking for or not, but she did have twins, and there weren't too many twins born at Brownsboro. It was a small hospital, you know.'' She gave a helpless shake of her head. ''Lord, thought we might lose her, she took on so bad. It was typical.'' Lillian heaved a big sigh.

It must be Abby, Laura thought. It *had* to be! How many twins could have been born at a small hospital like Brownsboro on a stormy night? ''How so?''

''Even though a mother's made her decision, sometimes when she gets a look at her baby, there on the spot she decides she can't give it up. Disappoints everyone. Had it happen all the time.''

''So she changed her mind? But why didn't she keep both boys?''

''There was a problem with one of them.'' The nurse frowned. ''Let me think. Jaundice? Rh incompatibility?''

''Think, Miss Hampstead,'' Laura urged.

''I just don't know,'' she murmured. ''But seeing that little mother crying nearly broke my heart—that's it! One of her twins had a heart condition.''

''Heart?'' Laura was taken aback.

Lillian reached over and took her hand, oozing compassion. ''Oh, honey, she did the best she could. They were dirt poor, she didn't have a husband, and that baby was so sick. The adoptive family was well off enough to care for the little fellow, see he got the best doctors, and she knew it.''

The breath left Laura at the picture Lillian painted. Abby had chosen to give up Jake because she couldn't afford his medical bills. Abby had wanted the best for him. Maybe that would help ease his hurt. She shook her head. ''That's amazing. To look at Jake Lattimer today, you'd never guess there'd ever been a problem.''

"Then there's the blessing, isn't it?" They were both silent for a moment, then Lillian smiled sadly. "I guess that little girl made a very courageous decision."

"We've got her."

"You'd better be right this time, Shoes." The voice over the phone was tinny, irritated, deadly.

Shoes leaned into the pay phone in the line of booths at the DFW airport. Chatter and pedestrian traffic nearly drowned him out, but at least he was anonymous among the crush of travelers. He was beginning to feel the deal he'd made wasn't such a bargain after all, and he urged a heartiness into his voice to hide his fear.

"No, this is it for sure. Someone's been to her apartment, took some things out. Women's things. Nice stuff, like you'd wear to court."

"You followed them?"

"Yeah. Right to her old partner's apartment. He's going to make the pickup for sure. Then we snatch her quick, take her out of the picture until after the Grand Jury hearing, and you're home free. All we have to do is wait."

"That, my friend, is something I am extremely tired of doing."

Shoes gulped. "Yes, sir."

"And Shoes? Unless this assignment is completed successfully, you understand that you will be seeking new employment—on a permanent basis?"

Shoes gagged on his own bile, and perspiration sprouted under his arms and around the shoulder holster hidden by his sports coat. "Sir, don't worry. Nothing can go wrong now."

"I wish I shared your optimism."

The receiver went dead in Shoes's sweaty palm. He left

it dangling as he dashed for the men's room to relieve his heaving stomach.

Jake had been awake a long time when the phone on his bedside table rang the next morning at dawn. He grabbed it, barked a quiet, "Yeah?"

Shelby rolled over to gaze at him with a wary frown, looking tousled and touchable in the rose-trimmed gown he'd bought her an age ago. No one would have ever known they'd spent their first night without touching. Jake knew he ought to be grateful that she'd been asleep in his bed at all when he'd finally decided he'd had enough of Attila's company and retired for the night. But the mound of pillows and her on-the-edge-of-the-mattress position had sent a message more clearly than words that he was still to "back off." Maybe now that she'd had time to sleep off whatever was eating her...

He frowned at the deep voice grinding questions in his ear. "Yeah, Zach, I hear you. You want to talk to her? She's right here."

Zach Rawlings paused on the other end of the wire, cleared his throat. "That's what I thought."

"It's none of your business," Jake growled.

"She's my best friend."

Irritated by Zach's proprietory interest, he snapped, "You should have thought of that before. Here she is."

Shelby took the phone, shoving back her hair and coming up on one elbow. "It's too damn early in the morning for social calls, Rawlings."

Jake watched as her expression changed, her belligerence faded. Nodding, she mumbled assent a couple of times, then murmured, "I'll be ready."

Jake's look was questioning as he took the receiver from her and replaced it in the cradle. "Well?"

"The judge is convening a secret Grand Jury at ten o'clock in the morning. Zach will be here by five today to get me."

"I can take you into town as well as anyone."

She kicked off the chocolate-colored sheet and rose with a negative shake of her head. "No. He said something about precautions. He's going to hide me out somewhere—somewhere plush with room service if he knows what's good for him. You know Zach, always overprotective, but I'd best humor him."

"All right, so I'll go with you both when he comes."

Shelby rounded the end of the bed and came to an abrupt halt. "Why?"

The very question raised his ire. "Because dammit, I don't want you facing this alone."

"I don't need a cowboy on a white horse charging to my rescue."

Jake flung himself from the bed and reached for his jeans. "Don't give me that crap about your taking care of yourself. Everybody needs somebody sometime."

"Spare me the bad lyrics, Jake."

"They're true enough. And, angel, you need somebody now."

"I don't know what you're talking about."

He grabbed her hand, turning it so that they could both see the ragged edges on several newly chewed nails. "You're turning into a nutcase again right before my eyes. Let me help."

She snatched her hand free, and the gaze she turned on him would have turned a lesser man to stone. "You've got a helluva nerve."

Then she stormed into the bathroom and slammed the door. Jake scrubbed a palm down his night-stubbled cheek in pure frustration. Hell, what was with the woman?

You'd think she'd welcome a little support, but it was as though he was offering her poison. They'd gotten off to a bad start again. He had to talk to her calmly, rationally.

Going downstairs, he made hasty ablutions in the powder room and brewed two cups of instant coffee. Shelby was still in the bath when he returned. He knocked softly.

"Coffee's ready."

She emerged wrapped in his white terry robe, her mouth still puckered, but her eyes suspiciously bright. Had she been crying? Jake cringed. *Oh, hell.*

She took the cup. "Thanks."

"I'm sorry. I don't want to fight with you, Shelby."

It was almost as if he'd struck her. She stiffened, turning a defensive shoulder as she stood at the window and watched the world brighten to gold and lavender with another hot Texas sunrise. She held the mug like a shield against her chest, not drinking.

"We're not fighting," she said finally. "I knew this was coming, and I thought I'd be able to handle it better, that's all."

"Look, you're doing great." Jake set his own mug down and leaned a hip against the dresser. "This Salvatore will be sent to a place where he can never hurt anyone again, thanks to you, and—"

Shelby turned then, her mouth twisting with disbelief. "Are all men so stupid, or is it just cowboys? I can face the Salvatores of the world. That's my job, my life. I'm not dumb enough to pretend I'm not frightened at times, but I've got what it takes."

"You're just about the most courageous person I've ever known."

She blew out a shaky breath. "That's where you're wrong. I'm a wreck. Because, as the walrus said, 'The time has come.'"

"For what?"

"To end it, Jake." She raked fingers through her hair. "I'm leaving today, and it's best to make a clean break, so…"

Her words stabbed him, mocked him, turned him mean. "Uh-uh, lady."

"Jake, please." She cast him a furtive glance, then looked back at the window, her lips trembling. "It was great, but it wasn't real, so please allow us to end it with a little style and class."

He crossed the room before either of them realized he'd moved, grabbing her arms and pressing her against the wall, his expression savage. "No way, baby. This is as messy as it comes. Don't think there's an easy way out."

"But there's no point." She broke off with a gasp as he caught her jawbone and snapped her head back, forcing her to see what was in his dark eyes.

"Don't try to deny what we have," he growled.

"Chemistry, that's all."

"That, and everything else. Dammit, woman! Are you blind? I love you."

"Don't." The word was almost a moan, and her features blanched, white and stricken. "It's just a word that seems to fit for what's now, but when I'm gone, you'll see the difference."

"How do you think I can let you go?" He kissed her then, gently, feeling the shudder of her mouth beneath his. His whisper was harsh against her lips. "You belong with me."

"Don't make it any harder than it already is," she begged. "You've helped me heal, but now we need to go our separate ways again. If you care about me at all, you'll see that."

"Care? Didn't you hear me? I'm in love with you! And

I know you're in love with me, so don't try to deny it. That's all that matters. And this.''

Digging deep in his jeans pocket, he plucked out Retha's engagement ring. The tiny diamond glittered in the early-morning light, and Shelby's eyes widened in both wonder and dread.

"I've been trying to say it right," Jake said, his voice gruff. "But I'm just a cowboy, and the words don't always come easy for country boys. So here it is—I love you. I want to make a life with you. What do you say, will you marry me?"

Chapter Twelve

It was so unfair. So damned unfair. Just like a cowboy to change the rules in the middle of the rodeo, take the eight-second bell and make it into a five-alarm catastrophe.

Shelby looked at the old-fashioned ring Jake held, knew it wasn't the rock that had graced Georgia's finger for two years. Her heart twisted with the innate knowledge of what this truly meant.

"It's your mother's, isn't it?"

He nodded. "And you're the only other woman on earth who could wear it." His voice was warm as velvet.

Ah, she wanted it. She wanted everything it symbolized—hearth and home and a lifetime commitment. And it was as distant and phantasmagorical as a leprechaun's pot of gold disappearing beyond a rainbow's horizon. She hated Jake at that moment for showing her heaven, tempting her with paradise while she knew in her heart of hearts she'd never deserve it, and certainly never live the dream.

"Damn you." Her throat was so thick she could barely choke out the words. "Don't you dare do this to me."

Jake's dark brows drew down in a scowl. "It's not hemlock, Shelby."

With a strangled laugh, she reached down for the last of her resolve, pushed away the glittering dreams reflected in the tiny diamond and shoved out of his embrace. Tossing back her hair, she took a deep breath. "Not for you, cowboy. But a guy like you, a girl like me—get real. It would be the kiss of death."

His jaw worked. Deliberately he set the ring down in the middle of the uncluttered dresser, then shot Shelby a level look. "People do it all the time—get married, plan a family, grow old together."

"Not people like me."

"Dammit, Shelby, that's a load of horse manure and you know it. Despite what you think sometimes, my head isn't filled with hay. Everything you are or were or will be makes you the woman I want."

Oh, he was good. The pain sliced through her like slivers of glass. And suddenly she was afraid he'd seduce her with more than his body, with those impossible irresistible words, and if she gave in to her heart, succumbed to what she most desired, she'd end up destroying what she held most dear—this man with his dark eyes burning, his velvet mustache pulled down in a scowl that would have melted lead. And that she could not bear.

He'd given her so much—his strength, his healing and, yes, she knew, his love—but he deserved so much more than a battered cop with a bad attitude. He wanted it all, too—the wife, the mother to his kids, the helpmeet for a lifetime, and she knew to her utter, unworthy center that she could never live up to those expectations. Somewhere, somehow, down the line, she'd fail. Something within her makeup and background would cease to be what he needed and wanted.

To have the dream, even briefly, then to watch it disintegrate and die through her own fault would be so much worse than never experiencing it at all. At least she'd had a brief taste of paradise. They would both have to be satisfied with that. Someday Jake Lattimer would thank her for being the stronger one and making the hard choice.

So she groped for strength and prepared herself to hurt him.

"What *you* want is not necessarily the issue, cowboy. But I suppose spoiled only children can't help but want their own way."

"Don't try to bring it down to that level," he growled. "Don't trivialize what's going on."

"But do you even know? What about what *I* want, Jake? What about that?"

He massaged the back of his neck. "Hell, I thought...the way things are between us, how could I not believe this is something we both want? God, I want you with me, woman. It's as simple as that."

"A month ago you wanted Georgia the same way."

"It's not at all the same."

"Isn't it?" She made her voice scathing. "You say you love me. How can I trust a cowboy who's proven himself so fickle? You like to delude yourself that you're above it, but you're no different from any man. You were on the rebound, looking for some solace, a little ego building, and I was available. Don't kid yourself that it's going to last. Next month it'll be someone else."

The muscle worked in his jaw. "If you can say that, then you don't know me at all."

"It works both ways."

"Meaning?"

"That I'm not ready to pledge my troth or whatever the phrase is. I've got a life to go back to, and I'm not ready to give it up for the various bucolic pleasures of the boondocks."

"I never said I'd ask you to give up your work! There are ways to compromise. That's what people who love each other do."

"Oh, so I'm supposed to be satisfied chasing an occasional rustler? Maybe giving a few parking tickets to the local buzzards?"

"Only if you want to. You're creative. What about that family counseling degree? There are options—"

She silenced him with a scowl. "Aren't you listening? Look, after what happened, I've got something to prove—to myself. The only way I'll ever overcome it is to face the fear, and that means performing my sworn duty. Until I'm sure of myself, I'm not good to anyone—least of all you."

He shoved fingers through his hair in frustration. "That's a load of psychobabble. You're fine, and there are opportunities for you and me that don't include your getting back on the street."

"It's what I know."

"It's not *all* you know." Face intense, his fists clenched as if resisting the urge to grab her and shake some sense into her, he said, "You've proven it to yourself already, Shelby. Look at how you fit in at the Lazy L. I've never seen anyone so taken with the life here. The hands love you already. You fill this old homestead with life and laughter and all your energy—just like my mother did. I saw it work between my folks, angel. We can do it. It's as if you were born to it—as if you've always belonged right here. With me.''

He was doing it again—painting the picture that was too good to be true.

Belonging. To someone. To someplace special, just hers. To always be accepted right or wrong. It was heaven and hell rolled up in an impossibility. Her fear escalated, changed to the old defense—the self-preservation of anger.

''You think you've got all the answers,'' she snapped. ''Well, you really don't know squat about me, Jake Lattimer. Not if you think I could ever be satisfied cleaning the cow dung off your boots, playing the dutiful little society wife, PTA and the garden club. My God, can you imagine!''

''Who's asking you to plant posies? Hell, you can be the president of the hunting club for all I care. Who's trying to rein you in?''

''You, that's who. You want someone at your side who'll do you proud, look the part, act the part. Well, cowboy, I can't do it!''

''That's nonsense. We can do anything as long as we're together.''

Weariness made her voice rusty. ''Just stop, Jake. Don't make me say it.''

''What is so hard about this?'' he shouted. ''I love you. You love me.''

''No,'' she lied coldly, using every talent she'd learned on the streets to make him believe. ''I don't. And to spend the rest of my life with a man who'll bore me to tears within no time is something I'm not willing to do—even if you are the hottest thing in the sack I've ever experienced.''

His lids flickered at the poisonous barbs, and his jaw clenched. "Don't go there, Shelby."

"I tell it like it is, cowboy." She tossed her chin in defiance. "You won't call it quits like a civilized man, so fine. I'm not against a little tumble anytime you come to town. Who knows, maybe when you finally latch on to that perfect little wife you want I can still be in the picture. Always thought I'd make a terrible wife, but a great mistress. At least we won't bore each other that way, so—"

"That's enough!" He was on her then, clasping her shoulders in a grip that could have crushed bone. "Hellfire and damnation! I don't know what kind of act you're trying to pull—"

"It's no act."

"And you're a damned liar and we both know it."

Her eyes gleamed more golden than green with ire. "Believe what you like—just leave me out of it."

His big hands framed her face, threading through her hair to force her gaze to his. Anger washed off him in waves. "Is that what you really want?"

She forced the bald word out of her throat, meeting his eyes unflinchingly. "Yes."

"Then prove it."

He ground his mouth down on hers, holding her still while he ravaged her lips. She hadn't expected it, hadn't anticipated the surge of heat that exploded between them—anger, hurt, desire, a bundle of emotions going off like a nuclear explosion. Instant flash point; no containment; utter destruction.

Jake pulled her to him, molding her closer than thought. She moaned, but whatever will to protest she'd possessed had already been consumed in the battle, and suddenly she was kissing him back, hungry for this, for what she knew was the last time.

His tongue was rapacious, consuming her. He shoved the gown off her shoulder, and the thin batiste parted with a ripping sound as his palm cupped her breast. At his touch, her nipples puckered, and fire ran like a hot wire to her core, igniting every passion. Somehow she was all over him, arm wrapped around his strong neck, knee slung over his lean hip. A broad palm cupped her bare buttock, grinding her against his denim-covered manhood. The groan that tore from his throat was something urgent and primal, not to be denied.

He picked her up, and they tumbled into the rumpled bed, tearing at the remainder of their clothing. The torn gown floated like a cloud to the floor; denim sailed across the room. Jake's anger was still palpable and yet even in his roughness and urgency, Shelby knew that he'd never hurt her. It made it all the harder to bear, even as she welcomed the force and the power of him, reveled in his strength like a glutton breaking a forty-day fast.

They came together with muted cries, the pleasure mixed with a nearly unbearable agony. Blood pounding, bodies misted with moisture, they strove together toward that perfect bliss. With everything that was in him, Jake took her to the edge again and again, until she was begging for release. And then he pitched her over the edge of a bottomless canyon and catapulted them both into oblivion.

She came to herself slowly, only to find that she was weeping.

Jake levered himself from her, his arms shaking, his face a mask of rage and love and desperation.

"You can't deny it, Shelby. You can't make me believe this doesn't mean anything."

She gasped for air, her head spinning. "It doesn't. It *can't*."

He looked at her, his eyes going nearly black. "I was wrong. You *are* a coward. You're gutless where it means the most."

Then he pulled himself away from her love-dampened body, snatched up his jeans and left her alone in the big bed with only her tears and the knowledge that he was absolutely right.

She lay there for a long time, too stunned to move, too brokenhearted to even berate the universe for its perfidy. Finally, when the floods stopped coursing down her cheeks, she rose and splashed water onto her fevered face, trying to shock herself back to life and sanity. Wrapping herself in Jake's robe, all she could remember was how close he'd come in those last final moments of completion to wringing the truth from her. How with just a little more time, a little more pressure, Jake Lattimer could undo all her good resolves. As long as he didn't know she loved him, there was hope he'd write her off as a bad investment in the same way he had Georgia. He'd already guessed the truth, but if he *knew,* well, then the stubborn cowboy wouldn't give up and he'd eventually wear her down. She couldn't let it happen.

The panic that filled her was a hundred times worse than waking up with Salvatore's fingers around her neck. She knew she had to get out—and fast—before she made the biggest mistake of her life.

Going to the phone, she checked the time, then dialed Zach's office at Ranger headquarters.

"What do you mean he's not there? Well, beep him for me, dammit!" Desperation made her voice edgy.

There was no way she was waiting until five o'clock to leave the Lazy L, not if she had to walk every step back to Dallas barefoot. She waited, listened with impatience as the clerk tried to explain the complications of modern technology and that Zach had left only minutes before but would check in before long.

"How about his partner? Is Will there? I need a car—"

The clerk sounded more and more frazzled. "There's really no one available at the moment, Ms. Hartman. In fact, Zach's got three people waiting to see him now, including Officer Spaulding, who's sitting right in front of me—"

There was the sound of muted conversation, the receiver changing hands abruptly, then a new voice. "Shelby! Is that you?"

"Harve!" Relief flooded her at her partner's familiar drawl. "What are you doing there?"

"Trying to rescue my partner from Coventry. Heard you were due in and wanted to see if I could help. That Ranger of yours sure has kept you under wraps."

"Well, it's the grand reopening of the new and improved Shelby Hartman today, pal." She blew out an unsteady breath. "Listen, you've got to get word to Zach immediately for me. I'm not cooling my heels on the Lazy L for another minute."

"That's the Lattimer place?"

"Yeah. Zach's brother. Tell Zach to come get me *now*."

"Is something wrong?"

"Just do it, Harve."

"Yes, ma'am. We'll be there ASAP. If I can't locate Zach, I'll come myself. Pick you up where?"

"The main house. Don't come in. I'll be waiting."

Zach Rawlings strode down the ramp in the parking garage of the Dallas County Court House. The meeting with the D.A.'s had gone well. It would all be over soon.

Unlocking his car, he tossed his Stetson in the back

seat with the neat pile of Shelby's clothes Georgia had picked up the night before—royal blue suit, navy pumps, even pearl earrings. Shelby could look the part of competent professional policewoman when the chips were down—and this was it.

He'd arranged for a suite for her at a top-of-the-line, but utterly unprepossessing hotel, complete with fruit basket, flowers and a magnum of champagne. It was the least he could do to make up for her enforced stay in the wide-open spaces. Zach's jaw clenched. He only hoped whatever was happening between his old partner and his twin wasn't going to leave either one of them with permanent damage. Then, he'd have a lot more to answer for than what had possessed him to use the Lazy L as a hideout in the first place.

Zach pulled into the heavy downtown traffic, shaking his head. No, it was futile to second-guess himself at this point. Still, something prickled at the back of his neck, raising hairs. He glanced at his watch. It was still before noon. Just a few more hours. He cursed under his breath. If the waiting was giving him the willies, just think what it was doing to Shelby.

But the closer he got to his office, the greater the gut sense that something was wrong.

The stoplight turned green, but Zach stared at it. He ignored the sounds of horns and curses, trying to focus. Premonition formed a knot at the base of his throat, the sudden dread nameless and faceless but far more potent than any adrenaline rush he'd ever experienced in the heat of battle.

Did a competent, rational cop follow procedure, tell himself he was seeing demons where there were none? Or did he trust a gut instinct, an otherworldly sense of "not right" that dimmed his vision and made his ears ring?

Zach shoved the blue light onto the dash, hit the siren, made a blatant U-turn across the curbed median, barely missing an eighteen-wheeler. Reaching for the radio, he gunned the engine and headed south.

"We got her."

"Where?"

Shoes gave the information.

"I'll meet you."

"Sir?" The word rattled from the henchman's dry lips. "I can handle it."

"And indeed you shall."

"Shelby, Shelby! Come see, quick! I—" Leza skidded to a stop, her brown eyes full of reproach. "Where ya going?"

"Nowhere, sweetie." Shelby dropped the sheer drape on the front parlor window, touched the little girl's curls and forced a smile.

"Mama says don't ever fib," Leza said solemnly, then gave a pointed look at Shelby's duffle on the carpet by the front door and the jeans and denim jacket she wore.

Something punched Shelby in the heart. She dropped to her knees in front of the little girl. "Your mom's right. I'm sorry. I have to leave today."

"Now?"

"Soon."

Like a coward, the gutless wonder Jake had accused her of being, she'd written out her notes to Ben, Rosie, and even a stilted one to Jake, and left them on the foyer table. All was quiet before lunch, so if Zach would just arrive, she could make her craven escape unscathed except for her own self-recriminations.

"But you can't! You haven't seen—" Leza grabbed Shelby's hand in protest. "We just found them, and you just can't—"

"What is it?"

"Elizabeth!" Leza's eyes shone. "She's had kittens!"

The little burst of joy at Leza's announcement was all the more poignant for knowing she'd miss out on the antics of a litter of Elizabeth's and Attila's offspring.

"That's just great," Shelby murmured. "They're in the barn?" No way would she risk running into Jake!

"Of course not. A barn's not grand enough for Elizabeth." Leza's laughter burbled over. "Come see! She had them in the doll room!"

Shelby gave an anxious glance outside, but the drive was still empty, so she gave in and raced with Leza to Retha's sitting room.

"Mama's gone to fix a better box for her," Leza explained, then pressed a finger to her lips. "Shh. Look."

In the corner behind a wing chair, tucked into a basket of hand-needlepointed cushions, Elizabeth blinked at them with a Madonna's eyes while several small squirming bundles of fur mewled and blindly sought their mother's teats.

"There's seven of them," Leza whispered. "Enough for everyone to have one. You can have first choice, Shelby."

Shelby's throat constricted. She knew she couldn't take anything back with her from the Lazy L, not if she expected to survive, not if she expected ever to get on with whatever was left of the shambles of her life.

"I'd like one, but I work so much a kitten would be lonely at my place," she told the little girl.

"We could keep him here, for when you come back."

The child's guileless offer nearly brought her to her knees. "I don't think I'll be back, Leza."

Her eyes got wide. "Not ever?"

How could she crush the child with the truth? Shelby tried to smile. "Well, of course, sometimes it's hard to say…"

The crunch of gravel outside alerted her, and she went to the window. A typical department-issued blue sedan trundled down the July-parched drive in a cloud of buff dust.

Zach. Thank God.

"There's my ride." Shelby knelt again and gathered Leza into her arms for a final hug. "You be good for your folks, okay? And take care of all those kittens for me."

With a final squeeze, she bolted down the stairs, grabbed the bag and raced outside to the waiting car. She didn't look back, and she didn't see the little girl waving forlornly from the upstairs window.

Jake unloaded a final feed sack into the barn's feed room and bent over to catch his breath. Five hundred pounds of horse feed and some honest sweat had brought his rage and hurt to tolerable levels and his mind into focus again. He glanced at his watch. Still early for lunch, but he had let Shelby cool her heels long enough. If that little heifer thought this shooting match was over, she was dead wrong. Wiping his brow with the back of his arm, he headed for the house. He'd get cleaned up and stay calm.

The hell I will. It was time he shook Shelby up just as she'd shaken him to the core.

Everything Shelby had told him was a bunch of so much hooey, of that he was certain. That she'd had the utter gall to lie straight-faced to him, after all they'd grown to mean to each other, made him want to chew nails. He couldn't read her mind, but he knew she was scared—of more than Salvatore's threats. If only Jake could convince her that being together wasn't such a fearful thing. Maybe the knuckle-headed woman somehow thought she was protecting him. All he knew was that she was frazzled again by this court business, and not thinking straight. He was a patient man—at times. He could wait to sort things out permanently. But by golly, he was going with her today and would stand at her side to support and protect her whether she liked it or not. So forget the shower, he was telling that to Miss Shelby Hartman now.

But as he walked into the house, he found a new problem—Leza, sitting in the middle of the tile floor, sucking her thumb and sniffling.

"Punkin, what's the matter?"

Leza snuffled, crystal tears streaming down her face. "Shel—Shelby didn't wave goodbye."

Thunderstroke slapped Jake like a giant hand. He caught Leza up in his arms. "Goodbye? You mean she's gone?"

"In the blue car."

"Hellfire and damnation!" Jake's shout reverberated to the rafters, but his thoughts were quiet and deadly. *Gone—just like Georgia.* And Zach had a hand in it this time, too.

Jake cursed. "That damnable brother of mine—I'll skin him alive for this!"

"*Madre de Dios,* what's the ruckus?" Wiping her hands, Rosie hurried into the kitchen, only to have her child practically thrown at her. Ben appeared from his room, tucking in a shirttail that indicated he'd taken a mid-morning snooze.

"What's going on?"

"Did Shelby tell either of you she was leaving?" Jake demanded.

Rosie looked puzzled. "She was in her room—"

"No, Mama," Leza said, "she went in the car just a little while ago. She didn't even want a kitten."

"I'll pound that sorry Zach Rawlings to within an inch of his life," Jake raged. "Once wasn't enough. Damnation, if he thinks he can snatch my woman from right under my nose without so much as a by-your-leave—"

"Zach wouldn't do it that way," Ben objected. "He wants to build the bridges, son."

"Sure, he'd have come in, no matter what," Rosie agreed.

"Not if Shelby had her way. His first loyalty is to her—especially if he thinks I'm hurting her," Jake said in a raw voice.

Just like Georgia. But this wasn't anything like breaking it off on his wedding day with Georgia. This was Shelby. He'd stood on his pride, taken it like a man and let Georgia go without a fight. But his heart had known then—if not his ego—that she was right, that Zach was the man for her.

But this was Shelby. And what mattered pride or ego if you lost the woman you loved? This time he'd fight. Hell! He'd grovel if he had to, but he wasn't letting this one get away!

"I'm going after her." Fishing truck keys out of his pocket, he bolted toward the door.

"Take the Little Mesquite Road," Ben shouted after him. "You just might beat her to the main highway."

"I really appreciate this, Harve." Shelby stared at the fence posts flying past.

"No problem." Harve Spaulding snapped his gum and shifted his sports coat on his narrow shoulders.

"Zach—"

"Was tied up in pretrial. No problem, I said."

"It'll be good to get back to work."

"Missed the bright lights, did you?"

She could answer honestly now. "No. Not at all. They have a good life out here."

"You sound envious."

Her laugh held no humor. "Yeah."

Harve poured on the gas through a curve, wooded on one side with pin oaks and bounded on the other by a pasture with a rutted road. "Well, the grass is always greener for the rich folks, I always say—"

A powerful black automobile pulled out of the oaks right into their path. Cursing, Harve stomped the brake, fishtailing them into the side of the other vehicle. Shelby hung on to the door handle. The jolt snapped her neck, but as soon as she could draw breath and realized she was okay, she saw red.

"Arrest that SOB, Harve!" she ordered, fumbling with her seat belt. "I swear—"

But Harve sat slumped over the steering wheel with blood on his forehead.

The door on the passenger side popped open, but the hand that latched on to Shelby's throat and dragged her into the sun didn't belong to a concerned accident victim.

Shelby looked up into the cold reptilian eyes of Gus Salvatore and plunged back into her worst nightmare.

There'd been an accident, he could see that much. Jouncing at a dangerous pace across the rutted Little Mesquite Road, Jake squinted through the dusty truck windshield. Then he saw it.

The man with the gun. Shelby's white face. Her being dragged from one car to another. And she wasn't even fighting.

"No!" The howl took him like a mad demon.

One hand on the bucking steering wheel, he couldn't even wrestle down the rifle on the rear gun rack in time. He stomped the gas pedal. The truck tore through the gate separating the pasture from the pileup, twisting the metal into an S and sending it flying like a cannonball.

The gunman spun, calmly aimed at the speeding truck.

"No!"

Shelby came out of the nightmare into something far worse.

Jake. Coming to her rescue. She could almost laugh, except that it wasn't ludicrous, it was deadly. Salvatore was a marksman, even with a handgun. Jake didn't stand a chance. Salvatore's grip on her windpipe tightened, and he aimed.

She went deadly calm, fear of this killer forgotten in the all-important need to protect Jake. Desperate, she chopped at his gun arm, bringing it down as his weapon fired. Salvatore growled, caught her with the hilt of the gun against her temple. Her pain didn't matter. Instead of recoiling, she attacked again, two fists to his exposed groin. Her air was going and her ears screamed with sirens and alarms, but still she grappled.

And then someone else was there, rolling into them, knocking the weapon loose. She was free, air gusting into her starved lungs, Salvatore falling facedown in the dirt from a blow to the jaw that produced the sickening crunch of splintering bone. The sirens were upon them now.

"Shelby." Jake's voice was ragged. "You all right?"

"Jake!" She scrambled to her feet, saw him wobble,

saw the crimson staining his chambray shirt. "Oh, God, Jake—you're hit!"

He looked down in surprise, then began a slow slide to the ground. Shelby barely caught him, cradled him to her breast as they both found the earth.

"Don't worry, angel," he said. "My brother's brought the posse."

The surgery to patch the hole in Jake's shoulder was a bit tricky and took the afternoon, and by the time they'd let her see him, out of danger but still doped up in recovery and knowing no one, it was well into the wee hours. Knowing Ben and Rosie would keep vigil, there was nothing for Shelby to do—except her duty.

Which she did, promptly at ten o'clock the next morning before a secret Grand Jury who would see that Gus Salvatore, now resting in intensive care at a maximum security hospital facility with new attempted-murder charges against him, would never see the light of day again.

She and Zach arrived back at the Ft. Worth hospital to find Jake had been transferred to his own room—a good sign that made Shelby breathe a sigh of relief. She wanted to see him but was hesitant. After all she'd said and done, Jake had a perfect right to hate her. Maybe he wouldn't even want to see her.

"I still can't believe Harve was mixed up with Gus Salvatore," Zach was saying. "God, I can't stand a dirty cop."

Shelby shrugged. Even the knowledge that her partner, who Salvatore called Shoes, had sold her out couldn't move her after nearly losing Jake. "He was a chump, thinking Salvatore would forgive those gambling debts."

"Or that he'd just hold you until after the Grand Jury."

Zach looked at her hard. "Gus was going to kill you both. Shoes would have been history."

"Then Harve's a lucky man."

"If you consider spending the next decade or so learning what it's like on the inside lucky." Zach grinned as they located the right corridor. "Convenient."

"Convenient you showed up when you did."

Zach rubbed his nape, his mouth twisting in baffled consternation. "Hell of a business, this twin stuff. Somehow I knew there was trouble. It was Jake all along, not you. And if that bastard Harve had had his way—"

"I don't want to think about Harve anymore. Look, there's Ben."

Shelby straightened her shoulders and lifted her chin. There was no way to put things right between her and Jake just now, but she'd faced her moment of truth with Salvatore and triumphed, so could she do less than come clean with the man she loved? He at least deserved the truth. After all, the dadblamed cowpoke *had* saved her life.

Ben glanced up and saw them approaching. He looked a bit haggard, but he wrung Zach's hand soundly and kissed Shelby's cheek. "He's resting, but why don't you go on in, Shelby?" he suggested. "He asked for you earlier. I need some coffee, and Zach here's going to pay for it."

Trepidation and eagerness and dread pounded a nervous rhythm through her blood as she cautiously pushed open the hospital room door.

"Damn, woman. You look like a million bucks."

Jake's voice was low and husky, his dark head on the white pillow a startling contrast in the dimly lit room. Shelby glanced down at her city-slicker suit in surprise, realized he'd never seen her gussied up. It was a wonder he recognized her.

Her voice wobbled dangerously. "Yeah, I wash up real nice."

"Come here."

She was leaning over the bed rail in an instant, clutching at his good hand, her eyes wet as she took in the bandages and IV drip. "Oh, damn, I told myself no waterworks."

"Honey, if those are for me, you can dry your eyes. I'm okay."

"Jake, I'm so sorry, for everything."

He raised his hand, threading strong fingers through her hair, stroking the unique angle of her jaw and a shadow of new bruises so that she shivered. "Yeah, when you mess up, you do it big-time, don't you, city girl?"

Her laugh was strangled. "You noticed."

"Well, get this, Shelby. It's okay. No matter what—I love you, anyway."

The acceptance and the unequivocal trust in his gaze demanded no less than complete honesty from her—at last.

"I love you, too, Jake. God knows I do. Forgive me for being too much of coward to say it, but—"

"You're still running scared, Shelby."

She swallowed. "It's very hard…seeing you hurt, and it's my fault. How can I ever live with that?" Her throat was raw with emotion. "I could never forgive myself if I made you unhappy, and I know I would—"

"So you can just take care of yourself. You've said so often enough."

"Yes." She hesitated, uncertain of his drift, yet somehow her fingers were entwined with his as if she'd never let him go again.

"So can I." His dark eyes burned. *"But we don't have to."*

"I don't understand."

"You saved my life when you went after Salvatore like a tigress."

"No, you saved me," she protested. "If you hadn't been there…"

"So we took care of each other, angel, just the way people who love each other should. Don't you see how right that is?"

And suddenly she did. Life was a risk, but to be without Jake—to have nearly lost him by tossing away his devotion through her own cowardice—would be the most unbearable waste imaginable. The most frightening thing in the universe was facing the rest of her life without Jake. It was as simple as that. All she had to do was trust Jake's love and her own. With a shaky breath, she took the leap of faith.

"You must be very tired of dealing with a damned fool."

Leaning back, Shelby stripped off her suit jacket down to the silky shell, then lowered the rail and very gingerly eased onto the narrow bed beside Jake. His good arm came around her like a lifeline.

"Shelby…"

She stretched to kiss him, softly, with every tender feeling swelling in her heart. "I'm not afraid anymore, Jake," she whispered. "Not if you love me. Not if you can forgive me. Not if you still want me…"

His groan was wrung from the heart, not his physical wound. "God, woman—how can you ever doubt it?"

She drew a deep breath. "Then marry me."

"Done," Jake said. He cupped her chin, brushed her

lips in benediction and promise, and they smiled into each other's eyes, seeing the future.

"This looks too familiar."

Jake and Shelby looked up to find Zach and Georgia hovering in the doorway. Reluctantly Shelby eased to her feet, her hand still clutched in Jake's.

"Just had to see for ourselves you're okay, Hoss," Zach said, his tone a bit rough, but a quirk of a grin splitting his cheek. "We'll come back."

"You might as well stay, you outlaw," Jake said, "and offer congratulations. We're getting married."

Georgia's soft gasp was both relief and joy. "Oh, Jake. Shelby. I'm so glad."

"Thanks, sugar," Jake said. It was enough for all of them—peace and forgiveness and an unspoken acknowledgment of mutual affection and blood bonds that would never again be threatened.

Zach cleared his throat. "We spent our wedding night watching over Shelby. You want me to go find the hospital chaplain? As twins we appear to do certain things alike—"

"Not this time." Jake held on to Shelby's hand, kissed it. "I'm still due a church wedding. Suit you, angel?"

Shelby's throat grew thick with love and the rich promise of tomorrow. "Anything you say, cowboy."

Zach and Georgia shared an awkward glance, but Jake's smile shone with warmth.

"And I'd like my brother to be best man."

Epilogue

Radiant.

In an understated ivory suit and orchids, that was the only word to describe Shelby Hartman Lattimer as she clung to her new husband's arm. Fresh from the simple church service, Jake in his wedding tux had the typical besotted bridegroom's expression, and Zach and Georgia Rawlings, as best man and matron of honor, couldn't stop beaming.

Laura Ramirez lifted her champagne flute to the happy couple as a crowd of well-wishers flowed through the Lazy L, offering congratulations. Outside, the August heat had relented with sundown, a country-western band played at poolside, and a lavish Texas spread and three-tiered marzipan wedding cake filled the dining room. Leza, decked out in peach lace as befitted a flower girl, flitted here and there like a butterfly, rice bags and one black-as-the-ace-of-spades kitten tucked into her basket.

Just over a month after the Salvatore story, which had set Laura solidly on the fast track at work, the wedding was a testimony to a certain cowboy's determination to hitch himself to his lady.

Laura smiled again, thrilled to see them so happy. If anyone deserved it, these two did. And she had another reason to feel satisfied. As soon as she'd spoken with Lillian, Laura had called Zach to tell him what the old nurse said about why Abby had kept him and given up Jake. Relieved, but not really surprised, that it was concern for her child's welfare that had prompted Abby to do what she'd done, Zach had suggested that Laura wait until the wedding reception to break the news to Jake— sort of a wedding gift. Laura had agreed. Putting an end to that mystery would set the stage for a new beginning, and, looking at Shelby and Jake, Laura knew that today was a day for just that.

She spotted a distinguished silver head in conversation with several guests. She might as well start the ball rolling by having a word with Ben. But as she made her way to the periphery of the group, a familiar name caught her attention.

"I'll be damned if I'll let that crook Tom Barnette slide into the state house without a fight." The tall sandy-haired man wore his suit with the elegance of old money, but his craggy features and unusual amber eyes held an element of hardness that could chill bone.

"Logan, really. Must you talk business now?" The chic, dark-eyed brunette in shantung silk placed a maternal restraining hand on his arm. "This is a social occasion, son."

Ben Lattimer laughed, his eyes twinkling appreciatively. "Don't be too hard on the boy, Valerie. You and Black Jack depend on this bulldog lawyer, don't you?"

"I haven't let Jack dictate to me in a long time." Her tone was as neutral as her ring finger was bare.

"Barnette's an old grudge," Ben said.

Logan's cool amber eyes narrowed. "One neither Dad nor I intend to forget."

Ben's glance flickered to Laura. "Then you ought to meet this little lady. She's a heck of a reporter, been looking into a few things for us, including ole Tom. Laura Ramirez, meet Logan Campbell and his mother, Valerie Gaspard, of Gaspard Enterprises and Campbell Drilling."

Shock slammed into Laura. She struggled to hide it as she shook hands. "Campbell Drilling?"

"You know the company, Ms. Ramirez?" Logan asked.

Laura nodded, swallowing hard. "I covered an oil field fire about six years ago—"

"The Odessa blowout." Logan Campbell looked at her with respect and not a little calculation. "I remember now. Your coverage was excellent, although at the time the whole world began to think my brother had a death wish."

Laura had known the truth instinctively, but it didn't stop her stomach from plummeting with the memory of fire and light and intense emotion. "Russ Campbell is your brother?"

"Yes. You know him?"

"Not well," she lied.

Only for the most intense six weeks of my life. Only for the hardest, sweetest, best and worst times I've ever known.

Her voice was shaky. "I remember he was a hero."

Valerie made a soft noise of exasperation—or perhaps a mother's fear. "Or a reckless boy who still takes too many chances, my dear. Thank God Russ and Bliss are scouting for Jack down in South Texas these days. Maybe he can stay out of trouble.''

Ben chuckled. "Wouldn't count on it, Val darlin'.''

"And that, you sweet talker," she replied with a fond smile, "is why, after I've hugged that boy of yours—and his new brother, too—I'm off to nurse my gray hairs at my favorite spa for a few days."

"Gilding the lily," Ben said gallantly.

"You Texans!" Valerie smiled, then caught her son's eye. "Logan, I'd like a piece of wedding cake."

"Of course." Logan excused himself to follow his mother, stopping to hand Laura his card. "I'd like to discuss Barnette with you, Ms. Ramirez. I'll call."

Dismay warred with a reporter's anticipation as Laura took the creamy business card. "But—"

Logan Campbell's eyes were steely. "I'm going to bring him down. Believe me, there's going to be a helluva story in it for someone when I do."

He left her gaping and tantalized and despite everything that screamed a warning—tempted. A man to watch, her instincts told her. Before she'd fully recovered her equilibrium, the newlyweds had come to join Ben.

"I think we're supposed to take some more pictures, Dad," Jake said. "Got to toss posies before I can carry my bride off on a honeymoon."

"Hope they got room service in Aledo, Shelby," Zach quipped.

Flushed and beautiful, Shelby shared an intimate look with Jake. "Oh, I think the Louis Quinze can rustle up a waiter or two."

"Paris!" Zach stared.

"Georgia's idea," Jake acknowledged. *"Merci."*

The strawberry blonde winked. "You're welcome, Jake."

"Cowboys in France," Ben boomed, looking at the two men as proudly as if they were both his sons. "Now I've seen everything. It's a great day—a fine one to get a new daughter, a damn fine one to see you boys together."

"It is a fine day," Zach said. "And Laura has a bit of news for Jake that'll make it even better."

Ben, Jake and Shelby looked at Laura expectantly.

She smiled and took a deep breath, anxious to end Jake's concern. "I spoke with Lillian Hampstead, the nurse at the hospital the night you two were born. It took some prodding, but she finally remembered what happened." Laura beamed at Jake. "Your mother didn't give you away because she didn't want you, Jake. She gave you away to the Lattimers because she couldn't afford the bills that went with your medical problem."

"What medical problem?" Ben asked. He and Jake stared at her in total bewilderment.

Laura's feeling of euphoria began to evaporate. She frowned. "His heart condition. Lillian said…"

Jake shook his head. "I've never had any trouble with my heart in my life."

All eyes swung to Zach. "Neither have I."

"Then there must be some mistake…" Head spinning in confusion, Laura could only blink as the photographer gathered up the wedding party.

In a moment Jake was sliding Shelby's frilly blue garter off her slim thigh. When he tossed it into a party of hooting bachelors, it was a rather annoyed Logan Campbell who came up the winner. Then it was the ladies' turn to clamber for the wedding bouquet.

Laura hung back as Shelby performed the festive duty amid peals of laughter, for her mind was a daze of questions. It was back to square one on all fronts.

But Laura's natural curiosity brimmed over, not to be denied. With a deep breath, she rallied. There was a story here, and no matter what, a good reporter would find it....

* * * * *

Coming this December 1997 from
Silhouette SPECIAL EDITION®

AND BABY MAKES THREE: THE NEXT GENERATION:

The Adams women of Texas all find love—and motherhood—in the most unexpected ways!

The Adams family of Texas returns!
Bestselling author **Sherryl Woods** continues
the saga in these irresistible new books.
Don't miss the first three titles in the series:

In December 1997: THE LITTLEST ANGEL (SE #1142)
When Angela Adams told Clint Brady she was pregnant, she
was decidedly displeased with the rancher's reaction. Could
Clint convince Angela he wanted them to be a family?

In February 1998: NATURAL BORN TROUBLE (SE #1156)
Dani Adams resisted when single dad Duke Jenkins claimed
she'd be the perfect mother for his sons. But Dani was
captivated by the boys—and their sexy father!

In May 1998: UNEXPECTED MOMMY (SE #1171)
To claim his share of the White Pines ranch, Chance Adams
tried to seduce his uncle's lovely stepdaughter. But then he
fell in love with Jenny Adams for real....

Available at your favorite retail outlet.

▼ *Silhouette*®

CHRISTINE FLYNN

Continues the twelve-book series—36 HOURS—in December 1997 with Book Six

FATHER AND CHILD REUNION

Eve Stuart was back, and Rio Redtree couldn't ignore the fact that her daughter bore his Native American features. So, Eve had broken his heart *and* kept him from his child! But this was no time for grudges, because his little girl and her mother, the woman he had never stopped—could never stop—loving, were in danger, and Rio would stop at nothing to protect *his* family.

For Rio and Eve and *all* the residents of Grand Springs, Colorado, the storm-induced blackout was just the beginning of 36 Hours that changed *everything!* You won't want to miss a single book.

Available at your favorite retail outlet.

36HRS6